Chasing Freedom

Chasing Freedom

a novel

Gloria Ann Wesley

Roseway Publishing
an imprint of Fernwood Publishing

HALIFAX & WINNIPEG

Editing: Sandra McIntyre
Design: John van der Woude
Printed and bound in Canada

Published in Canada by Roseway Publishing
an imprint of Fernwood Publishing
32 Oceanvista Lane
Black Point, Nova Scotia, B0J 1B0
and 748 Broadway Avenue, Winnipeg, Manitoba, R3G 0X3
www.fernwoodpublishing.ca/roseway

Fernwood Publishing Company Limited gratefully acknowledges the financial
support of the Government of Canada through the Canada Book Fund, the
Canada Council for the Arts, the Nova Scotia Department of Tourism and
Culture, the Manitoba Department of Culture, Heritage and Tourism under
the Manitoba Publishers Marketing Assistance Program and the Province of
Manitoba, through the Book Publishing Tax Credit, for our publishing program.

Library and Archives Canada Cataloguing in Publication

Wesley, Gloria
Chasing freedom / Gloria Ann Wesley.

ISBN 978-1-55266-423-0

1. Black loyalists--Nova Scotia--Birchtown--Fiction.
2. Women, Black--Nova Scotia--Birchtown--Fiction.
3. Slavery--South Carolina--Fiction. I. Title.

PS8595.E6295C53 2011   C813'.54   C2010-907222-7

In 1783, after the War of Independence in the United States, Britain evacuated thousands of people who had fought on their side to the remaining North American colonies. Among those transported to Nova Scotia were a number of freed slaves. These Black Loyalists had no idea of the tremendous hardships awaiting them. They arrived in Port Roseway (present-day Shelburne) and were forced to settle outside of the town, in an area they named Birchtown. They were promised land and the supplies needed for survival, but these promises were not kept. Soon, poverty, the harsh climate, disease and isolation, combined with racism, became their curse. In 1792, many of the Black Loyalists took the opportunity to leave Nova Scotia and sail to Sierra Leone to start a new life in Africa.

For Grandmother

And for Adrienne, Brian, Bessie, Ellie, Amberly, Garnet and Alphie

SPECIAL THANKS TO

Beverley Rach for believing in my story.

Sandra McIntyre for guiding me through the world of editing.

Brother, Larry, for advice.

Byron Jones for kind assurances.

Finn Bower, Shelburne County Museum, for wonderful resources I could not have done without.

Fred Leigh and Stephen Hart for reviews and encouragement.

One

E VERYWHERE BEAUTIFUL FALL COLOURS MELTED INTO A thick stew of forest greens. Lydia and Sarah Redmond stepped carefully over the tree stumps and sharp rocks threatening to slice through the worn soles of their boots as they walked through the trees along the shore of Birchtown Bay on the northwest arm of Shelburne Harbour. Their route stretched past the growing clusters of Birchtown shacks and connected to the Port Roseway Road which, after three miles, would bring them to Roseway itself. The heavy fall frost caused their breath to steam and their hands to ache. Sarah pulled down her hat and fastened her thin, grey coat.

Lydia forged ahead, keeping up a good pace, balancing a weighty basket of potatoes on her head. A white kerchief tied in a knot at the back of her neck framed a coffee-brown face that was deeply wrinkled, but smooth and shiny around the bones. She had good teeth. The empty corn pipe on which she constantly sucked hung from her mouth. On her left hand she wore a ring made of wood and decorated with an intricately carved olive branch. As she walked, her feet came down hard and fast.

Sarah followed the five-foot body of thick flesh, watched it wobble inside an array of colourless cotton. Her grandmother was old, the guess was fifty, but a slave's age was hard to tell. Sarah viewed the woman with an uneasy tension—the kind that always exists between the young and old.

"Hurry along now. Time's a wasting." Grandmother waved her arm like a sergeant, a bag of laundry and rag purse swinging wildly by her sides while the basket of potatoes on her head sat motionless.

"Morning comes too early." Sarah yawned. Her chestnut face was fixed in a knot—too pouty and childish for a girl of sixteen.

"We got lots to do this morning. Our first stop is at Prince and Beulah's. Oh Lord, Prince is down with the fever. It has been a few days since our last visit and there's no tellin' what to expect. The fever's carryin' folks to Glory one after the other."

"Prince is strong. He'll be alright."

"I hope so. I prayed this morning. We got a lot on our plates today. We also have to trade these vegetables at Cecil's store and then go down to Roseway with Mrs. Cunningham's wash."

Sarah swung her baskets of beets, carrots and cabbages. She mimicked the old woman. "Get along, get along," she murmured. "Being in Birchtown is the same as being on a plantation, someone always giving orders." She pressed on, knowing that talking back would make her the worst of human beings—a sinner. She wanted to ask why Reverend Ringwood didn't have prayers with her uncle, but old folks did not like questions—you got hard looks instead of answers. The one thing they did like was giving orders. Sarah had more to say, but she rolled her eyes and sucked her teeth instead.

But Grandmother was quick. "There's no need for sass," she said. "We have to make Roseway before the sun gets to burning. I hope it's peaceful down there."

Grandmother looked directly at Sarah and came to a sudden stop. "Hush," she whispered. An unfamiliar noise disturbed the stillness and the forest shivered. Grandmother and Sarah struggled to slow their thundering hearts by hastily puffing in the cool morning air. Danger lurked all around. It could come at a moment's notice in the form of slave hunters or other wicked men about. Saying or doing the wrong thing could get you whipped, jailed or shot.

They stood staring at each other in the dimness when the noise came again. Together, they stepped carefully from the trail into a stand of tall birch trees and crouched behind a huge rock. There, in a small clearing, was a white man on horseback. A long rope was tied one end to the saddle, the other around the neck of a Negro whose hands were chained. The women strained to make out who the men were, but they were too far away and dared not get closer.

Sarah gasped and in a low tone murmured, "Do you know them?"

"No," Grandmother said. "Stay down."

The white man dismounted and untied the rope from his saddle. He strained to pull the Negro along, for the man dug in his heels and had to be dragged. The white man pushed hard and forced his captive up onto the horse, which he then led under an oak tree with low-hanging branches. He tossed the long end of the rope over the thickest branch, tied it to his saddle and slapped the horse.

Sarah's teeth chattered and the veins in her neck jutted out. The Negro rose up from the horse and dangled several feet in the air as the two women watched in horror. The white man pulled out a long musket and stuffed it with shot. No sooner had they turned their faces away when a loud bang startled the air and the foul smell of gunpowder spread throughout the clearing. Off in the distance, the sound of cackling like a banshee hen rang through the woods.

It was some seconds before Grandmother came to herself. "The poor man refused to go along quietly," she said. "And that man … Oh, Girlie, what kind of man laughs after taking a life?"

When all had settled, two pairs of eyes searched the deep woods. Deciding the danger had passed, Sarah stood up and sighed deeply. "What good is freedom, Ma'am, if all we can do is live in fear? It's not right that we get treated this way, not here." Her anger flared and she exploded with a gutsy squeal.

"You are right, but you must learn to hold that anger, Girlie. Choose the time to speak your truth and always with caution." Steadying the basket on her head, the old woman cast her steely eyes on Sarah as she turned back to the trail. "And another thing, Girlie. Keep those eyes peeled. I hear that ol' Boll weevil Carter is sniffing around for stray Negroes. It could have been him back there." Her pipe rested in the small indentation in her bottom lip as she grunted between sucks. "He aims to take Negroes without certificates to the South and sell them back into slavery. We got our papers, but we can never be too sure. Wish it weren't so, but this here freedom only lasts from minute to minute. Folks are disappearing faster than a fresh loaf of bread."

"Yes Ma'am." Sarah quivered at the mention of heartless Boll weevil. A devil, the slaves called him. Always something or someone to fear, she thought. This crazy life sure had its ups and downs.

SARAH KICKED A ROCK TO THE LEFT OF THE PATH. THE SMELL of gunpowder lingered, stirring an image in her that prompted an all-too familiar flashback: a troop of raggedy people and soldiers, deathly quiet except for a moan or two, their faces long and heavy with grief.

Sarah's flesh tightened. Tiny goose bumps peppered her quivering skin as her heart beat in double time. In the swarm marched Grandmother, Uncle Prince, Aunt Beulah and herself. She strained to find Papa, but as usual, he was missing. In a short time, the figures evaporated into a blur of washed-out colours. Sarah let out a string of curses at the nagging memories. The past was always stirring the present like an angry wind swirling a pile of leaves.

It was the end of September 1784 as best Sarah could tell. Fifteen months had passed since their arrival in Nova Scotia from St. James Goose Creek, a settlement outside war-ravished Charles Town, South Carolina. For Sarah, there was no more hauling water buckets to the fields on a yoke. She didn't have to plant crops, weed the fields or work at the Big House. She was free from the thick sweat of summer's heat and from Cecil MacLeod breathing down her neck and treating her like a beast. Had she not been able to fill her belly this morning? And as far as happiness... well, that was just a step away now that she had Reece Johnson's eye.

The first golden rays of dawn trickled through the thick canopy of towering trees. Here and there, Birchtowners were starting to fill the trail, on their way to Roseway in hopes of finding a day's pay. They greeted Grandmother with a nod and moved quickly past. It was not long before the old woman burst into her vibrant strains of "Go Down, Moses." Sarah joined in as she watched a flock of grey birds darting among the pines. She was inspired to say, "I wish I was an eagle soaring above the clouds. I would find me a safe place and have a fine time. Oh yes, I would."

The old woman responded in a tone that was gruff. "Birds are blessed all right, but a bird finds trouble if it's not on guard. I pray trouble never finds you, Girlie."

"Papa said that we shouldn't fear trouble. That trouble is shackled to change."

"Trouble is shackled to change all right, and a whole lot of other things."

"Trouble does not scare me. Not if it can make things different."

The old woman fired back. "Don't be getting big ideas, Girlie. Could be I'm wrong, but change does not come easy."

"Why doesn't it?"

"Because old habits die hard. They run deep—right to the marrow in the bones. Folks didn't leave their old ideas and feelings behind in Carolina."

Sarah nodded. "I suppose not," she said.

Grandmother caught an expression of arrogance in the girl's attitude. She too, had been full of confidence at one time. Yes Lord, a stubborn fighter. But she learned. A sad thought brought fear for the girl. Life's lessons do not come easy, she thought, they always come with a price. The ridges on her back proved that. Her next words dragged mournfully. "We have more pressing things to dwell on this morning. Prince and Beulah's baby is holding back. I don't know what's holding the child. She's carrying low. It's her time now."

"The baby will come soon. And I'm sure Uncle Prince will be just fine."

"We have to stay on our knees, keep sending up prayers," Grandmother said after another long suck on her pipe. "It's our job and the Lord's order, Girlie, to keep this family strong."

The pair continued on, knowing that something else was bound to catch them up, for in the heart of Birchtown lay misery so thick it stank like rotting flesh. The miserable makeshift shacks sprawled in all directions. To the left was the Thomas place. Across the way was the Joneses' and, further on, the Haywoods'. Birchtown was lively at this hour with folks cooking over outdoor fires and doing the wash while others hauled carts and lugged bags and goods on their backs.

Lydia and Sarah circled the maze of shelters, sidestepping the roaming chickens, hogs and sheep. It was then that they noticed

Dinah Haywood standing a few feet from her shack in a frayed blue dress with a yellow rag tied around her head, bawling.

"Troubles, Dinah?" Grandmother asked.

"A man came and took my Isaac," the woman wailed. "He accused him of being a runaway. He didn't ask if he had papers, just shackled his hands. And he put a rope around his neck. Off he went with my man tied to the back of his saddle. It makes not a drop of sense. We free people," she wailed. "We free."

Sarah watched as Dinah fell to her knees in the mud, feeling the sharpness of the woman's pain. She thought of the man hanging from the tree. Isaac Haywood? But she held her tongue and suppressed the tears, waiting to hear what Grandmother would say to the grief-stricken woman.

"What did the man look like?" Grandmother asked as she reached out and touched Dinah's shoulder.

"He was tall. A lanky-looking fella in a brown coat."

"No telling, but it could be Boll weevil Carter," Grandmother grunted. "They say he's here in Scotia. Ah, that devil. He's up to his old ways, sneaking about looking for mischief or to make money."

"Yes, yes. You said a mouthful there," Dinah wailed, not letting up.

"I know your pain. The troubles never tire of finding us. I got them too. You've heard, no doubt, about my son."

"Yes, Ma'am, I heard."

"I'd stay awhile, but I'm in a hurry this morning. We will send up prayers for you and Isaac," Grandmother said as she turned to go. "You're welcome to come by tomorrow, Dinah, if you feel like talkin'."

"No need to steal her hope. She's got enough on her plate," Grandmother said when they were far enough off for Dinah not to hear. "That ol' Mr. Misery is as excited as a Manhattan pickpocket in a crowd. You never know who he's goin' to rob next." She was silent for a long time before she turned to Sarah and muttered, "This place is as cruel as the weather."

Sarah looked at her hard, for everything about the place was a betrayal of promises. She longed for something better, but dared not speak it or even dream it. "Yes, it is, Ma'am," were the only words she could rally.

Two

To Sarah's torment, gunshots, smoke, wailing, murder and Boll weevil Carter were as much a part of her life in Nova Scotia as they had been on the plantation.

Sarah had been no more than thirteen when life on the Redmond estate had changed from what had felt normal to one of strange happenings and unknown fear. It had been a hot July night when Papa suddenly awakened her from a sound sleep. "Don't be afraid," he said as he stirred her. His voice was anxious and came in gentle whispers. "Be quiet and don't wake the others."

Sarah stumbled sleepily into the darkness around the back of the hut. The scent of honeysuckle and magnolia glided on a light night breeze, calming her senses.

"A visitor's coming tonight with news about the war and slaves," Fortune said. Sarah did not question her father, but stood staring into the uneasy quiet. A visitor at this hour? Whenever the quarters stirred at night, there was trouble afoot.

"I need you to keep your eyes and ears open. Boll weevil will be making the rounds soon." He patted her on the shoulder as they stood in the chilling darkness. Fortune took out a long candle and lit it.

It was not long before a man came sneaking around the side of the quarters. It was Ebenezer, a former Redmond slave. "You got word that I was coming?" he asked.

"There were murmurs."

"Are there others wanting to hear the news?"

"No, not here, but two the next hut over."

Sarah was nervous. She watched Ebenezer pull a piece of paper from his jacket. "I have a notice," he said. "This here is a copy of a proclamation." Sarah marvelled at the Negro in uniform. Excitement flickered in her dark brown eyes as she gawked at the stranger.

"You know that battles are raging to the north," Ebenezer said. "The British have taken Boston. It's a good sign. But the Patriots are making gains and the British cannot hold the colonies without more men." Ebenezer pointed to the paper. "It says here they are offering freedom to slaves who escape and join their army."

Fortune's eyes glowed like hot coals, but the idea of slaves taking up arms troubled him. Sarah had heard similar news at the Big House. The call of a hoot owl caused her to jump. She searched the eerie blackness. Seeing nothing unusual about, she turned again to listen.

"This is our chance, Fortune. It may not come again," Ebenezer said.

Fortune scratched his head.

"When the war is over, it says here the British will grant freedom to your family. Yes, freedom. Imagine that. But the prize is that you will get land and provisions in one of their colonies. That's the promise."

Fortune ripped off a piece of tobacco and chewed fiercely. He didn't answer, but looked at Sarah, then stared at the ground. Could he trust such a promise? Freedom, land and provisions— it sounded too good to be true. The bright flame from the candle flickered across Fortune's ebony face and Sarah saw worry wash over it like a sudden storm.

With his eyes darting about the woods, Ebenezer added, "The slave owners are still fussing over whether to let their slaves join the fight. The slaves want their freedom now. They are not waiting for permission."

LONG DAYS AND NIGHTS BROUGHT A HEAP OF AGONY. Freedom stole Sarah's thoughts. She found it hard to imagine being free to think for herself and act like white folks or like Mr. Thompson, the old Negro who'd bought his freedom and delivered feed to the plantation. But she'd heard terrible stories of those who stole away. And yet, her head buzzed with Ebenezer's words. "This is our chance. It may not come again." Which would Papa choose?

Not until the full moon night, when Sarah stood under the sweeping cypress behind the sleeping quarters, did the answer come. The moon glowed bright, but the crickets, owls and frogs were silent, making the stillness feel unnatural. Fortune held a small brown sack in one hand and hugged her shoulders with the other. "I'm leaving tonight to join the British army, the Black Pioneers," he whispered. "Watch yourself, Babygirl, and don't be afraid." He squeezed her tighter. "I promise we will be together again. I'll find you when the war's over, no matter how long it takes. You and Grandmother will have to be strong. I'll pray for you every day."

"I am going to miss you, Papa," Sarah murmured. "I'll pray, too."

"This war will not last long. Everyone is hungry to get their due. I'm doing this to earn our freedom, but if something happens, you must look after your grandmother." Fortune's face clouded with sadness. "She's been carrying a heavy burden all these years. She has a lot balled up inside, things that she has kept to herself. It's all just waiting to spill out."

"What's she got all balled up?"

Two soft whistles drifted across the magnolia-sweetened blackness. Fortune gave Sarah a long hug. "It's time to go," he said. "Say good-bye to the old woman, Prince and Beulah. No matter what happens, try to keep this family together."

Watching her father slide quietly away into the darkness, Sarah whispered, "Be safe." She swelled with pride, but it did not stop the tears.

The next morning, Sarah and Grandmother were busy polishing silverware at the Big House when Sarah turned to Grandmother and asked, "Will there be much to do today?"

"Yes, Chile. British officers are coming for lunch in the grand dining room." She looked away towards the window and Sarah could see that she was troubled. "I don't know what came over Fortune. He just up and left without a word."

In a low voice, not to be overheard, Sarah said, "Papa wanted to say good-bye, but they kept you here at the Big House."

"Yes, Lord. People coming and going. Everyone talking about the war and losing slaves." Grandmother looked about, then said softly, "What are these slaves thinking, running off to join some black army? Freedom. Well, well. It could even be the uniforms."

"Papa did it for us."

Grandmother slipped her pipe into her mouth and chomped down hard. "Can any of this be true? Has everyone lost their senses?"

"Everyone is talking about freedom. The slaves just caught the fever. Uncle Prince says the men are tired of the whip, of being called boys and animals. They long for a chance to prove they are men." Sarah's voice turned dreamy. "They want a chance to gain their freedom. That's all."

"Oh my. Can we gain anything without a fight?"

"I heard Master Redmond say he'd rather be ruled by the king than a bunch of rebels with nothing to offer but gab and blood."

"A Loyalist, he calls himself. Prince overheard a man in town say, 'Loyalists are traitors.' Some have even been murdered."

"I'm worried, Ma'am," Sarah said.

"Oh, Chile, something's in the wind. Something frightful."

UPON HIS RETURN FROM A SHORT STAY IN NEW YORK, Mr. Redmond gathered his family in the parlour. He asked that Grandmother and Sarah join them. His news was unexpected: They were leaving Goose Creek. He had joined a group called the Port Roseway Associates—Loyalists who were promised property and provisions in the British colony of Nova Scotia.

Sarah's heart sank when he ordered them to ready his prized belongings to store on *Jupiter* in Charles Town Harbour. He explained that when the crops were finished and accounts settled, he, his family and slaves would go to New York, then on to Port Roseway.

After that, Sarah found the plantation more worrisome than usual. It was in the air and in the way Master Redmond walked and looked at the slaves with the most despicable snarl. Sarah noticed that visitors were rare now. And Boll weevil Carter and Cecil MacLeod, the foreman and overseer, were meaner than usual. Now they were counting the slaves morning and night and watching their every move, and Sarah was terrified her father's absence would soon be noticed. Finally, one scorching day, footsteps pounded the dirt outside the hut with loud thuds. The door flew open and there stood Cecil, face twisted, eyes bulging red balls.

"The devil," Lydia murmured and drew back, for the overseer was in a hot rage.

"Where's that boy of yours?" he howled. "We were one ploughman short today!"

Sarah was on guard, watchful of every move and word. She imagined herself or Grandmother dragged behind Cecil's horse to the wheelhouse and beaten until the truth oozed out of them. She feared that every breath would be her last. Man, woman or child—none was safe from Cecil's hands.

"I don't know, Sir," Lydia replied with her eyes cast downward.

"It won't do you any good to protect him. Tell the truth, woman!" He hauled back with a short whip and struck her across the face.

A terrible sickness came over Sarah as the blood streamed down her grandmother's face. Her stomach knotted and her legs went weak.

"I was busy at the Big House," Lydia sobbed, "what with the British coming and going."

Sarah took a deep breath. She had to stay strong, like Papa said. She stared at the floor, combating the rising sobs and sudden stomach cramps.

"Your lies won't protect him or you," Cecil sneered. He turned to Sarah, keeping his gaze on her for a long time before turning back to Lydia. "We plan to take the dogs out in the morning and you better pray that we don't find him."

Sarah's head was spinning, but she willed herself to stand tall and keep the terror and pain at bay until Cecil left. Then she collapsed into a heap on the dirt floor.

Three

THE RAIN STOPPED AND THE EASTERN HORIZON SETTLED into long streams of pink sky above the fields where Sarah was picking cotton. Out of nowhere sounded the call of a blaring bugle announcing the Patriots' charge. Suddenly, Goose Creek filled with the exploding echoes of cannons. Fumes from gunpowder and smoke swallowed the air. Sarah cut short her picking and dropped her bag on the ground. She ran as fast as her legs would go to the quarters. Standing on the step for a moment, she watched soldiers plunder everything they could find: pots, utensils, bedding, equipment, horses, cattle, feed and hay. As streaks of blue, white and gold dashed in and out of the stables, barns and Big House, panic claimed her and her heart skipped a beat.

Inside the hut, Sarah found Grandmother grabbing up the few treasures she had hidden under her bunk—a small wooden box, papers, some coloured head rags, pipes and shoes. Sarah got her counting stick, a bone-handled hairbrush and ribbons and they tied the things in blankets.

The next minute, a loud shot and bone-chilling screams cut through the troubled air. Outside the quarters, Sarah and Grandmother watched as flames shot from the Big House windows. Missy Redmond and her daughter, Margaret, left the grounds in a carriage with several soldiers riding beside them.

Two soldiers carried Master Redmond's bloody body from the Big House veranda and dumped him in the woods not far from the house.

Grandmother started to sob—a reaction that puzzled Sarah. Slaves were not so fond of their masters they would grieve so openly, so deeply. It was as though she had suffered the pain of the bullet herself. Sarah had no time to ponder dark secrets all mixed up in the crumbling house.

"They had no right to kill Master Redmond," Sarah blurted.

"It was done out of hatred," Grandmother said.

"What will they do with Missy Redmond and Margaret?"

"Hand them over to the British, I expect. That was the promise."

"And us?"

"I don't know," Grandmother said. "I don't know."

Danger hung on the evening air. The two women were jittery and anxious. Sarah watched Cecil MacLeod, his wife and Boll weevil Carter come from around the charred stable and flee into the woods in a wagon loaded with goods.

The soldiers set fire to the barns, the stables and the storehouses. Only the slave quarters remained.

"Grandmother," Sarah said, "The fire has set us free. Master Redmond is gone. We have no master."

There was not a moment left to think. The thick air filled with screams of slaves hustling in and out of the quarters. "Run. Run. The soldiers are coming."

It was a wild run. They scattered unarmed like frightened squirrels into the night. Crouching in the river reeds, cowering, Grandmother, Prince and Beulah squatted beside Sarah. They watched the soldiers move about. "Take the Loyalist slaves to Charles Town for evacuation!" their captain directed.

Sarah strained to smother her gasping as the old woman's

body trembled and her prayer became a series of mumbles. "Dear Father, show us mercy … Deliver us … Amen."

So many soldiers raced along the river's edge, their eyes searching, searching. How they sniffed about like wild dogs yearning for a feast of flesh. Sarah ducked lower but the soldiers foraged with muskets and bayonets until they found their reward. Despite the captain's strict orders to hold their fire, the soldiers discharged their guns on any slaves who dared try and escape.

"Twelve miles to Charles Town. Move along. March." They left the dead, feeble and injured behind, ignoring their pitiful cries, leaving them without any means to survive.

A long, dry road stretched ahead. Two lines, thirty-five slaves in total. They marched, their heads down, some shoeless and ragged. Sarah fell into step. She dared not speak, but she worried over what would become of them in Charles Town. Would they be set free or forced to work on another plantation? Perhaps the soldiers would shoot them as they had Master Redmond and the other slaves.

The moon hid. The wagons squawked. The slaves moaned. In the torch light, Sarah watched Brodie motion to his brother Bill with a nod that said, "Join me in an escape." Bill turned his head away, but for a second something stirred in Sarah … the idea of an escape intrigued her. The thought came late, for just as she was thinking it, Brodie turned and ran. In a patch of hickory to the left of the road, a small musket ball lodged between his shoulders and he was felled like a deer. Sarah cringed with revulsion and shock. It could have been her lying in the woods.

She marched on, the future a huge, grey, worrisome space. Everything she had ever known was gone. Five miles along, the parade halted. Ahead lay a small clearing surrounded by trees and bushes. One of the soldiers said, "The men are exhausted, Sir. We've been on the road for days with little time to rest."

The captain answered, "We will make camp here and take a break before going into Charles Town."

Sarah could barely move her feet. Her grimy clothes stuck to her back. Her aunt and uncle leaned like bent willows. Grandmother drooped from exhaustion and thirst. One of the soldiers approached her, pointed his musket and barked, "Stand up tall, old slave woman." A wide grin strained his face. Sarah's heart went still. Grandmother's eyes held the eyes of the soldier. "Better not get too close," she gasped. "I still got the fever from the pox. It took a lot of folks to the Glory Land."

The soldier's grin faded. He shouted, "Stay away from the old woman. Had smallpox." Sarah laughed quietly. She was cunning, that old woman. No doubt about it.

Sarah was amazed by the noise and activity that filled the camp. Chains and leg-irons rattled as the soldiers secured the slaves. Hammers pounded the soil to erect tents for the officers. Soldiers secured the livestock and guarded their spoils. The stench of scorched beef tainted the air. Owls screeched, whippoorwills called and neither Sarah nor Grandmother could rest. They kept watch throughout the night, huddled together for protection.

With morning came a meal of hard biscuits, beef and tea so strong it looked like molasses. With the sun climbing over the horizon, the weary soldiers screamed and cussed as they readied their loads and unchained their captives.

It was a slow trek across a once-beautiful countryside. War had spread its ugly hand over Carolina, seeding a bitter hatred. It left a long red trail of stubborn resisters. Everywhere, bodies lay blood-soaked, some with holes as large as melons. Rancid odours smothered the thick heat. Sarah wondered if the price for freedom was always blood. She wondered if her papa had paid the price.

When the band of slaves reached Charles Town, it greeted them not only with unsightly rubble and confusion, but also beautiful stately homes and buildings that mesmerized Sarah. They camped on the side of the road with the free Negroes, military men and white Loyalists. They lined the torn-up roads and docks at the Charles Town port, receiving rations from the British. Even though she was tired and often hungry, Sarah rejoiced in her new freedom, wandering about and marvelling at new things. This alone boosted her spirits. At night, she stretched out on the grass and felt almost weightless—a bag of fluffy cotton. As she gazed at the stars, she imagined a glorious fate. If preacher was right, freed slaves went to the Promised Land where all their needs were met.

Two weeks dragged by. In that time most of the white Loyalists had sailed on, leaving the rest in a cloud of worry. Then, finally, a British Red Coat hung an announcement on a lone, charred tree. Steppin' John, the Redmond blacksmith, stared at the notice. Beside him stood a tall young slave.

"Look here," Steppin' John shouted, rallying the scruffy flock with his bullish yells. "It says we will be taken to Manhattan, New York, on February 12, 1783, and from there to a British settlement." Then he added, "That's in another week. The ships will be coming soon. May the good Lord be with us."

"New York." Sarah choked back the words. Her heart was numb. Where on earth was New York? She wondered how far it was from Carolina.

The young slave looked out at the crowd and shouted, "The British have promised Steppin' John more blankets, food and water. Remember to carry your belongings with you at all times."

Sarah could not turn her eyes from the young man. He was muscular like most slaves, maybe eighteen, and fair with golden skin like the wheat in the fields. His eyes flashed as he spoke. The curve of his jaw was like her father's—square with a fat round ball for a chin. A new and glorious feeling rose from the pit of her stomach, a feeling so profound that in the midst of all that commotion she felt warm and lightheaded. The slave shifted uneasily. As he scanned the crowd, marvelling at such a number, their eyes met for an instant and, to her surprise, he smiled. Sarah wondered if they would go to the same settlement.

THE SHIP CARRYING THE EX-SLAVES FROM CHARLES TOWN crawled up the mouth of the Hudson River amid hundreds of sailing ships and men-of-war. At the huge city of Manhattan, Sarah and her family disembarked, joining the thousands of Negroes who relied on British provisions. They slept in parks and roamed the Negro areas or stayed on the docks while awaiting send-off to a British settlement.

Companies of British soldiers were everywhere. Sarah ignored Grandmother's advice to stay put and roamed up and down the long wharf and nearby streets focusing on her one task—finding her father. She was cautious, very cautious, keeping her eyes open for slave masters and hunters roving about to reclaim runaways without certificates. Those with their master's brand on their foreheads, arms or necks had no choice but to go with their rightful owners. Sarah saw men seized who produced certificates, only to have them torn up and be led away in shackles. She could not look in their faces. Such a short taste of freedom, she thought. She moved like a cat among the buildings, wondering if her father, perhaps out of uniform or without a certificate, went back to Charles Town in chains as well. In her prayers, she pleaded for a sighting. After days of searching, her prayers went unanswered.

Drained from all the uncertainty as their wait stretched from fearful days to weeks and then months, the ex-slaves grew anxious to move on. Finally, in early spring, after three months of waiting, the day of departure came.

The air was warm and humid inside a dilapidated building on the wharf. A line stretched and coiled like an enormously long black snake for several blocks. Men in long black coats and soldiers sorted through the masses. A British soldier directed Sarah and her family to a table where a man in a red and white uniform dipped a long white quill in a bottle of ink and wrote their names in a large ledger called "The Book of Negroes."

She watched as he added all four of them to the list.

Book Three, Inspection Rolls
Brig Molly, *bound 16 May 1783 for Port Roseway*

Prince Redmond, *32, stout Negro man, formerly slave*
   to Edward Redmond, Charles Town, South Carolina.
   (Certificate from General Birch)
Beulah Thomkins, *26, ordinary wench, thin. Formerly*
   slave to Edward Redmond, Charles Town, South
   Carolina. (Certificate from General Birch)
Lydia Redmond, *50, stout Negress. Formerly slave to*
   Edward Redmond, Charles Town, South Carolina.
   (Certificate from General Birch)
Sarah Redmond, *15, likely girl. Formerly slave to*
   Edward Redmond, Charles Town, South Carolina;
   goes with grandmother, Lydia.
   (Certificate from General Birch)

A man in a white wig with a long speaking trumpet startled her when he announced, "You must have your name recorded in order to board a ship." A second man at the table assigned them to travel with a company of Black Pioneers. They each received a certificate and a ticket to board the vessel, *Molly*, headed to Port Roseway, Nova Scotia.

Grandmother gazed at her Certificate of Freedom for a long time. "My, my! Oh my Lord. A Certificate of Freedom." The words kept rolling off her tongue. When Sarah received hers, she longed to be able to read it. She held it tenderly, for it was the first piece of writing she had ever held. Grandmother took both certificates, folded them into neat squares and opened her raggedy bundle, but instead of putting them in it, she searched out a long hatpin and attached them to the inside neck of her dress. Sarah saw a wide smile capture Grandmother's face as she patted the papers tenderly. They both knew these prized papers owned their futures. To have something so valuable was not beyond their grasp.

In the early morning of June 18, 1873, Sarah, her family, other former slaves, military men, white Loyalists, slaves and servants by the thousands readied to board the transports. A man on the wharf shouted, "Thirty sails. Three thousand people." Another said that upon landing in Port Roseway any Negroes not on their list were to be shipped back to New York. Captain Randall Smith stood on the bow of *Molly* awaiting the completion of his inspection. The inspector finally presented Captain Smith with a certified list of whites and Negroes: the time had come to depart.

"We are casting off for Nova Scotia," the captain finally screamed. "All Loyalists ticketed for *Molly* come aboard. Negroes go below deck."

Suddenly, *Molly* was pulling away. Below deck, Sarah envisioned the flapping sails as great white wings stretched across the sea. It was a slow, choppy ride at first. Soon, the voyage turned into a bad dream. Overhead, high winds howled as they lashed the sails and salt spray blasted through slits in the boards. Things rattled and rolled and hit the floor above. As *Molly* tossed about like an empty canister atop fifteen-foot waves, Sarah's heart rose and fell with it. The screams of white Loyalists sent chills along her spine as she ricocheted back and forth, struggling to stay alive and keep from being sick.

On the fourth day the weather calmed. Sarah strained her eyes and neck in search of familiar faces. She found Aunt Beulah and Uncle Prince standing at the far side of the hold, clinging tightly to each other. By the fifth day, the crowded space in the ship's belly had bloated with heat and unbearable odours. Sarah's empty stomach heaved continually and she nibbled on bread and salt beef, only sipping the stale water. As Sarah fastened her arms around Grandmother's shoulders, she imagined the flow of memories the old woman must have of another Atlantic voyage. There were no chains this time and neither were the men and women separated, but true feelings of horror revealed themselves on the old woman's face.

Despite the hardship, all around, those who were not sick engaged in chatter about getting land and provisions and making a new life in the land of plenty. There, in the disgusting hole, tears of joy crept through. But this new and faraway place held little charm for Sarah when it was not of her choosing, when all it brought was much uncertainty for a former slave. Would freedom bring a return to humankind, a chance to make her own decisions, to live and breathe without fear and to one day have a family?

four

O N THE NINTH DAY, THE NOVA SCOTIA COAST CAME into view. *Molly* sliced through the rising fog to a shoreline of wharves, scattered buildings and huts. The ship headed in to moor in Port Roseway harbour amid the disquieting awe of the passengers.

Sarah was anxious to leave the ship, breathe fresh air and get a glimpse of her new homeland. When at last the time came for the Negroes to disembark, they raised loud, boisterous cheers. Sarah blinked hard and fast when she emerged from the ship's belly. Her confidence abandoned her. The contrast with her former home was extreme. A vast breastwork of slate and rock and sand stretched along the ocean and inland to meet thick greenery. All of it merged into a palette of every muddled shade of green, grey, brown and blue. This was it? The place Big Moss, the preacher, spoke of as "The Sweet Freedom Land."

Sarah hesitated and stepped back, terrified of leaving the ship, afraid of perishing in the wilderness, for the only signs of existence were several clusters of buildings and rows of houses in lines that cut across each other. The land was rough, covered in boulders, trees and underbrush. Tents and pole huts were pitched everywhere. "Uncivilized," she heard someone say. Her fear amplified as she envisioned some great creature lurking within the steamy woods, ready to snatch her up.

Sarah stood on the wharf, drowning in the persistent cheers and chatter. How the white Loyalists' tongues wagged about starting life over and becoming prosperous. They spoke of their determination to create a great city to rival New York. Sarah listened and watched in dismay at all the commotion. The sight of the town paralyzed her — her expectations had been of greater things.

A Roseway Associate, a plump man in a red coat, approached them with a long sheet of paper. She listened carefully as he welcomed them. He gave his name as Joseph Pyncheon, a founding father. He said that the people he called by name from his list were to go with him. He read only the names of the highest-ranking white officers, lieutenants, captains, colonels and sergeants. Sarah's eyes followed as this group left with their families, slaves and indentured Negroes. They scattered about the new settlement and disappeared into the meagre dwellings of Port Roseway. Shortly after their departure, servants came and quickly unloaded the furniture and other household goods belonging to the first lot of settlers.

Mr. Pyncheon returned and met separately with the remaining white Loyalists — disbanded soldiers, southern estate owners whose lands the Patriots had confiscated, tradesmen and adventurers. He informed these men that Port Roseway could not accommodate them until more lots were surveyed. He offered them lodging aboard the ships and sloops in the harbour and gave them permission to pitch tents on the Public Ground. The grumbling and cursing that followed became so out of hand that a band of Red Coats was called in. After assurances their wait would be short, that surveyors were hard at work and building materials were arriving daily, the settlers left to make arrangements.

Mr. Pyncheon finally dealt with the remaining settlers— the free Negroes—ordering them to wait on the wharf and be patient. Sarah and the others sat in the welcome warmth of the blazing sun for most of the day, hungry and bewildered. The nearby streets sloping upward from the wharf were full of Negroes going about their business—women walking with white children, going in and out of shops and homes; men working on new structures, carrying lumber on their backs or piling supplies onto ox carts. The activity reminded her of the plantation.

At last Mr. Pyncheon returned. He came with soldiers and barrels of water, boiled salt pork and bread. Sarah was grateful that she could finally stomach food. Pyncheon looked over the sorry lot with sharp blue eyes and a furrowed brow saying, "I regret that Governor Parr has not issued orders for your settlement. You'll receive some relief until separate land is set aside. Until orders come, you can stay at the black quarters here in Port Roseway. Be mindful that any caught roaming, begging or stealing will be whipped … What is your company and who is your leader?" he asked a man standing nearby.

Before that man could answer, a man in brown military dress stepped forward and said loudly, "Colonel Septimus Black at your service, Sir. A disbanded member of the South Carolina black Loyalist unit, the Black Pioneers, and the appointed leader of this company of Negroes."

Pyncheon frowned and asked, "Can you read and write?"

"Yes Sir."

"Well, well." Pyncheon faced the crowd. "Any complaints or needs will be handled by your leader, Colonel Septimus Black." He raised his hand to his forehead and wiped the sweat from his brow. "Your rations will be distributed through him," he puffed.

Sarah's family settled into the black quarters while hundreds of others arrived daily on ships. Two weeks later, they gathered in a group to hear Benjamin Marston, the chief surveyor. His news was good. The provincial secretary had issued an order to the magistrates to situate the Negroes on the northwest arm of Shelburne Harbour. He joked and laughed and Sarah warmed to his friendly tone. The next morning, Marston filled his sloop with free Negroes. This time Sarah stood on deck. A place to call home at last, she thought.

Such cheering as Marston's boat approached the arm! Sarah's spirited shouts of joy mingled with the rest. But when the anchor was lowered, Sarah's jaw fell. To her dismay, there was neither a building nor a hut in sight, just rocks and woods so thick not a bit of light came through. She waded ashore with the others where they were met by Pyncheon. He informed them that this was to be their new home. Then he ordered the Negroes to take to the woods and do what they could to survive.

THE CHATTER, THE PRAYERS AND THE SERMONS ... IT HAD ALL been about "gettin' some of that 'sweet freedom land' and riches." Well, Sarah was fast realizing that this new Birchtown was a far cry from that.

Colonel Black, being of high rank, built a comfortable house with a garden on a large lot. The remaining Negroes would have to wait for surveyors to lay out their land.

When winter came, unfamiliar cold took many lives, for they had nothing to fend it off with. Sarah and Grandmother gathered materials, sought rations and tramped back and forth to Roseway to work. They scavenged for usable materials, goods and clothing in Port Roseway. They made baskets, and Uncle Prince built make-shift carts and sleds to transport things. They pooled their money and got themselves chickens and a pig. With no buildings for shelter, they lived in a pit house—a hole in the ground supported by rocks and a roof of long poles and spruce branches.

With the first spring came hope, more rations and shacks.

Prince and a few Birchtown men helped Grandmother build a small dwelling. Sarah helped too. They used rough logs and poles stuffed with mud and moss, and put up a pitched roof. The only door opened into a tiny rectangular room with one small window fitted with a thick sheet of canvas, a fire pit made of rocks in the floor, a table and chairs shaped with an axe, two shelves holding dishes and pots and a table for water buckets. Along the opposite wall was a small wooden bunk. The air was always thick with smoke and the aroma of food cooking. A canvas curtain partitioned off a space at the back for sleeping. There was barely room for two small bunks, a washstand and hooks for hanging clothes. Behind the hut was a dug well and a small dump.

They enjoyed fish, sometimes a little wild meat, venison, rabbit or porcupine, and gathered wild apples and good-tasting berries in season. They often received vegetables, dairy goods or bread in exchange for work.

Grandmother kept to herself, though Sarah preferred company. She tried hard not to complain, at least not aloud, but she could see how the worry and strain creased Grandmother's face in ever-deepening lines as she tried to keep their spirits up, pleading with God to spare the last of her "brood." Sarah worried too. There was no telling if her father would ever return.

Under the bleak clouds of poverty, Sarah watched with interest as the settlement began to take shape, what with its endless paths, hustle and bustle, and strange goings-on. Hundreds of unsightly shacks sprang up as more freed slaves, runaways and rough characters came to Birchtown, many with all manner of disabilities attributed to the war or misfortune. Fifteen hundred free Negroes. It was not a safe place, but as time pressed on, a little of the fear and some of the daily aching lifted from Sarah's spirit. In all that squalor and misery, she was grateful and managed a smile from time to time.

Five

THE MORNING AIR WAS WARMING AND THE DARK SKY brightening as the frost lifted from the Birchtown trail. At first a mere footpath cut through the trees, the trail was now worn and widened from the daily travels of hundreds to and from Roseway—a bustling town with homes, businesses and warehouses.

It was only a mile more to Prince and Beulah's place. Sarah stepped aside to let a man hauling a cart filled with wood go by. She turned to Grandmother and out of the blue said, "I never dreamed of such a dreadful place. There are days I yearn for home."

Grandmother looked at Sarah, her face drawn tight. "Why on earth would you do that, Girlie?"

"I miss having chores and good food—sweet potatoes, melons, peanuts and greens, and I miss the music and dancing. Such fun. And the sermons and singing at the camp meetings, too. Do you miss it?"

"I do think on it sometimes." Grandmother stopped for a minute. "Oh, that revolution. War shakes things up and brings about something different. Maybe the Lord was telling everyone that it was time for a change."

"Nothing left but the memories," Sarah droned.

"Yes, yes, the pain of memories. You be careful, Girlie. Things we thought we left behind will haunt us. We must think on mending our lives like patching an old pair of breeches. We must find our way here." She rubbed the wooden ring on her finger and said, "We must keep the bad juju away." Grandmother slowed down and her voice softened. "Some of mine never got to see this old world. Others be snatched from me. Oh Lord, I pray that one day I will get to see all my children ... before I go to Glory." Her words trailed off and there was no mistaking the pain behind the grief.

Sarah was confused. Grandmother had two sons: Sarah's papa, Fortune, who had gone off and joined the revolution, and his younger brother, Prince, who was married to Beulah. Were there others? She looked off in the distance and brushed aside her eagerness to learn more about the past and this woman who seemed just as much a stranger as any of the other Birchtowners.

Sarah shifted her baskets. Slavery had denied them their right to have a real family. They had been the master's property and he had the right to sell children, mothers and fathers, scattering them to the wind. She wondered if there was any chance of the old woman's longing coming true. Would it be possible for her to find her other children? Was it possible that they might be here in Nova Scotia?

"There's not much family left," Sarah said.

"We have each other and your Uncle Prince and Aunt Beulah for now."

"There are four of us and one more on the way. That's five." Sarah grinned. It was her mother who had taught her numbers and words. How different her mother had been from the woman marching ahead with her feet coming down hard on the ground. Grandmother's words were always sharp, to the point, while Dahlia's light-hearted nature had caught people up.

Sarah pictured her mother in the driving heat of the midday sun. Saw her walking the mile-long rows with her dress drenched in sweat as she filled her bags with cotton. Saw her scooping out food and placing it in hollowed gourds from the barrels Mr. MacLeod brought to the fields. By day, she lit up the fields with her spirituals. By night, while Sarah kept watch for Cecil, slaves gathered round to hear Dahlia spin magical tales of Africa, of casting out spells, of romance and of people gone missing in the middle of the night. "A sweet woman," Papa had said. "She be the scented sap running through a honeysuckle vine."

Dahlia had loved to read. She learned how by sneaking off with Mingo, an escaped slave who returned to the plantations late at night. He taught them by drawing numbers and letters on the ground. One day Dahlia and another slave were standing by a wagon loaded with barrels of rice. The words on the barrel rolled off her tongue: "Carolina Rice, Finest Quality, 25 Pounds." When she turned and saw Cecil, she knew there was trouble. He grabbed her hard by the arm. She tried to tell him that she was just repeating words she had heard. Cecil sneered, tied her to his horse and dragged her to the wheelhouse. "Chop one thumb off," he told one of the slaves. Sarah had gathered wild herbs and made a potion to bathe the thumb.

Sarah shook her head to toss off the memory, slowed her pace, for her heart suddenly grew almost too heavy to carry.

Grandmother took a long drag on her pipe as Sarah plodded along. Pointing upward, she said, "The sun's far from overhead. We're making good time. I trust Prince is holding on."

The wooden ring on her finger, polished with pig grease, caught the light and shone like a diamond. The ring unsettled Sarah. Where had she seen another like it?

"What are you thinking about now, Girlie?" Grandmother asked, for she had never known anyone as busy in the head as Sarah, always with a clever thought or something new to say.

Not wanting to mention the ring, and trying to lighten the air, Sarah said, "Oh, I'm just thinking about the get-togethers for the big feeds after harvest. When the music from the spoons, washboards and calabashes got our feet to stirring. Do you remember ol' Plenty Fat, what a good dancer he was? That slave sure could make the dry earth crack with his stepping." She envisioned the man's high jumps and twirls and how he could kick up his heels like a crazy mule, and she chuckled.

"The Lord will remember all that carrying on. He sure will. He cannot step his sorry self into heaven. There's none of that allowed up there." Grandmother let out a turkey chuckle. "Yes Lord, none of that goin' to be allowed up there."

With that, Sarah stopped her chatter. Surely freedom was not so narrow—some stuffy old woman smothered in snarls and fear. Sarah wondered if Grandmother had ever felt the belly-shaking joy of laughter in her pitiful and cruel life, always with child and nothing but work.

The pair tramped along cautiously, crossing Ackers Brook. Now walking with baskets swinging, Sarah joyfully turned her thoughts to the Charles Town slave, as she called him. It had been several weeks after their arrival in Nova Scotia before she'd had a sighting of him. The first had come after finishing a day's work for Mrs. Atkins. She had been making her way up a dusty road past the Anglican Church when she spotted him several yards away. She'd hurried to catch up, but making her way along a street packed with folks rushing back to Birchtown proved difficult. When the crowd thinned, he had vanished. It upset her that folks had to rush, but she did not want to be found in Roseway after the six o'clock curfew. Just two months earlier, the white residents of Roseway, accusing the Negroes of lowering wages, formed a huge mob and rioted. With clubs and arms they wandered the streets for days, pulling down or burning Negro houses and chasing them out of town. Finally, the magistrate imposed a curfew from dusk to dawn to keep order. Thinking about it made Sarah cringe. It was so unfair to use a curfew to punish the Negroes instead of those who caused the trouble.

Another time she had seen him at the Roseway Wharf, where she had gone after work to look for fresh fish for Grandmother. He gave her a quick nod with a tip of his cap That was the day she learned his name—Reece Johnson. On this September morning, his name played a thousand times in her head. Perhaps today she would run into him again.

She and Grandmother had walked a good distance when Sarah stopped to watch a blue heron gracefully swoop down and skim across the bog. She looked kindly at Grandmother. Why it was so difficult for her to enjoy life or to talk about the past? Papa had been right. All her living was balled up inside.

Unbeknownst to Sarah, Grandmother had been keeping a close eye to her. Grandmother's mouth squeezed to the side of her face. "You best let go of the past and think on getting ready for this life in Scotia," she exclaimed. "It won't be soft candy." Surprisingly she added, "Good times do come around once in awhile, but don't be thinking the way some folks do. Look over there, Girlie, lying in the grass. My, my. Such a pitiful sight."

"It's just Cato."

"Yes, and drunk no doubt from the poison and goings-on last night. How is acting like that going to raise us up? Good times, all right. Being strong is better than being weak. You remember that, Girlie."

The noise of an approaching cart forced them to the side of the road. Four Black Pioneers sent out a loud greeting as they moved slowly past.

"The Pioneer uniforms remind me of Papa," Sarah said.

"Fortune joining the Red Coats was a sad day. No need to be talking about him now, Girlie. I swear your mind is like a bee going from flower to flower."

"Maybe Papa made it. Maybe he is somewhere in the colony. No one is saying he was killed."

"Maybe so, but Colonel Black has already made it clear that he has no knowledge of the missing soldiers. They got scattered, the healthy and the wounded, and put on different ships at war's end. So slow your hopes down, Girlie. Don't you get carried away with the tide."

After rounding a huge boulder, the pair came across some men raising the rafters on a small hut. Sarah's heart raced when she saw that one of the men was Reece Johnson. She stole quick glances in his direction, knowing that if the old woman had any inkling of the thoughts in her head, she would drag her down to the river for a confession and a quick baptism. Reece was busy passing poles to one of the men. Sarah was thinking she must look a sight with a big blue bonnet pulled low on her face and a long grey coat in need of cleaning.

"Look," she suddenly said after spying the fish man. "Over there. Is that Enos? I hear folks saying the mackerel are running. Maybe he will come by, if you ask."

"I believe so," Grandmother said, wasting no time in leaving the path to hail Enos.

"Where are you going today, Miss Sarah?" Reece asked as Sarah approached the men.

"I'm going down to Roseway. I see you've found work."

"Work, yes. Pay, no. I was hoping I'd be able to use my trade."

"Trade?"

"I forged nails for the blacksmith, Steppin' John, back home."

"I saw you with him in Charles Town, but I never saw you on the plantation."

"That's because pretty girls weren't allowed around the black-smith shop."

Sarah warmed to his compliment. "There aren't many jobs now. What will you do?"

"I'll head up north, go whaling … there's good money in that."

Sarah sighed. "I see. Do you plan on leaving soon?"

Reece chuckled. "I'm waiting for a spot to open up." Reece twisted his stout shoulders and wide frame uncomfortably, like a little boy. "I can't talk now. Rod's giving me the eye. But I'll be at the camp meeting on Sunday."

A smile as long as the Mississippi stretched across Sarah's face. "I'll look for you." Sarah tingled in the bizarre feelings taking charge of her. Well, well, the Birchtown girls would wag their tongues on that since they all had their eyes on Reece.

Grandmother took several drags from her pipe as she made her way back to Sarah. She stared long and hard at Reece and cast a sour sneer in his direction. Then she turned her head and looked at her granddaughter, her face hardening with sternness. "Be careful about getting friendly with strangers, Girlie. Do not get lost in foolish feelings."

Sarah frowned and said nothing. Little did Grandmother know that she was already hopelessly lost.

Six

THE DOOR AT BEULAH'S HUT STOOD AJAR. LYDIA AND Sarah stood on the wobbly step of the crumbling shack, while Lydia bowed her head in prayer.

Fibby, Birchtown's midwife, sat at the table cutting out coloured squares from old rags for her quilt making. Her face was drawn and thin. Her short black braids pointed in every direction like the spines of a sea urchin. "She's resting now, waiting on her time," Fibby said, pointing to a narrow wooden bunk in the corner of the room.

"And Prince? How is Prince?"

Fibby pulled Lydia aside. "Hush, Lydia," she whispered, putting a finger to her mouth. "Beulah is taking it hard. Quiet now. Best not to excite her again. It will be two days. No one came by to take you word that Prince passed on. Come, I'll show you the pile."

Lydia followed Fibby quietly to the rear of the hut. Sarah trailed behind. There they saw a pile of rocks just barely covering a body. Lydia knelt beside the pile. She covered her face with her hands and sought comfort in weeping. Sarah knelt beside her and put her arms around her grandmother. Then followed the long moans and praying. And when all the suffering subsided, she and Sarah quietly went about gathering rocks to deepen the pile, making it so neat and high it looked like a tomb.

Back inside, Lydia let out a long, disturbing sigh and patted her chest several times as though she was preparing for a huge event and wanted to be ready.

Lydia looked at Beulah, who was sitting up now, and said softly, "You're carrying low. That is a good sign. Oh my, it will not be long." The old woman's fat fingers rolled around the mountainous belly. Her voice was gentle. "Everything will be alright," she cooed. "Yes it will." She continued rubbing Beulah's belly, staring, trance-like, far off, in a different world ... *A stout wench, broad and strong, good breeding stock*, the auctioneer had said.

She turned her face to Beulah and spoke in a low murmur, "I have to go now. I got to stop at Cecil's and then go down to Roseway this morning." She patted the belly once more saying, "I asked the good Lord to keep His eyes on you. He hears ol' Lydia." Then in a tender voice that was thin and not so matter-of-fact, she said, "This baby has a special calling, Beulah. It will be the first one in this family to be born free. Imagine that. Born free. A miracle, that's what."

"It's true, Mother Redmond. But it's not right that the child won't have a papa." Beulah pushed her tangled hair back. A tiny smile unfolded as she said, "Prince and I got married as soon as we got here. We had plans. We dared to dream. This place was going to be a new beginning. We planned to raise our children ... like proper folks." The soreness of her loss made her lips quiver. "Why did the Lord have to take Prince after getting free ... after all we came through?" The tears streamed down her face leaving long salty stains on her brown skin. "I keep trying, but I don't know how much more I can take." Beulah swallowed hard and her misery forced her to sob, and then more pain, and more sobs.

No one spoke. They waited for Fibby to get up and get some rags and the washbasin of warm water. But no, she sat tight and

Beulah kept sobbing until Lydia broke in saying, "Fibby, best get things ready. This must be her time."

"Not yet, Lydia," Fibby said. "I know the birthing pain. Those wails are not about the baby. They come from a dark place. She's heartsick, always thinking on Prince."

Lydia stroked Beulah's face. "Hush now. It will not be long before you are holding your child. There is joy in that." She was silent for a minute and then she said, "We made it this far. We got through the first winter. This family is growing." She looked at Sarah and smiled, "There will soon be four. We must always give thanks for that."

She placed her hand gently on Beulah's hair, patting it with her cupped palm as gently as a mother bear. "Don't you be worrying. This family sticks together. You won't have to raise your child alone, no Lord." She cradled Beulah's head in her lap and wiped her wet face with her coat sleeve. "Oh yes, Beulah, everything is going to be alright. You will see. God is good." The strains of old spirituals drifted from her lips.

Beulah dabbed away the tears with the edge of the blanket. She was ashen and pale and kept rolling the coarse blanket in her fingers as she rocked back and forth. The old woman squeezed her tightly, with joy hiding somewhere in the creases of her mouth, but her happiness did not last. For a second, she caught a strange look in Sarah's eyes. The girl was studying her intensely with a look of loathing. She knew the reason and felt guilty for withholding such tenderness from the young one. She knew it was another custom, a slave's way of avoiding attachment. She shrugged off Sarah's venom with a smile, for deep down she knew the girl could never hate her.

She turned back to Beulah and as much as she wanted to stay, she said, "Oh my, Beulah, we got to be on our way. The longer we stay the further Roseway gets."

"You're leaving?" Beulah asked.

"We will stop on the way back. You just might be a mama 'tween now and then. I guess that child is taking its good old time, but it cannot stay back forever. The Lord is good. Put your faith in Him to see this through."

Beulah's eyes strayed to the corner of the room. She turned to one side. Her face became mean and she said, "There's no God, Lydia. They made God up to keep folks like us from having our rightful place on this earth."

The old woman's eyes stretched three times their size and she said, "You rest, Beulah. You need more rest."

Beulah continued to stare away. "Your God makes no sense to me. Why would God allow so many folks to have so little and all this suffering? Why should we believe that we have to wait until we get to heaven when everything for our joy is right here? All this religion, it was the master's way of controlling the slaves, but who controlled the master?" Her eyes lit up like a firefly. "We were sent here to die, to rot in this hell." Beulah's head fell on her chest. "Say what you like, this place is going to be the death of us all." Her voice was sharp and angry. "You can have your God, Mother Redmond."

Fibby spoke up. "She gets this way. Oh my, ever since Prince passed she has been ranting and cursing God. The dear soul even curses me. I don't know how much more I can take, but after that baby comes, Old Fibby will be gone. I will see that the baby comes into the world, but after that, she is going to need someone to come and stay and help with the child."

Lydia was stunned. "Cursing God?" Her hands shook as she raised them up to heaven. "Sweet Lord," she said, "Pay her no mind. She is tired and angry, Lord. You got to be patient with this one. Amen."

Beulah's sudden change frightened Lydia. Maybe she was scared. Giving birth was a worrying thing. She thought about losing children, about Dahlia. How on one jet-black night she had awoke from a deep sleep to horrible screams. Screams so loud they could crack bones. A horrible birth, the worst see had seen. She saw Dahlia's newborn briefly, before the midwife declared the tiny bundle was off to Glory. She recalled that it was One Eye and Soldier who took Sarah's mother and the child away in a rickety cart. All the slaves in the quarter gathered in the yard and wept hard until the cart disappeared into the night.

Lydia turned to Fibby. "You do your best for her. She's not herself and needs your patience. This is her first."

On the trail, Lydia lagged behind, struggling with her thoughts. The sun was brighter now and the autumn leaves glistened. She looked through the trees up at the patch of blue sky and gave her fears and aching heart to the Lord, for the pain was too severe for her alone to bear.

Seven

T HEY WERE MAKING GOOD TIME. STREAMS OF BLACK smoke from the hundreds of crooked shacks streaked the sky. The busy sounds of wood-chopping, hammering and sawing hung in the air as they neared the Roseway Road. They waded through a stream where the women and children usually filled buckets, but this morning there was a line of men that stretched beyond to a nearby hut. "The water brigade," Grandmother said. Sure enough, within minutes, they could see wild flames shooting through the roof and walls of one of the shacks. It was devoured even as the men tried to dose it with water.

"I don't know why they bother trying to save these shacks," Sarah said. "They go up like pieces of paper, a couple every week. You never know the cause with so much hatred goin' on. I hope no one was inside."

"Not likely at this hour. Whoever it was has probably left for Roseway."

"Mrs. Atkins was saying last week that in Roseway someone started a grass fire during high winds and burned down two homes."

"Oh Sweet Lord, where are the people's senses?"

As they strolled through the centre of Birchtown, Sarah pointed to the men working on a large structure. "The new meeting house is going there. Everyone gets charged up on Sundays at Reverend Ringwood's camp meetings and then pours out the spirit during the week in their singing. Finally, there'll be a place for worship."

The old woman grunted. "Singing to the Lord to cover their sins."

"Still, maybe we could go to a camp meeting and get some of that spirit."

"My religion is between Lydia and the Lord. That's all I got to say on that."

Sarah held her tongue. She was accustomed to Grandmother's thick demeanour — a wall of bricks, tightly cemented without a crack. To Lydia, people were either God fearing or godless. The Birchtowners disliked her attitude and so they kept their distance, acting formal in their greetings, but always polite, respecting but not embracing her. They held their dances and drinking parties on the other side of Birchtown. "Sinning," Grandmother called it. A strange thought came to Sarah. She wondered if Grandmother had ever sinned. Sarah blurted out, "A good sermon could cheer you up. The Lord wants us to be happy."

"Don't you worry about Ol' Lydia. She knows the Lord better than any Christian." Her chins wobbled as she held her head back and let go a turkey chuckle. All the while, the empty clay pipe held steady on her lip as she sucked the stem like an old man sitting on a porch veranda in Charles Town.

Sarah's face brightened and broke into a wide grin. She laughed at the crazy sounds coming from the old woman. Grandmother had her own way of appreciating the Lord. She called upon Him when things got rough and she called him out when He went against her grain.

The sun suddenly drifted behind a span of dark clouds. From the top of a high knoll, Cecil MacLeod's store stood in full view.

He was a respectable Roseway Associate now and proud of the new store he built shortly after arriving.

Lydia lowered the vegetables from her head. She put her hands on her hips and straightened her back. "I want you to stay out here with these vegetables and laundry, Girlie, 'til I tell you to come inside. Whatever you might see or hear between me and Mr. MacLeod, you keep it to yourself."

Sarah did not trust Mr. MacLeod, even now. She hated the very sight of him. A grubby squat man, balding with sparse grey hair and a cruel smile that cradled a bully's sneer. And his eyes. Oh, those narrow, cold eyes that peered through puffy pockets of fat.

The air felt magically warm. She unbuttoned her coat and breathed deeply, delighting in the strange aromas drifting outside from the store. Through the open shutters, she saw kegs of West Indian rum and molasses, barrels of corn meal, flour, beans and wooden containers of loose tea and coarse salt. There were tools, guns, dishes and cloth. On the counter were blocks of dark brown chewing tobacco. She could see Papa ripping chunks from the hard plug with his teeth, see the yellow drool as he spit the big mouthfuls of tobacco juice far out into the yard. "A farmer's gold. Good stuff for killing Boll weevils," he would laugh. "It keeps the little critters from chompin' down the cotton."

A large scale hung above the counter. Grandmother moved about, stopping beside the vegetable bin. Her grumbling was deliberate. "The vegetables are past their time, Mr. MacLeod." She looked over the shrivelled cabbages, turnips and soft potatoes with sprouts a foot long. Shaking her head, she laid her rag purse on the counter, and picked up a handful of crinkled carrots, then put them back. "How old are they?"

"They are from the storehouse." Cecil had an eerie look to him—with one tooth sparkling on the edge of his lip, dirty hands and a crumpled shirt from weeks of wear.

Lydia snickered. "Well, Mr. MacLeod, I have fresh vegetables I got in exchange for a little house work at Missy Dawkins. Can we do a trade today?"

Cecil's brow tightened and his approach changed. He smiled his arrogant smile. "That Mrs. Dawkins has good luck with this thin soil. Yes. Yes. Fresh vegetables will fetch a good price."

Lydia ignored his chatter. She walked to the door and caught Sarah's attention. "Bring those vegetables in now, Girlie."

Sarah put her baskets on the counter.

"Help yourself to some sweetmeats," Cecil said.

She reached into a glass jar and scooped up some nuts and dried fruit. Lydia replaced the vegetables in the basket with a small sack of corn meal and a pound of Navy beans.

Leaning forward over the counter, Cecil winked at Lydia. "A little something extra for your troubles." He added a small sack of flour to the pile of goods. "Half the cost."

"All right, I'll take it. Is it okay to leave these things until I get back from Roseway?"

"No trouble, Lydia. No trouble."

"Good. I'll add a chuck of that salt pork when I return."

Lydia focused now on a shelf lined with bolts of cotton. The sign under the bolts said two shillings a yard. "How much is the cotton, Mr. MacLeod?"

"For you, Lydia, three shillings a yard." He grinned inwardly, knowing Lydia could not read. Never hurt to make a little extra off the Negroes, he thought.

"Could you add a yard to my parcel?"

"You are paying for the cloth, right? That's not covered by the vegetables."

"I will be paying for it," she said bluntly.

Lydia quickly shoved her goods far back under the counter,

as though she thought Cecil might change his mind and take them back.

Cecil, who had been watching Sarah, strolled over to her. "I'd like to speak to Lydia alone. Go outside now and wait." He shooed her with his hands, then turned to Lydia, "I have been waiting for you for weeks." His eyes sparkled like fool's gold.

"Yes sir." Lydia kept her head down, avoiding his eyes.

Sarah positioned herself beside a long window to the right of the door. She could see the back wall and Mr. MacLeod talking to Grandmother. His voice was low and she had to press her ear to the shutter to hear.

"You should come by more often, Lydia. You seem to make yourself scarce. I give you good deals, allow a little trade or credit if you need it. I treat you right. It seems you are forgetting how things were between us. Nothing has changed."

"You have been good, Sir. But you know I have the child."

"My soul, she's a woman now. She can do for herself."

"Not yet, Mr. MacLeod. We have some unfinished business. No disrespect, but there's something I been meaning to ask."

"What is it?"

She drew a deep breath and waited for her courage to come into full bloom.

"After Master Redmond bought me, you took it upon yourself to go behind his back and breed me, knowing he did not approve. You took the light-skinned children from me. There are two that I am anxious to find."

"I have no idea what you are talking about."

"The children, what did you do with my children, Mr. MacLeod?" She raised her head and looked him straight in the face, eye to eye. Her anger swelled her up like never before and she wrestled to get comfortable with it, yet at the same time, it was filling her with courage. It allowed her to say, "Master

Redmond put you in charge of the buying and selling of slaves, not the breeding, but when you saw that the light-skinned slaves fetched more money, you bred me on the sly, then took my light babies to sell. I need to know what happened to my children. You took three of them. I know where one of my children is and I am not concerned about her. But what of the other girl, the one Master Redmond kept awhile then sold ... do you know where she is?"

She paused to catch her breath. She stared at Cecil for a long time and tried to read his thoughts. His face was blank. "And the fair-skinned boy, you took him as well. I see a man here who might be my child." She was studying Cecil hard now, her eyes swollen and red. The release made her feel strong and her voice grew louder, "Do you know if he is here, Mr. MacLeod?"

Cecil leaned in close to her. He was puffed up and his eyes were empty and cold. His voice was stern. "Never raise your voice to me again. Remember that." Then his tone changed. "There's no need to stir up trouble, Lydia. No need to be digging up yesterdays."

"They are our children, Mr. MacLeod," Lydia continued. "Master Redmond loved one like his own, and treated the other well until he sold her, but you ..." She kept pushing. "Are you so heartless ... not to care about them, to keep a child from its mother?"

"Don't be a fool. They were not born out of caring. The slave children were all bastards. Never mention this damn mess again. Let it go. If this gets out, it will bring disgrace to both of us." He touched her arm. "Well then, that's enough of that. You are not on a plantation now, so you just remember to keep your place." He moved from behind the counter and glanced around the store, then pressed himself in against the old woman. His thin hand went inside the big brown coat.

Lydia jumped back. "No sir. I am not an animal," she stammered. "It's time you done right by me."

"You have been my girl since our days in the south. I do not expect that to change." His arrogance inflated and his face tensed. "Let it be, Lydia. Do you understand?"

"Yes sir. I understand." She caught his eyes and held them. "I understand how it was back then. Yes sir, I do. Breeding slaves to get free workers or for your pleasure was common. You could take a slave and do what you liked and the law protected you. You treated me like an animal because I did not have any rights. That is all behind me. I got my papers now." Her anger blasted through her words. "You can take your hands off me. The law might still protect you from your evil ways, but I will spread the word about you. Oh, Lord, I'll let the people know all about Cecil MacLeod."

"What's gotten into you, Lydia?" Little beads of sweat clustered on Cecil's forehead. "You were just a slave. You better stop and think before you do something foolish. This is just between me and you. We must protect ourselves. No one needs to know about our past."

"I need to know what happened to my children."

Sarah stepped back from the window, numb. There was no doubt about the past always stirring up the present. To her surprise, the old woman was speaking her truth, standing firm against Cecil. Papa was right. All that hatred and pain was just waiting to spill out. Sarah steadied herself against the wall. Had Grandmother forgotten her own words about speaking with caution? Had she forgotten who Cecil was, a fearless and vicious killer? Without warning, her mother's words came to her: "After the red tide comes, you let the men have their way with you. You are their property, their girl. You have no choice in the matter."

Sarah inhaled deeply. Here was the truth at last. There were other children, Cecil and Grandmother's children. She was not shocked. She was terrified. Cecil was a bully. If he could not whip the skin off your hide, he would torment your soul. He would keep the whereabouts of the children to himself. And Grandmother could count on him striking back. After another breath, she eased along the wall away from the window, mumbling as she went, her heart racing like a raging river. She could not bring herself to listen further.

Inside, the old woman turned her back to Cecil and with her eyes squashed together tried hard to quell the jitters that were making her hands shake. Cecil worked to regain his composure as well. When he spied Lydia's rag purse on the counter, he thought about the papers … former slaves were never without their papers. He reached for the purse while her back was turned and quickly rooted inside. So much trash. He felt a small pouch. In seconds, he unfolded one of the certificates. "Yes, yes," he snorted and stuffed the pouch inside a large pot on a shelf behind the counter.

Lydia turned. Her words came fast. "I will pick up my things when I get back." She snatched her purse from the counter.

"No problem, Lydia. They will be waiting for you."

Cecil swelled with anticipated victory. Things were not as bad as they appeared. Lydia would pay for her brazenness. She would soon learn her place.

Eight

ONE OF THE FIRST LOYALIST HOMES BUILT IN PORT Roseway belonged to Captain William and Margaret Cunningham. It stood one and a half stories with a gabled roof and two brick chimneys. Outside it was framed in timber with white clapboard siding and blue trim. Inside, it had paneled walls of plane boards with a chair rail and wainscoting. At the rear was a barn for cattle, sheep and two horses. Beside the barn, smaller buildings housed chickens and pigs. Along the walled walk, flowers drooped from the heavy frost. There were several black men in the fields behind the house. Simon, a middle-aged black man, was tilling the remains of the meagre garden to the left of the house, which had produced oats, barley, flax, gooseberries, raspberries and strawberries. Two tortoiseshell cats wandered about like miniature guard dogs.

Exhausted from the long walk, Lydia and Sarah proceeded to the back, the usual entrance for servants, and rapped on the porch door. A stout Negro woman opened the door saying, "Oh Lord, it's you. Good to see you," her head bobbing from side to side. "I'll take that laundry. You sure can do a bright wash. Missy Cunningham will see you in the parlour. She's got something to speak on. She said to bring the girl along as well."

The pair followed her down a long hallway. "The streets are quiet today, Fanny," Lydia said.

"Yes, yes. This place had been in a roar for a week, it being the king's birthday and Governor Parr arriving in his sloop to appoint the new justices. Oh, the noise with all the gun salutes booming from his ship and the cannons goin' off every half hour down by the shore."

"I suppose there were fancy suppers and balls. This lot knows how to entertain, but work, that's another rag."

Fanny let out a hoot. "You speakin' the truth on that," she snorted. "There has been no work here for days, just the drinking. Oh my, the drinking. Shameful! And every night the bonfires, dancing and fighting."

"They do love a good time to act the fool."

"Have you heard? The governor has renamed this hell-hole, calling it Shelburne. Well, Mr. Cunningham, oh Lord, that man, he's bitter for namin' the place after the prime minister of Britain, the man who signed away their rights to their country and their property to the Patriots. I heard him say he wasn't calling this place anything but Port Roseway."

"And right he is."

Off from the hall to their right was a small library and a tiny room with a spinning wheel and piles of fleece and yarn on the floor. To their left was the dining area and a large kitchen. Ahead, at the end of the hall, lay the parlour. When they reached it, Fanny said, "Ma'am, the Redmonds are here to see you."

Mrs. Cunningham was a wisp of a woman with long black hair pinned under a white cap. Her smile was broad and her face so golden it looked like fresh butter. From her chair by the window, she called, "Come and sit, Lydia. We have time to talk since no one is hurrying about today."

The splendour of the parlour reminded Sarah of the Big House. There were long velvet drapes, red velvet chairs, a rug, candle stands and a small table with graceful legs holding a glass decanter with six gold-rimmed glasses. Along the back wall was a china cabinet with glass doors filled with the heavy porcelain dishes she had washed so many times before. It was all so lovely, except that the size of the rooms and the low ceilings paled in comparison to the Big House. Of course it made the little hut in Birchtown feel even more like a shack. Sarah stood by the doorway, her thoughts drifting as she amused herself by thinking that one day she might have a few nice things to call her own.

Sarah's absence of mind prompted Mrs. Cunningham to ask, "Is Sarah feeling alright?"

"She's just taken with your place, that's all. Please excuse her, Ma'am."

"Excused," she laughed, then said, "Lydia, I wish you would call me Margaret. The time when you couldn't call us by our names has passed." She went to Lydia and placed her arm around the woman's shoulder.

"I know you don't see harm in it, but, oh Lord, it could lead to being careless with someone else. I could find myself locked up or whipped. Some things never change. No, Ma'am. I can't start bad habits, for your sake as well as my own."

"I'm so sorry, Lydia. Of course, you are right." She removed her arm. "The world is a shameless place for the way you are treated."

Sarah was looking about the parlour now and enjoying the warmth from the long yellow flames in the fireplace. A large blue and white jar, delicately crowned with a black wooden lid, caught her eye. "It's beautiful," she said. "I'm sure I saw one like it at the Big House."

"It's a Double Happiness Jar, a favourite. It's the same jar, a gift from William when we were courting. He found it in a little market off the Thames River in England. I'm so grateful Father had most of our possessions taken away in time."

"It would have been terrible to have such beautiful things destroyed," Sarah said.

Grandmother was beside herself. "Mind your manners, Girlie. You have no right to be asking questions and going around Missy's things."

Sarah, so distracted, did not respond, forgetting about the rules for servants.

"She's all right, Lydia. Let her look."

Ignoring the old woman, Sarah bent to look at the jar. "I'd give anything to have such a thing." She wanted to hold the delicate object, study the detailing up close. Without thinking, she reached for the jar.

Grandmother swallowed and her anger erupted with a shout, "Leave that, Girlie! That is not your concern. Come back and stand here beside me."

In an instant, Sarah straightened. In turning to face Grandmother, her hand dusted the jar with a soft sweep, knocking it from the table. Abominable silence. All eyes focused on the jar, forever falling down, down, down. Sarah's heart pumped fast as she watched the jar land … in one piece … on the thick rug where it rested. The old woman's eyes rejoined their sockets.

Sarah, ever so gently, returned the jar to its coveted place. "I'm sorry, Ma'am, for being so careless." She hung her head and waited for Mrs. Cunningham to haul off and slap her, or say that she would have her charged with some offence.

A composed Mrs. Cunningham leaned forward and embraced Sarah, saying, "There, there. You meant no harm, Sarah. It was an accident. It's a reminder to move the jar to a safer place." Turning to Lydia, she said, "Do not be afraid, Lydia, the jar is fine."

Fanny, who had been standing inside the doorway to announce the meal, slowly came to herself and sputtered, "Your lunch is ready, Ma'am."

"Come along," Mrs. Cunningham said in a kind voice, extending her hand to the kitchen.

Sarah was silent. Her eyes twitched with confusion. Why such unusual kindness towards Grandmother, inviting them to her table when the custom was for servants to eat separately? And such mercy and understanding when she nearly broke a precious object as the vase? There were Negroes serving time in jail for the careless handling of property.

In the kitchen, fresh bread and large bowls of corn chowder made with new potatoes, fresh onions, corn and bits of bacon awaited. Blueberry-gooseberry pie and tea followed. After the meal, Mrs. Cunningham reached into a green jar on the window ledge and placed two shillings in Sarah's hand, then handed two crowns to Lydia. "You both are a godsend. I've never forgotten the promise I made to mother to look after you, Lydia."

"We are grateful for your kindness, Ma'am."

"I never dreamed our lives would come to this, that we would have to leave our southern homes and start over in a foreign place. The war was a wicked display of hatred and unjust for those of us who wanted nothing more than to support the king."

"Oh, Lord, I worried for you when the soldiers came. I saw you looking back from the carriage. It was a terrible time."

"We tried to be brave, but with William away at sea and Father's death, we were defenceless. Then Mother passed away during the trip here … The strain was too much for her." She reached out with both arms and hugged the old woman. "I was so happy to see old friends after I arrived. It's a challenging place, this Roseway. These settlers are a quarrelsome lot. Tempers are hot. Everyone is worrying about class and privilege, not fully understanding the hard work and grit needed in a place like this. Now with the laws in the colonies forgiving us and returning

Loyalist property, many are giving up and leaving. I believe things will improve."

"All of our lives have changed, Ma'am. Nothing will ever be the same no matter what anyone decides. I appreciate all you and the mister do for us. I sure do."

"There is no need for that." She extended her gaze to Sarah and then back to Lydia. "I must get to the point. I have an offer to make. Sarah is grown now. It is time to send her to work. Poor Fanny has such pain in her joints and back, she says she will not be able to work much longer. Perhaps I could indenture Sarah. I will speak to William about this when he returns and get him to draw up an agreement. Fanny works for her room and board. However, Sarah might be happy to work for wages. Two years sounds reasonable. Times are hard, but we will do what we can for her."

"The girl is a good worker."

"Yes she is. I was always fond of her."

Grandmother excused herself from the table and nodded to Sarah to do the same.

"There's another bag of laundry waiting to be done by the porch door, Lydia," Mrs. Cunningham said. "By the way, I hear Mr. Carter is here in Nova Scotia working as a slave hunter. You must always have your certificates with you. Please be careful."

"Yes Ma'am." Grandmother patted the rag purse. "I aim to be safe."

They took their time going back to Birchtown. Sarah poked along, understanding that work was scarce and positions hard to come by, but somehow becoming indentured was not what she had imagined for herself. While the thought made her sad, her mouth produced a smile—she had to admit she liked this little woman, though the way she treated them was so peculiar.

Nine

SARAH WORE HER FAVOURITE CREATION, A BUTTERY-YELLOW gown with frilled sleeves over a white petticoat, a brown wool cloak and a green bonnet. She held her head high and strutted down the path carrying a small basket of apples. It felt good to be on her way to the Methodist camp meeting in the clearing. Throughout the colony, worship services were being held in every corner. There were plenty of ministers coming to Birchtown to preach to the desperate souls. Together, they agreed to build a meeting house, but until it was completed, they met in a valley between the hills in a place they called the clearing.

This was a day of blessings. Sarah felt it in her heart. In no other place could you feel more free or more at home than in the clearing. *Steal away, Steal away to Jesus; Steal away, Steal away home; I ain't got long to stay here.* How sweet the words were! She hummed them repeatedly. It saddened her that Grandmother refused to attend the meeting. She said all the jumping and shouting wouldn't bring her closer to the Lord, but Sarah loved the merriment. She would ask for much needed blessings for her family, especially for her Aunt Beulah, for it was three days since the visit and still the baby was holding back.

Sarah had agonized over the need to look after her aunt. Beulah was family, and hadn't her father insisted she look after the family, keep it strong? In Birchtown, you could easily perish without their love and support. The importance of strong ties was leading folks to marriage—one of the prizes of freedom. Sarah could not help but smile. Like many men, Uncle Prince had married as soon as they arrived. "I can't wait to get myself a wife," they would say, as if they were earning a medal or some kind of reward, as if getting a woman compared to bringing home a deer. She thought about Reece. There would be lots of time and besides, Beulah's needs would have to come first.

Sarah left the main trail. She could hear the commotion before she reached Big Mama Hagar's shack. Sunday morning didn't make a spot of difference to Big Mama. The cursing and screaming were flying out the windows and the open door. It wasn't long before ol' man Hagar came running out and sped past Sarah, with Big Mama in pursuit, cast iron skillet waving in the air. Her tongue feasted in a trough of vulgar names. Sarah wondered what the old fella had done this time. Sneaking around with the widow Jane again? Sarah chuckled and kept walking.

A large crowd milled about in the clearing. It was the one place where Negroes could legally gather, a place where they were free to let themselves laugh, sing and dance. It seemed all of Birchtown was in this place of healing. The air was full of the sweet scent of hemlock and the clearing dazzled with cheerful colours and laughter.

She found Reece among a group of Black Pioneers. They chatted while Reverend Ringwood delivered the greetings. Old plantation songs, "Bringin' in de Sheaves" and "Hear de Angels Callin,'" brought the crowd alive. Reverend Ringwood stood atop a wooden box. "Lay your burdens on the Lord," he screamed. "Lay your sins down, you Lambs of God and repent. You are the children of the Lord and He will give you what you need. Put your trust in Him to heal you, trust in Him to feed you, trust in Him to take away all your sorrow. Rejoice in Him."

Enthusiasm grew into frenzy as he encouraged the outpouring of hardship and grief. Bodies trembled. Words flowed from the depth of their hearts. Reverend Ringwood held each one with outstretched arms, offered them hope, told them to keep praying, to have faith and look to the Lord for salvation. Slaves who could not read rhymed out scripture word for word. Their moans and hallelujahs rose up to heaven. Then how they danced and sang. This festive rejoicing in the spirit was the one true testimony to gaining freedom.

At last a break came. Sarah took her apples to a large canvas sheet on the ground. It was time for lunch and everyone dove into the abundance of food spread out in the clearing, for all hoarded during the week to bring something and all indulged in the offerings. She ate quickly. "I wish I could stay longer," Sarah said, "but I promised to meet Grandmother at Aunt Beulah's place. Did you enjoy the service?"

"It sure got me going," Reese laughed, "and I'm not much on religion. All it does is keep a man down, encouraging him to rely on something other than himself. We have the tools to direct ourselves and a conscience to guide us. Fools have no conscience. That is what accounts for sin. What a man needs to get ahead is not prayers, but a good fight."

"A fight?" Sarah raised her eyebrows. He was sounding like her Aunt Beulah.

"The slaves believed God helped Moses free the Hebrew slaves. They figured that God would set them free, too. But it took action, a good old rebellion to free us."

"Well, I never heard it put that way before. I believe that their faith gave them courage."

"I don't know about that, Sarah. I do not plan to sit still and pray for change. I figure you should fight for it, like the Patriots. That's what a good man does." He winked at Sarah. "I'm not hanging around waiting for rations and a blessing." He blew warm breath into his hands. "Can I walk you to the crossroads? Beulah's is just across the field, isn't that right?"

"It is." Sarah concentrated on putting one foot in front of the other. "What do you mean you won't sit still?"

"Miss Sarah, if a man does not work, he will surely die. There is not enough work to go around. It's time for me to move on." He reached over and slid his fingers along her cheek. "It sure would be nice if I had me a pretty miss to take along. It would be nice to think about more than a job."

A soft gasp fell from Sarah's mouth.

"Sarah Redmond," Reece chirped liked a sparrow. "I've been thinking about you a lot. Have you thought about marriage? We can marry here. It's not like before, you know."

Lord. Lord. The thought of running off with Reece put Sarah's head in a spin and she could not stop grinning. Her mind stirred like a hornet's nest, scattering her thoughts in all directions. He was ready, but that was not the thing. She needed time—time to know him better, to know the kind of man he truly was. She didn't know much, but she knew some men could be kind one minute and brutal the next. "Reece Johnson," she said, "Such thoughts."

"It's lonely here without any relatives to count on. I grew up feeling like an orphan. It is hard to explain how a man yearns to connect to his blood. The need and the wondering never go away."

"I was lucky to have a family, but even mine is broken. I know how that can hurt."

"A family is your foundation. I used to see free Negro men in Charles Town when Steppin' John took me along to buy supplies. They would walk through the streets with their wives and children, heads held high. The children always looked happy. I want that happiness, too. A slave named Rose cared for me until

I was five. Then Mr. MacLeod put me to work with Steppin' John to learn a trade. He was good to me, but he didn't treat me like family."

"I don't know if you can ever find your true roots when you come from slaves. That part is sometimes a mystery. No telling who or even where you came from most of the time."

"So true, Miss Sarah. Right now I am thinking of putting down roots with you."

"Are you?" Sarah gave a wide smile. "That makes me happy, Reece."

"I can't make any real plans just yet, because a call may come any day to go whaling. Colonel Black has gotten assurances of jobs for several of us. The ship may leave any day, but I want you to know that I care a lot about you. Will you wait for my return?"

Sarah nodded and slipped her hand in his. He raised it to his cheek and kissed it gently. When they reached the crossroads, she said, "No need to worry. I am not going anywhere."

"Can I see you again, maybe here tomorrow evening? The Birchtowners come here to gamble, to wager away their few belongings and their hard-earned money. The folks in Roseway are so upset by the Negroes gambling they have banned it and sentenced those they catch to the House of Corrections, but out here in the clearing, folks feel safe. I have heard they have dice games like craps, cards and even cock-fighting. I don't play, but we can watch. Will you come?"

Sarah laughed. "I am sure I will see you again before you leave."

THOUGH IT WAS ANOTHER COLD AND FROSTY MORNING, Fibby held the door open. "I was expecting you," she said. "Lydia told me to keep a look-out." She did not display her usual indifference. Instead, she was bubbly and welcoming. Sarah hoped for good news.

Beulah sat upright on the cot. She turned slowly to face Sarah. Her "good morning" was a long, drawn-out affair. Sarah noticed the change in Beulah's belly and knew the ordeal was over, but where was the baby? Her eyes darted about the room from corner to corner in search of a small bundle. Suddenly, she filled with a familiar pain. The pain that came from losing her mama, from seeing chopped-off limbs, from having loved ones die. It all came in one big ball. It stuck in her throat and she could not speak. She walked to the window and stood, holding back the tears, preparing for the bad news yet hoping she was wrong.

At first, the cry was soft. Then it grew until tiny wails filled the room. Beulah pulled back the grey and blue quilt to reveal not one, but two beautiful, bronze faces. Identical faces, each crowned with thick black curls.

In her excitement Sarah screamed loud enough for all of Birchtown to hear. "Twins! Oh my Lord, twins!"

Beulah said, "A boy and a girl, Sarah."

"Have you named them yet?"

"I surely have. My girl is Destiny and my boy is Prince the Second. His name means 'first place' and that's what this place is to us, the first place where we are free after slavery." She turned to Grandmother and nodded her head.

"The names are beautiful and fitting," Sarah said.

Grandmother leaned in and stretched out her arms.

Beulah placed a tiny baby on each of Grandmother's palms. The old woman held both babies up, high up into the air.

"Bless this child, Destiny, and this child, Prince. They are born out of slavery. Born here to become a free man and a free woman in Nova Scotia. That is the gift to these children. For this blessing, we give thanks. Amen." Grandmother put the babies down beside their mama. With a scattering of water from a mug, she sprinkled their foreheads. She grinned proudly and her skin glistened as though the Rapture had caught her up. Sarah wondered what else she would say. She wondered if the old woman would dance—delight in the highest expression of joy.

"We are rich, Beulah. So rich. We got gold, Sarah." Grandmother sounded almost delirious.

Sarah grabbed the old woman and swung her around gently. "This day has brought wonderful blessings!"

"Will you stay for a bite to eat?" Fibby asked. She brought out the small mugs and filled them with pale yellow tea. "Bread and moose meat," she said, "The meat is from the Mi'kmaq, Joseph Joe, who camps down by the river. I helped deliver his son awhile back. We sure could use some fixings to go with it, but we will make do."

After eating, Grandmother snuggled the bundles against her breasts as though she had given birth to the twins herself. Her joy was real, but so were the tiny tears that gathered in the corners of her eyes and the soft moans that surfaced from a place buried deep. But Lydia being Lydia, she veiled her feelings and did what she always did to ease her despair—she belted out another hymn.

Ten

I T WAS A GOOD END TO A LONG WORKDAY. AS THE SUN
set, it spread bright ribbons of orange, gold and red along the
horizon. In Birchtown, the trails and paths were deserted. All
was quiet, but for the uproar coming through the walls of the
partly constructed meeting house.

The indentured Negroes from Roseway, who regularly
fled their cruel and cheating employers to seek the safety of
Birchtown, had gathered to voice their concerns. With much
shouting and fist waving, they were letting Colonel Black know
they were tired of the continued hostility and unfairness of the
white settlers. It was a rowdy gathering. Lydia and Sarah stood at
the back observing the ruckus.

Harris Clark, a carpenter, said that when some tresses fell on
him and injured his back, he received only half of the pay he
deserved for the time he worked. Priscilla Hayward complained
that her employer turned her out with no pay or provisions from
the King's Bounty and refused to pay what he owed her. Thomas
Wheaton alleged that he had to use his wages to pay for the
rations his employer received for him and for tools to do his
work. Hagar Primus found herself hired out to other citizens
without her permission.

And so it went. The list of injustices continued: beaten
for disobedience, forced to serve extended time through false

contracts, sentenced to hard labour or shackled in leg irons for neglecting assigned work and even starved for displeasing behaviour. Public whippings and hangings were issued for theft of the smallest items like shoes or butter, indentures were being passed on in wills illegally and children stolen.

At the front of the room, Colonel Black listened graciously, letting them speak their minds well into the night, promising that he would take the matter before the local justices of the peace. But this enraged the crowd further. Many had already appealed to the General Sessions Court and local magistrates for justice, only to be ignored. Taking matters into their own hands, the angry gathering settled on a course of action: A march through Roseway, as the white labourers had done, to show their unity and discontent. They demanded Colonel Black lead them.

Sarah listened with great interest. Colonel Black grew weary as he argued that an illegal gathering to show their frustration would only serve to stir up violence, not bring sympathy or justice. His refusal to support them or even to offer a solution angered the crowd. And when Harris Clark stood up and screamed that such a leader deserved a tar and feathering, Sarah saw Colonel Black slowly sneak along a wall and disappear into the night.

On the way home, Sarah said, "It's Colonel Black's responsibility to seek justice for all the wrongs we face. It seems he's still bound to the master with his loyalty."

Grandmother said, "Master Redmond once said that for the sake of a little privilege and money, most would sell themselves to the devil." She let out a long turkey chuckle.

"Why are you laughing, Ma'am?" Sarah asked.

"If you had an angry crowd ready to tar your behind, you would run too."

Sarah shook her head. She could not bring herself to smile. "The man in him is weak," she said with disgust. "Our people have lost all respect for him now."

Grandmother walked along, changing the words of her favourite hymn to a newer version, her version: *Come back Moses, way down in this free land, Tell old pharaoh it's time, oh Lord, time to let my people go.*

When she finished several rounds, she said, "This place needs prayers. Everyone in this colony has forgotten why we came. Lord, Lord, will we ever learn to work together?"

THE WORRY, ANGER AND SORROW THAT WERE OVERWHELMING the Birchtowners also nibbled at Lydia. On an early October evening, she sat soaking in the washtub. She looked at her feet, all lumped up with corns and bunions, swollen and rough. She remembered a time when her feet danced to tribal rhythms and ran along the banks of the Niger. She also recalled the long march to the West African coast to board a slave ship. Her slave's feet had travelled thousands of miles in all her years, sometimes covered, sometimes bare.

She gently touched her face, felt the hollows in her cheeks, the winkled brow, the sagging pockets of fat along the jaw. How many times had her mouth endured the slaps and spit of overseers? She looked at her sore hands, all puffed up, chapped and rough like tree bark from chores and lye. They were work hands. She rubbed them kindly with a little pig grease from the pot at the side of the tub. She rubbed her shoulders, marvelling at the softness of a slave woman. She pressed her fingers through the tight wad of crimped grey hair and massaged her scalp. It felt good.

A slave woman, she thought, never fully realizes the joy of her heart nor the sweetness of her body. All these years, her body has served others. It has known the work of a man and a woman, the cut of the lash and the forced bearing of children, but never the tenderness of love. She stared at the back wall and mouthed the name given to her by her mother: *Abena*. The name was in a place beyond her memory. "I have lost the way to go home," she whispered.

"Just a slave," Cecil had said that day in the store. The hateful words stirred a pain in Lydia that gnawed and ate, but could not find its fill. There it was—three cruel words to sum up a lifetime of bondage. In the pain, she found her voice and it was loud and sharp. "Just a slave. Is that what he thinks? I am just Lydia, an empty soul, something to claim and abuse. No, Cecil, never again." The days of being afraid of Cecil MacLeod had passed. But having secrets was dangerous. She must be on her guard, forever watchful. She sat in deep thought, looking back at her past until the water was icy cold. She wiggled her toes in the water and prayed, then dried herself with an old blue rag.

The next day was cold for a fall day. Mrs. Cunningham had paid Lydia with a piece of jewellery, saying her funds were low and there was hardly a coin to be found in the colony. She had insisted that Sarah accompany Lydia home; one of her servants had disappeared the week before. Daylight was fading into darkness when Lydia swapped the valuable brooch for goods at Cecil's store. Her bag was heavy with cornmeal, molasses, beans and a pickled beef tongue, enough to share with Beulah.

The air was damp. It felt like rain. "Best hurry," Lydia advised. Behind them, the grind of approaching cartwheels filled the air with a jerky rhythm. When the cart nudged slowly past and came to a stop at the side of the road, a man leaped down with a cap hung low on a face that sported thin grey whiskers. A Birchtowner, Sarah thought. His breathing was burdened and his footsteps heavy. As he drew nearer, Lydia stopped and reached for Sarah's arm. "It's Boll weevil, Girlie. Boll weevil."

Without warning, a brilliant flash of lightning streaked through the tall shadowy spruce. Heavy thunder rumbled. Lydia turned and her eyes fell on the willowy man with chalk-white skin in a worn brown jacket. He held a short rifle in his right hand. She knew the familiar stare, the piercing blue eyes. "Have mercy," she groaned and her knees went weak.

His voice was scratchy. "Do you Negroes have papers?"

"Papers?" Lydia's voice quivered.

"You heard me. Certificates. Certificates of Freedom."

"Yes Sir, I do. Why are you asking?"

"There are Negroes in the province without proper papers," he said. He eyed her sharply. "I aim to see they are returned to their rightful owners."

"You've got no worries about us. We are staying right here in Scotia." Her nervous turkey chuckle broke the tension, but only for a second.

"I was told about you and the girl." His lips fell into a sneer. "Told you were here without papers. I want to see them."

The words echoed through Lydia's head. Who could have told him such a thing? She laid her goods on the ground and fished deep into the rag purse. She fumbled eagerly among a heap of head rags, pieces of lace, yellowed scraps of paper, string, nails and other odd bits.

Lydia stopped digging and looked up. "Oh Lord," she said. "Save us, Lord." In an instant, the old woman fell to the ground with a thud.

Letting out a cry, Sarah ran to her grandmother.

Boll weevil took several steps back.

After kneeling and lifting the old woman's head, Sarah saw that Grandmother's eyes were open and her mouth hung to the side of her face. She shook the lifeless mass of flesh. "Grandmother. Grandmother," she cried. She cast a scowl at Boll weevil and swallowed hard. Her whole body trembled as she looked up and slowly announced, "She's dead."

Lingering thunder hovered over Birchtown. The storm did not produce a drop of rain. What was Boll weevil going to do next? The stillness was cruel and Sarah's face flushed with frightful anticipation.

"Dead is she? Good. This saves me the time and effort." Boll weevil's voice deepened to scorching anger. "All my troubles and for what, a dead woman? I won't be able to fatten my pockets with that."

"We have papers, Sir," she said. "I can look for the certificates." Sarah reached for the purse.

After a short pause, Boll weevil scoffed. "Never mind. I've had enough of you lot."

"What about my grandmother?"

Boll weevil turned to her and his eyes were biting, but he did not speak. He sauntered to the wagon and climbed in. He turned back then and shouted, "Let the crows eat her!"

Sarah watched until he was out of sight. She huddled over the limp body and from the old woman suddenly came tiny, feeble sounds. As they grew stronger, Sarah's mouth widened to a smile. She stroked Grandmother's face, shook her shoulders and rolled the body from side to side. Suddenly, the rigid form stirred. Grandmother jolted and sat upright as straight as an arrow. She wobbled to her feet and looked at Sarah.

"Boll weevil thinks he can outsmart ol' Lydia. We will have to guard ourselves better. Be mindful at all times. We must get a good stick to defend ourselves."

After Sarah found two sturdy sticks by the roadside, Lydia

steadied herself on hers and said, "Grab that bag. We best get along now before he decides to come back."

Lydia's thoughts gave way to suspicions. This night was all because of Cecil. Yes, it was he who had stolen her papers and set Boll weevil on them. It would take all she had to outsmart two such scheming men. They were the devil's hands.

Eleven

CECIL MACLEOD TOOK THE BLACK PIPE FROM HIS mouth and gave a long sigh. Sweat oozed from his ghostly brow as the yellow flames danced in the wood stove and poured out heat. It was two weeks now since his plan had misfired and he was still beside himself with anger. Lydia was still a free woman and still very much alive. He flung the Certificates of Freedom on the counter and cursed them. On the plantation, there had been an acceptable order: the master, the foreman, the overseer and then slave. That he understood. Slaves were property, like horses. You could do with them as you pleased. They had no choice but to follow orders.

Here Negroes were petitioning the court for rights and some were finding justice. He didn't agree with the judge for awarding payments to a slave for lost wages or that the Harding woman should be able to have her master jailed for beating her. Yes, times were changing. And Lydia—she was changing, too, going from being a submissive slave to a demanding fool, a woman of confidence now, bold and thinking herself smart.

Cecil plunked himself on a stool, inhaling hard on his pipe several times. Money was scarce in Port Roseway. Another long winter lay ahead. His missus was unhappy, wanting to return home. The supply ships were late again and he was struggling to get the necessary goods and supplies for the store. There was little to count on in a new colony. There was no guarantee of making money—people were resorting to all kinds of tricks to save their cash, such as lying about their incomes to claim rations from the King's Bounty. He jumped from the stool and stretched his short legs. The pile of belongings people had traded for goods lay in heaps on the floor. Amid the fancy shoes, patterned dishes and books, he grabbed up a sword belt, an Indian basket, a dictionary, a violin, only to throw them back into the heap. Who needed such things when food was scarce? Who could pay for any of it?

These were desperate times and so Cecil had turned to slave trading on the side. He had a keen sense of who the runaways were—they had a different walk, a scared look, always slinking down inside oversized clothes. Ridding the colony of intruders and troublemakers would be a profitable service. The meeting with Boll weevil had been brief. Cecil presented him with the names of several Birchtowners he suspected of not holding certificates, adding Lydia and Sarah Redmond to the list. The plan they devised was simple. Boll weevil was to round them all up, book their passage on a local schooner owned by his friend, Harold Lambston, and take them down to Boston where an agent would pay handsomely for the cargo, selling them in turn to former masters or at auction. Cecil and Boll weevil would split the profit fifty-fifty when Boll weevil returned.

"Such a supply of goods at hand," they had joked. But Cecil was not laughing now. He shook his head at the man's ability to botch such an easy job. He would try one more time. Without their certificates, Lydia and Sarah were vulnerable. It was inconceivable that a simple-minded woman like Lydia could outsmart Boll weevil. No, he could not let that happen again. He would give the man a second chance, but if that fool could not get it right this time, he would take matters into his own hands. Lydia might outsmart Boll weevil, but she would not dupe him.

He scratched his head and thumped the counter. Could he trust Boll weevil to return with his share of the profits? He figured it was worth the risk and besides, they were old friends. Two men cut from the same cloth. He sat back in his chair and thought about what it would mean if the old woman did not keep her mouth shut. He spit in a bucket near the counter. The devil would surely dance when disgrace fell upon him. He'd be the laughingstock of Port Roseway. They would call him "the father of Negroes," and to be called that would make him an outcast. He twisted his fingers deep inside his grey whiskers. There were others in the same boat, but they would hide behind their fine names. And stick together in condemning him. He had to shelter his missus from disgrace and protect himself from the hateful hornet's nest Lydia could stir.

Cecil added more water and coffee to grounds in the pot that had been brewing for several days on the stove. After it boiled hard, he filled a giant mug scarred with pasty stains, sat back in the wide chair by the heat and gulped the black brew like it was his last. This whole business—the threat of old secrets and his wickedness exposed—had brought him sleepless nights and great agony of mind. The audacity of Lydia to refer to the off-breeds as "their children" incited him more and he heaved the empty mug against the far wall, watching as several dishes fell to the dusty floor and shattered.

Her boy was in Birchtown alright. He had seen him several times, knew him from watching him grow up on the plantation. There was not a chance Lydia could pick him out of the crowd, there were so many mulattos. Maybe he did care for that one the Redmonds raised. She had the backing of old money and her husband's good naval name. As far as he knew, no one ever mentioned her background. Such a disclosure would ruin not just him, but also one of Port Roseway's most prominent families.

Twelve

A FRIGID COLD SWALLOWED UP THE COOL AUTUMN weather. The lakes froze as hard as iron. Snow was in the air. Everywhere the hustle and bustle in Birchtown heightened as the settlers prepared for the long winter. They were hoarding everything they could get, from heavy clothing, especially coats that could substitute for warm blankets, to food: flour, corn, molasses, potatoes and salt meat or fish, as well as ammunition and firewood.

It was early evening, the second Friday in November. The cold crept into the cabin through cracks and openings forcing the lumping on of heavy sweaters. The canvas window coverings fluttered from the draft. Sarah sat bundled in a blanket sewing the ties on an apron she made from scraps. The cabin filled with stinging smoke as Grandmother stoked the slow fire and added two blocks of dry wood to get it blazing. She checked the partridges bubbling in the kettle over the fire pit and set about preparing potatoes and carrots for the pot. She was thinking about the long winter ahead and with such scarcity how they would make it through. The heavy rapping on the door startled her.

Grandmother opened the door to a brisk wind and a tall man in a Pioneer jacket with a stuffed black satchel spread across his chest. She examined the stranger from head to toe. She was taken aback at first, cautious, and then she rolled out a loud turkey chuckle followed by a deafening squeal. "Sweet chariots. Is that you Fortune?" she shrieked. "Can it really be you, Fortune Isaiah Redmond? Come in. Come in." She grabbed the man and pulled him into her chest with a hard thrust, holding him so close he could barely breathe. Then the tears came, rolling, rolling down her cheeks and into his coat.

Sarah dropped the apron and turned to the door. Every memorable detail floated back—the earthy-brown skin, the tight curl of black hair, the moon-shaped scar on his left cheek. He was lean and drawn, but there was no mistaking his crooked smile. She ran and threw her arms around him.

The three entangled in a ball of confusion, Lydia with her arms wrapped around Fortune from the front and Sarah from behind. All were delirious and talking at once. They wept with no let-up until Fortune pulled them away and wiped their eyes with his hands. He was lost for words at first. When he came to himself, he said, "This is a day of miracles. Yes it is."

"Oh, my, I can't believe my eyes. I never dreamed this day would come. I never dared dream. The Lord is good." Lydia sat at the table now, holding her head in her hands. "There can't be anything better than seeing you, Fortune, except maybe seeing the Lord." Grandmother wiped her dress sleeve across her face several times. "We got a little place to lay our heads. I prayed every day for you to join us."

"You did good, Mama. It took courage for you and Sarah to leave Carolina. You make me happy and proud." Fortune turned and looked at Sarah for a full minute.

"You have grown, Babygirl. You are a woman now and as pretty as a magnolia." He looked closely at Sarah. "My, that's a pretty dress you have on."

"Thank you, Papa. I made it myself. Sewing helps to pass the time. I like turning something old into something new."

"I suspect you'll be looking to get out soon."

Grandmother jumped in. "Hush now, Fortune. There is no need for her to get out yet. Missy Cunningham is looking to indenture her. There's little else for a young girl here."

Sarah ignored the old woman's barb. She began singing one of the songs from the camp meeting: "Glory, glory, hallelujah. I feel better. So much better, since I laid my burden down. Feel like shouting, 'Hallelujah,' since I laid my burden down."

"Keep singing, chile. I got one less burden: one child has come home to roost."

The table filled with biscuits, tea and the watery stew. Grandmother told Fortune about the events that brought them to Port Roseway, of her resolve to make the best out of being in Nova Scotia. She told him about Beulah having not one but two babies who were fighting bravely to stay in the world. And the sad news also of the fever that had taken his brother, Prince.

"I wish I had gotten here sooner." Then, after a long silence, "Twins. Well, well. How is Beulah doing? It's been years since I laid eyes on her."

"She's holding up. There's not much to the poor soul. We try to help her as much as we can. We keep praying for her and the babies. I fear for them in the cold and the lack of rations makes life hard." Grandmother looked away to the fire. "I better warn you that Boll weevil Carter from Carolina is on the prowl, on the lookout for runaway slaves, always looking to make money off us. It seems it doesn't matter to him whether or not you have your freedom papers." She stopped talking and rested her chins in her hands.

Fortune shook his head. "That man will always be a crook. I guess you have all been tested. I suppose the good Lord only wants strong people up in Glory." He laughed, looked at his mother and winked, "I guess there's no one stronger than you." He turned to Sarah and asked, "Do you have plans, young Miss?"

"Yes, Papa, I do. I plan to make my mark in this colony, to be my own person. I will not spend my life being a servant."

"Slow down, Sarah. Those are big dreams for a Negro woman."

"A Negro woman has never had an easy life. She never had a man to depend on. Her life is what she makes it. Freedom lets us have dreams."

Fortune's face tightened. It would not do any good to try to change her runaway ideas, not with her being young and not with her being Dahlia's child. "And marriage?" he asked. "What of that?"

Sarah retreated for a minute to think about Reece and the idea of marriage. Girls as young as twelve or thirteen married in order to have earnings, inheritance and property. By the age of eighteen or twenty, an unmarried woman was called a spinster. But that was white folks. Those girls had something to gain. Marriage brought few benefits to a young Negro girl.

She smiled. "Everyone's anxious to jump the broom and they are mating like flies. There's been lots of weddings in the clearing. Marriage," she finally said, "perhaps in time."

Sarah cleared the table and refilled the mugs with weak tea. Fortune began telling tales of his adventures. "War is insanity," he said in his loud tenor. "The first thing the British did was to assign me to the Black Pioneers. We were not treated like the white soldiers." He looked down at the floor. "They used us to clear lines, tend to the wounded, cook and act as spies. We built bridges and made roads for the equipment and white soldiers, but not a rifle did we get."

Sarah sat back in her chair, unnerved by her father's unfamiliar tone. She fastened her eyes on him as she clung to his every word.

Fortune's mood grew heavy as his tone mellowed. "The Pioneers were falling everywhere, some got shot, others died from infection or disease." After a deep breath, he continued, "I heard a white lieutenant say us Negroes were no more than second-class citizens. Well, it was just as much our war," he drawled. "The cry was all about loyalty, liberty and money. We wanted the same and proved ourselves capable soldiers, but they drew the line at race, keeping the praise and rewards for themselves."

"Yes, yes. That they did," Lydia said.

Sarah sat still. She understood his anger. She pitied him. War could change a man's nature.

Fortune took a chew of tobacco. "Oh no, I did not intend to be a lame duck. I got myself a sweet pistol. Oh yes, and I killed me a few Patriot soldiers." His fist struck the table. The table bounced. "Lord, Mama, I didn't want to kill nobody." Tears rolled down his face and his words stalled. Fortune pulled a rag from his pocket and dabbed the sweat from his face. "All I got was the uniform on my back, passage to this colony and a head full of promises. We will see how they honour their word." He pushed his cup forward and his chair back from the table. "I want my land, my rations and supplies. Is it too much to ask after risking my life? Where are the rewards?"

Sarah piped up. "We were rewarded, Papa. We got freedom."

Fortune stared at Sarah. His nostrils flared as he gritted his teeth. "I want you to listen good, Babygirl. Did they promise the white man freedom or was he promised rewards?" His eyes blazed. "What would you call titles, honour and glory and large land grants? We are at the end of the line, getting the crumbs, if there are any left." He waved his finger at her and said, "It is your right to have rewards if you put your hand to the load. Don't think that the colour of your skin makes you less deserving. You are worthy." Then his voice softened, but remained firm. "Freedom is not a reward, Sarah. Freedom is a right. Never forget that."

"Fortune, you are right, but hush now and put that anger away. It will wear you down. Tonight calls for joy because you found us. You did us proud and because of your courage, you got your freedom. We are not worrying about anything else tonight. We got you back and we can work together to survive in Scotia. We got to look to ourselves as best we can."

"I guess it was the Lord's will that it happened the way it did. I went to war because I felt it was the right thing to do for my family. I did not do it for greed."

"You hush, now. The Lord will show the way, if we take the time to listen. We can help each other and stand up for our rights." She looked at Fortune with an inquisitive face. "How did you get to Scotia, son?"

"That's a long story," he growled as he took small sips of cold tea.

"We got nothing but time. Come on Fortune, finish the yarn." She loved a good story and besides, it would keep him from talking about the war. Her voice was sharp. "I know you been through a lot son, but come on now, tell us about your journey."

"That's a yarn to tell, but I'll make it short. Save some for another day."

"Just start at the beginning, son."

"Well, it was 1781 when I joined the British. I watched the surrender of Charles Town to the American rebels in '82. After that, my unit headed to New York and stayed for a year. We boarded the ship *Adventure*. She took us to Saint John, New Brunswick."

"All this time we wondered if you had made it."

"I got myself a little work, but it was not long before I got discouraged. I was worrying about you. Then, the strangest thing happened. One day down on the dock in Saint John I come across a long, lean fellow by the name of Hercules."

"Hercules is a funny name, Papa. Was that his real name?"

"Aye, that's his name and he was an odd man to go with it." Fortune stretched back in his chair. He grinned for the first time. His voice quieted and he began to laugh. "He was a slave hell-bent on getting freedom from his master. He had one eye and one ear and a back so ridged with scars that it looked like a ploughed field. Ol' Hercules just laughed off his misfortunes. He liked putting us to shame by saying it proved he had courage. It made him a man, not like the rest of us. He was always asking us, 'Where your scars be, you jellyfish?'"

"You don't have to wear your scars on the outside," Grandmother interjected.

Fortune nodded in agreement. "So true, Mama, so true. As I was saying, Hercules came to Saint John from Port Roseway. We got to talking about the settlement in Birchtown."

"That be a rag. Oh, Lord." Lydia chuckled.

"He said that he got separated from his woman and he searched this colony high and low, but could not find her. That Hercules. He came right out and said that he was glad to be rid of her. Said that woman was nothing but trouble. She had a split tongue like a snake, always speaking out of both sides of her mouth." Fortune hissed. "Ol' Hercules couldn't believe a word she said."

"A sinner, she was," chimed Grandmother. "There are plenty of them."

"Well now," Fortune grinned and added, "Then he mentioned an old lady and a girl in Birchtown."

"Did you figure it was us, Papa? What did he say?"

"Oh Lord, Sarah," Grandmother said. "How would your father know it was us?"

Fortune laughed hard. "Hercules said the old woman was as hard as a coconut shell. Everyone minded his manners around her. Who else could it be, but you, Mama?"

Grandmother sucked on her pipe with such a ferocious drag, she choked.

"I said that sounds like Lydia Redmond, all right. Well, he jumped up saying, 'That be the name.'" Fortune's laugh was long and hardy and it infected them. He looked at Sarah. "And the girl, well, Hercules said that she was as pretty as a field of peach blossoms."

Sarah's face beamed. This was the old Papa, always with a bit of mischief in his words and such a laugh.

"Fortune, how did you get by in Saint John?"

"I worked in the woods marking trees with the king's broad arrow … only the best and the straightest trees for the masts on British ships. I got me some money and took a lumber boat across the Bay of Fundy to Digby. After that, I hitched a ride to Yarmouth on a fishing boat, then on another to Port Roseway."

"That was a trip. It surely was."

"In Roseway, I came across a fellow playing the spoons at the wharf by the name of Cato. He gave me directions to Birchtown. I swear he knew the name and background of everyone here. He rhymed off names and places I never heard of. I never thought it would be that easy to find you. Sometimes a man gets favoured with a little luck."

"Yes he does. To that, I say Amen, Fortune."

Thirteen

Beulah greeted Fortune with an eerie smile. It was early morning and another snowy December day. She neither acknowledged nor commented on Fortune's return. She turned with just a quick hello and went to the bunk where Prince Junior lay crying, picked him up and gently pressed him to her breast. The child made ghastly sounds and sucked so hard, Fortune wondered if he was getting any nourishment at all.

He chatted with Fibby, who came by just twice a week now, to give Sarah a break. She was all talk. "Yes, Fortune," Fibby said. "I delivered the twins all by myself. It was a hard labour, but I pulled her through, not once, but twice. Yes, yes. It takes a good midwife to do that for two days." She beamed with pride.

"Yes, it takes a skilled hand," he agreed, stealing a glance at Beulah. She looked small inside the big blue dress. He was baffled by her strange reaction to him. This place had stolen her joy, he thought, for her eyes were as blank as a clear sky and her spirit was numb.

"You don't recognize your brother-in-law?" he said jokingly.

Beulah glimpsed quickly at Fortune, a solemn expression on her frail face. She clung to Prince Junior and kept patting the back of his head. She did not reply.

"Is she alright?" he asked Fibby.

"She's frail and heartsick over losing Prince. She's a broken woman."

Fortune looked at the broken woman closely. Beulah Thomkins came to the plantation in chains, one of the new arrivals, in the back of Boll weevil's cart. She walked to the quarters, not bent over like the others, but tall and upright in a dress that was stiff with dry blood. She was broken then, beaten bad to take the running out of her. However, beyond the rags and blood there was beauty—a face golden-brown like fresh molasses and eyes that mesmerized all the young slaves. She took chances that often brought her trouble. It was all gone now.

He shifted in the chair and broke the morbid silence by humming. When Beulah put Prince down, he approached her, reaching out his hand. "Don't be afraid, Beulah. You can't give up now. We survived worse times, didn't we?" He waited, but she did not answer. "You are a good woman. Do not lock yourself away from life. Let yourself feel again." He stuttered now saying, "Please, Beulah. Let me help you." He fumbled for comforting words. "I'll help you. Come on now and cheer up. Things will get better."

She leaned into him and placed her head on his chest. She wept without any explanation. He held her tight and hummed again. Fortune understood her silent grief, knew it was difficult for her to connect rightly to her feelings. She had trained herself to hold emotions back because crying was a sign of weakness. A weak slave made good sport for an overseer. Patience, he thought. A little kindness would help bring her around.

"You look a lot like Prince," she said finally.

"So they say."

A long silence swallowed the room. Fortune thought about the revolution, how it had displaced thousands. How it had separated men from their women, children from parents, slaves from masters. The reality was that no matter what happened, you had to march to the beat. If you lost step, you would fall down and get left behind. And no one would care. You had to hold on. You had to believe and trust that if you fell, God would find you. His mother had said it a thousand times: "Blessings will find you if you let them." He looked at Beulah. She needed his help to get in step and march. She was scared and lost and broken, sure. He quietly stroked her hair. His voice was protective: "It's going to be all right."

"I'm not myself, Fortune. I don't know what's come over me. Sarah and Fibby have been such a help, but there is so much to do. I'm tired and there's no money and so little food."

Fortune looked around the shack. If ever there was misery, he thought, it found its way here. How were any of them going to survive in this squalor? He looked at Beulah. Could she care for herself, let alone the twins? He looked at the two babies curled up tightly to each other. Their tiny faces looked ashen. He bent and picked up the smaller of the two. Destiny was frail and list-less. She was not much bigger than a large melon and weighed barely as much.

"I promise to help," he said, "starting with fixing up this place and building up the wood pile to heat it."

Fibby chimed in saying, "That will be good, but she needs food and a tonic, Fortune. That's what she needs to get her strength back. Cecil carries tonic at the store." She nodded her head. "And a little meat would be good. It's been a long time since we had meat."

"I'll see what I can do," he said as he headed to the door. "I'll be back."

The cold December wind caught Fortune's back and pushed him along the trail. He wondered about Beulah and thought about his future. He was thirty-seven. Sarah was grown and the old woman was getting along in years. Time was sliding along. It was time to settle down. Beulah was a good person. Behind her sad eyes, he knew there was a woman capable of finding herself again. The tonic would help. When she was feeling better, he would test fate.

After Fortune crossed the frozen brook, he came upon some Pioneers warming themselves around a roaring fire. He recognized Bill Abbot and Jake Whalen. He joined them with a yarn about his journey to Birchtown. They made small talk about the war and the weather, discussed the plans for a new church and talked about folks having to leave Birchtown to find work. When all that was out of the way, Bill said, "A lot of folks are getting picked up and shipped south."

Jake interrupted, "So I hear. That Boll weevil tried it with Lydia."

"What do you mean?" Fortune asked.

"Boll weevil is up to his tricks," Jake said.

"What's he done?"

"I was putting in a half day with Ramsey Lewis, the livery man, when I heard him say that Boll weevil rented his cart to collect runaways and that he tried to pick up Lydia and the girl."

"I heard it as well and that the old woman pulled a fast one," Bill spurted.

"A fast one?" Fortune asked.

Jake laughed so hard he took a pain in his side. "She faked dropping dead on the road."

"Yes. Boll weevil left her there on the side of the road for dead with her granddaughter. Lydia always has a trick in her pocket. She fooled him," Bill said.

"Well, I know this much, she's not dead," Fortune frowned.

"That Lydia," Jake said, still laughing. "She's a fox all right. And a clever one."

The news left Fortune unnerved. With Boll weevil lurking about, any one of them could disappear without a trace. He wondered why Boll weevil was after his mother and Sarah. He thought about his army pistol stored away in his bedroll. He would carry it from now on.

Cecil MacLeod kept one eye on Fortune and the other on the barrel of salt pork he was stirring. Fortune flipped the coins in his pocket and looked about the store. He could feel Cecil's eyes. He recognized him as soon as he saw him. Not wishing to be disrespectful, he spoke first. "Good morning to you, Sir."

"Good morning." The tone was condescending. "And who might ye be?" Cecil looked him over from head to toe. He tried to keep up on all the newcomers, if not by name, then by face. This one was new, yet there was something familiar about him.

"Name's Fortune Redmond."

"Redmond? One of Lydia's tribe, are you?"

Fortune bristled at the word "tribe." "Yes, Sir. Lydia's son."

"Well, well. Her boy has come home. She must be happy."

"Yes sir. She is happy to have the help."

Cecil made no reply. He kept his eyes on Fortune as he milled about. The missing slave. Another Redmond. One of his shameful offspring. This was certainly more than he had bargained for.

Fortune, aware of being studied, kept looking among the strange bottles. It would have been easier for him to find the tonic if he could read, but it was not long before he found a bottle of the right shape and colour.

"How much, Mr. MacLeod?"

"One crown," Cecil sneered. "I suppose Lydia sent you. Not feeling herself these days? Or, is she too busy to come by?"

"I don't know, sir. Folks can't get out and about in the cold."

Cecil swept his hand over his bald head. He squirmed and discharged a loud belch, leaving his face beet purple. He sized the boy up.

Fortune put the tonic on the counter. He was feeling uneasy and acutely aware of Cecil's eyes on him as he walked about, adding a small keg of milk, a half dozen salt herring and a small cut of chewing tobacco to his pile. He calculated the total and then reached into his pocket and placed the exact amount on the counter. Dahlia had taught him enough not to get cheated.

After Fortune departed, it dawned on Cecil that Lydia's Certificates of Freedom were still in the pot. He removed the prized papers and placed them inside the pocket of his thick, woollen vest. Later, when things quieted down, he would find a hiding place upstairs in the loft. For the present, he would work on his plan for Lydia. "Soon," he mumbled. "Soon, I too shall be free." His sarcasm produced a wide smile and his one tooth rested on his bottom lip.

When Fortune arrived back at Beulah's, Beulah was mumbling, holding her head in her hands at the table. Fortune placed his bundle on the table beside her, but she did not look up. He looked at Fibby, who was sitting on the cot holding a small bundle tightly wrapped in rags. Her eyes were grey with tears and her sobbing was long and sharp, like a child's whining.

"What has happened?" Fortune asked, already knowing the answer.

"Destiny," wailed Fibby. "Shortly after you left. Peaceful it be, in her sleep."

"Oh Fortune, my Destiny's gone," Beulah moaned. "She's gone. My child has passed on. She's gone to be with her daddy."

Fortune put his arms around Beulah. "Life will be good again. This grief will pass." After holding her for a few minutes, he started for the door and said, "I'll tell Mama the news."

The following day, the Redmonds stood huddled with their backs against the cold December wind. The frozen ground behind Beulah's shack did not enable a proper burial. Their hearts were as heavy as the stones Fortune managed to pry from his brother's grave. He piled them over Destiny in a spot next to her daddy.

Grandmother's words were brief. "Dear Lord, we commit this baby to your loving care, our child, Destiny Redmond. May she rest in peace. Amen."

Fourteen

AN UNRELENTING BLIZZARD ENGULFED THE BIRCHTOWN settlement bringing a frightful amount of snow, six feet deep in places. Every available hand turned out to shovel.

The sod roof on Reece Johnson's shack had collapsed through the centre. He stretched long poles across the gaping hole and piled the last of the spruce boughs over the poles. When he finished, he sat on a tree stump and finished off a chunk of salt deer meat as he took a much-needed break. He focused on a pair of noisy woodpeckers drilling relentlessly for moth larva. He was thinking how the birds had such a convenient supply of winter food and the tools they needed to find it, unlike many of the Loyalists, who were fending off starvation with little more than their will.

Sarah, who was on her way to Cecil's store, spotted Reece and slowly crept up from behind until she was close enough to reach out and place a hand on his shoulder. Reece jumped, then stood and turned about sharply. She giggled and was about to say, "A good wife would make you a nice lunch," but checked herself, as finding even a morsel these days would be hard. Reece looked into Sarah's sparkling eyes and said, "You should have on a heavier coat. This weather can make you sick if you are not dressed for it."

"I'm warm enough. I have a ton of clothes piled on."

"A good thing. So what are you doing out on such a day, Miss Sarah?"

"Cato came by with a message from Mr. MacLeod. He said that Grandmother took a dizzy spell on her way back from Port Roseway. She made it as far as the store and Mr. MacLeod has asked that I come and see that she makes it home safely." She squatted on a stump opposite Reece. "I only have a minute. I'm worried. Grandmother has never gotten sick, not that I can remember."

"Why didn't Cato help her back?"

"I didn't ask, but you never know his condition! He always smells of brew."

"Fortune could have gone."

"He left early this morning because Cecil asked him to do some carpentry work at the store. Nothing would stop Papa from a day's work. It's too hard to come by."

"True, but it's a poor day for outside work and a long walk in the cold. It is not safe for you to be out alone. I heard about your run-in with Boll weevil. I'd feel better if I went with you." He reached inside the door and grabbed a heavy coat.

"Thanks. I don't like being out alone, but I try to be careful. It's the cold I hate more than anything."

When they had gone some distance, Reece turned to her and said, "It's a bitter winter, just as bad as the first. I was hoping this one would be better. The winters last so long up here … they seem to last forever."

"I try not to think about it. There's something nice about the snow. It's so pure and fluffy; it reminds me of the cotton fields!" Sarah picked up a handful of snow and threw it at Reece.

"Missed!" he said, ducking fast.

"I hope Grandmother is alright. She's old and she's had a lot of worries lately."

Reece was quiet. The snow was heavy and walking was difficult. He was thinking that Sarah was strong and determined, like her grandmother. Now that they had settled into a friendship, they were nearly inseparable. He frowned at Sarah's insistence that they keep their friendship from her grandmother, agreeing only because she assured him it was for the best. He supposed there was no need for trouble.

They came to a place where the snow had filled in the path and they climbed over huge banks of snow. Beyond the drifts, they took a shortcut through a part of the arm Sarah had not seen before. A long rock wall stretched for about a mile and there were ruins: dilapidated buildings and piles of rocks outlining foundations where the wind scattered the snow—the homes of the French before their expulsion.

"It's hard to believe people were here before us," Sarah remarked.

"People move on, but they leave their mark."

Suddenly, without warning, Sarah let out a loud scream. She found herself sinking down into a wide hole. For a moment, Reece panicked. He approached the hole and managed to pull her out, but Sarah was shaken. She gathered her wits while Reece asked her if she was hurt.

Sarah straightened her bonnet, brushed herself off and said, "I'm alright."

"That's a relief. You must have stumbled into an old well. The snow's light, you went right through it."

"It gave me a fright. We better hope nothing else happens. Grandmother must be worried."

Sarah looked back at the ghostly ruins. A sudden emptiness and feeling of sadness for lost souls caused her to say, "I don't know what I would do without Grandmother. Death is funny. It comes unexpectedly most times, like a sudden fire alarm. Just go, get out, with little or no warning. I've seen so much of it."

"Death is hard to deal with, I imagine. I can't say that I've ever had to deal with it, really. I mentioned not knowing my parents. I feel like a ship adrift in the Atlantic. I have no idea who named me Reece. Reece who, I often wonder."

"Reece is a wonderful name. You told me your name was Reece Johnson."

"I did. It's funny how that name came about. When the man who was recording names on the Inspection Roll asked for mine, I said 'Reece.' He asked if I had a surname. I didn't think of myself as a slave or want to take on the Redmond name, so I said 'Johnson.' It was the first name that came into my head."

The path was slippery in places. Reece took Sarah's arm. "Careful," he said, and helped her over a spot of ice.

"You weren't alone. A lot of slaves just had one name."

"They did, but I named myself! My free name is Reece Johnson." He let go a roaring laugh that echoed throughout the woods.

"Well, at least you had the freedom to choose. This freedom is not all it was supposed to be. I'm indentured to the Cunninghams for now. Housework does not suit me. It's shameful to trade our freedom and souls for a hand-out and a bite to eat."

"In these hard times, we do what we have to do." He squeezed her hand, pulled her to a standstill and looked into her eyes. "I have news. I received my notice to go sea."

"When are you leaving?" There was sadness in her voice and she bit her lip and looked away, stepping faster, dreading the answer.

"In three days I will be heading up north on *Cape Blomidon*. I can't turn down a job, much less a good-paying one like this."

"And will you return to Birchtown?"

"I can't say how long I'll be gone for sure, perhaps a month or more. I suppose I'll return here to home port. There's no other place to call home."

"Grandmother says we have to put down roots. It's the only way to survive," she said matter-of-factly.

"She's right." That was all he said, until a crow cawed. "Sometimes I feel like your grandmother is sizing me up. She looks at me in the oddest way …"

"I have my own mind and my own heart."

"I have no doubt of that, Sarah Redmond. No doubt at all. We are almost there." Reece grabbed Sarah's hand. "You're a strong and brave woman. I'd work my heart out for someone like you. Honestly, I would."

Sarah smiled. "And what good would you be to me if you worked your heart out?"

Reece smiled a boyish smile. His eyes met hers. He felt manly now that he had a purpose and hope. He stopped and pulled Sarah forward and brushed the snow from her shoulders. The sound of Ackers Brook making its way under the icy covers filled the air. It was in that spot that Reece stopped and pulled Sarah close. Just as they were engaging in a gentle kiss, the sounds of fierce howling and panting jolted them apart. Suddenly a pack of wild dogs sprang from the woods and bared their sharp teeth. Their growls were vicious and their ribs bulged through their puny sides. Like lightning, Reece broke a spruce branch and waved it with much screaming until the dogs ran off through the thick snow.

Sarah's fright had turned to amusement as she watched. "They're starving," Sarah said. "There's nothing for them to eat in this snow."

With that remark, it came to her that she was starving too. As they hurried on, Sarah turned her thoughts inward. What was she starving for? Food? Excitement? Happiness? There was nothing for a lively spirit in this empty place. A picture of New York came into her mind with its tall buildings, hustle and bustle, smells and people going about with purpose. She was tired of the heavy-hearted wayfarers and gloominess of Birchtown. She looked at Reece, another adventurer, and the very idea of getting married felt like a sentence to the House of Corrections. Such thoughts. It was all too much, too complicated on a morning like this.

She had other pressing concerns. She could see the roof of Cecil MacLeod's store in the distance. Upon reaching the store, she and Reece parted company. She watched as he headed back to help other Birchtowners with their repairs. Knowing what had transpired between Mr. MacLeod and Grandmother, her fear of him transformed into a great lump in her stomach.

Fifteen

"YOU OWE ME TWICE OVER CECIL. WE HAD AN AGREEMENT." Boll weevil screamed, the spit flying from his mouth.

Cecil scowled. "We had a deal and you fell short. A man has to live up to his word, otherwise his word becomes a shallow reminder of how useless he is."

"Damn you, Cecil. I agreed to do your dirty work. You couldn't have managed without me this morning. The old woman and her son were a handful." Anger cut across his face. "An honest man keeps his word. It wasn't my fault the first attempt failed."

Cecil laughed and then grunted. "An honest man you say? Have you forgotten how long I've known you? You are far from that or you would have returned and reported what happened. Did you think I wouldn't hear the news of Lydia's prank? I've been terrified that she would reveal our plot. I was sick because of your blunder." Cecil was edgy, wondering how any man could speak of honour in times like these. He massaged his forehead several times. "I won't pay you for a botched job. This second attempt to capture Lydia and the girl will put an end to this blasted partnership. For that, I will pay." He held Boll weevil's gaze and gave him a poisonous sneer. His tone hardened. "We will talk after you honour your promise to return this evening."

Boll weevil eyed Cecil with contempt. Anger bloomed beneath his skin. "I need supplies and the least you can do is allow me credit. You owe me that. Business is slow with the Birchtowners on their guard, hiding runaways and sharing their certificates."

"I owe you nothing, man. I would be crazy to trust you in these anxious times. There is no credit here. What chance would I have of repayment? All you've got to barter with is a gun and a shabby horse."

"You're a miserable snake, Cecil. You'll pay for this." He was in Cecil's face with his right hand raised. "You can't cut a man down and walk away free."

Cecil smiled nervously. "Here's money to rent the wagon. Just be sure you are alone and back here by dusk," and he handed Boll weevil some coins. "We will strike a fair deal then. I'll pay for what you've earned."

When Sarah opened the door at Cecil's, Boll weevil stormed past, meeting her surprise with scorn. She watched him mount his bony charger, mumbling unintelligibly under his breath. Sarah grew faint, wondering if he would remember her, turn around, and come back. She watched as he steered the horse around. Her thoughts were also of Reece's safety. When Boll weevil headed in the opposite direction, her fear slowly subsided.

Inside, Cecil scurried about. His face was flushed with sweat though the small stove was barely heating the store. Sarah stood in the doorway watching as he nervously poked in the fire. He appeared distressed and she moved with caution towards him.

"Hello, Mr. MacLeod." She expected to see Grandmother sitting near the door, but there was no sign of her or Papa. She looked about. The stillness was disturbing. Something was amiss. The sight of Boll weevil caused her mind to fill with chilling thoughts while Cecil's awkward silence created even more uncertainty. Sarah spoke again, choosing her words carefully, "Cato stopped by with your message. I am here to see to my Grandmother."

Cecil was not himself. The prospect of keeping captives in his root cellar rattled him. Hatching his plan meant one more to join the others. The sheer weight of all the uncertainty filled him with exhaustion. This was turning into a nasty business. "She's down in the cellar, picking over the vegetables. Go down and give her a hand."

Cecil led her to the back of the store where he wrestled with a trap door bolted to the floor. Sarah had not noticed the door before. Why had he bolted it? Grandmother would need light, need to get back up. In her uneasiness, Sarah was trying to decide if she should stay or run. When the door was fully open, she could see a crude set of steps leading into the darkness. Cecil gave her a nudge, saying, "There's nothing to be afraid of."

Sarah hesitated. Cecil stood behind her motioning for her to go. "Lydia has a candle. She is at the far end. You go on now. Get along." She moved cautiously down the seven shoddy steps. When she reached the bottom step, the trap door slammed.

A strange sickness overcame her as she stood on the bottom step trembling, trying to adjust to the darkness. The cellar had a strange musty odour. It was bitter cold. Faint bands of light glared through the holes in the stone foundation crisscrossing at various angles. "Grandmother. Are you here?" She could barely mutter the words. Overhead, she could hear Cecil moving and the blows of a hammer pounding, pounding on the trap door. She held her breath and listened for signs of life—human or otherwise. A sudden tapping on the dirt floor spooked her just as muffled sounds came from the right of the stairs. Sarah halted. She searched through the darkness, adjusting her eyes to the dim light, expecting to see Grandmother, when instead of one figure, she saw two. They sat upright on the ground.

"Grandmother? Papa? Is that you?" The ceiling was low with thick beams that prevented her from moving quickly. She knelt and put her hand on the old woman's face. It was cold and clammy and her breathing strained. She untied the rag from around Grandmother's mouth, then struggled to untie the ropes that bound her hands and feet, but the knots were too tight. She turned to her father. A sudden flurry of mice scattered about his feet. She pushed her hand against her mouth. Would she survive even an hour in this hole? She worked the knots until Fortune's hands fell free. He stretched them behind his ears and untied the filthy rag from around his mouth. Slowly he untied the rope that bound his feet.

He stood and stretched as best he could. After freeing his mother, he turned to Sarah. "How was Cecil able to lure you here?"

"He got Cato to tell me to come. That Grandmother needed me. She had taken a spell."

"This has turned into a game for them, I believe." To his mother, he said, "Do you have any idea why they would want to do such a thing, when you have papers to protect you?"

Lydia was quiet, but shortly she responded: "Times are hard. Who can you trust?" Soft humming flowed from her lips while her mind was busy wondering how she was ever going to keep the truth to herself. What a morning. One minute she was looking at the shipment of used dishes and the next Cecil and Boll weevil were grabbing her from behind. They scuffled in the cellar as they tried to tie her up. In the process, she heard the words, "sail to Boston" and "money." When they brought Fortune down, it was then that she fully realized the truth. The two men had hatched this terrible plot to get her out of Birchtown.

Lydia gasped for air. "Forgive me. Forgive me," she moaned. She was a fool to believe she could leave her torment behind, that it could possibly not trip her up in a faraway place. So this was how Cecil's cunningness was to play out. If only she had revealed the truth about having children by him after arriving in Birchtown ... but she had hesitated, believing there was too much at stake. Here was the result of her stalling—and it was not just her life on the line, but Fortune's and Sarah's as well.

Sarah sat in silence, too overcome to speak. Her first thoughts were of Reece, wondering if he was safe and if she would live to see him again. Boll weevil and Cecil had the three of them caged like animals. She wondered how long they would keep them in the cellar. She wondered if Grandmother's God was watching. Impulsively, she cast her eyes upward and prayed.

Fortune took several deep breaths. Lydia's run-in with Boll weevil had something to do with their situation and he wanted answers. He put his hand on her arm. "Tell me what happened the evening Boll weevil tried to kidnap you and Sarah."

The demand irritated the old woman. She remained silent for a long time before saying, "Oh my Lord. He tried to say we were runaways." She snatched up her pipe from her pocket, and sucked air for several seconds. "He planned to ship us down to Boston. His living comes off the backs of slaves you know."

"You have your certificates. Did you show him your certificates?"

"I searched in my purse, but I could not find them because, oh, sweet chariots ... they were gone."

"What happened to the papers?"

"I don't know. I had them at Cecil's store that morning."

"How would he get his hands on your papers?"

"I left my purse on the counter when I went to look at the vegetables."

"Mama, of what interest was your papers to Cecil?"

Lydia stared at the light coming through the tiny holes in the cellar wall. She rubbed the back of her neck, felt the pain of a thousand beatings, the weight of long-held secrets when they came like thieves to steal her rest. It was her fear of Cecil and shame that kept the secrets safe. She was careful in her answer this time. "You know how Cecil loves the coin. He would sell his own mother if he could make a shilling."

"Seems like a lot of trouble."

"Oh, Lord, Fortune, that man is not worrying about who he catches."

"He planned this for a reason." He looked at his mother. "I believe that you know the reason. It is time now to be free of your worries. Tell what happened."

She sucked more air through the pipe. "I was bought to make slaves. I was breeding stock. Cecil bred me behind Master Redmond's back for the light-skinned babies to sell." Silence hung on her painful account and tears streamed down her face. "He fathered my children. He is … your father as he was Prince's."

For a moment, Fortune could feel nothing, then his heart rebelled and the pain was so intense, it was as if a sharp blade was passing through it. However, he came to himself and summed up the situation. "You suffered a lot. I saw how he treated you. That was the practice, selling, buying and breeding slaves without any regard for life or decency. But that does not explain why he wanted to get rid of you and Sarah. That's my concern."

"He is protecting himself because he has moved up in the world. He is afraid I will tell about his past. He will not lose what he has. "Cecil and I have a daughter in Roseway, perhaps a son in Birchtown, and another daughter somewhere."

"My Sweet Lord. Who are they, Mama?"

"I only know of the one for sure."

"Who?"

Her words turned to mumbles. The name would not fall from her lips. What right did she have to reveal her daughter's mixed blood without her permission? She thought again of the trouble that letting it slip in Roseway might bring.

"This woman, do I know her?" Fortune growled, impatient with his mother's stalling.

"The name is the least of our worries now. How are we going to escape from this cellar?"

Fortune realized now that, sadly, she and Cecil were entangled in a secret web. "I'll wait on your time to tell me. You are right about the cellar. We need a plan for when Cecil and Boll weevil return. I got my pistol." He reached down inside his long brown boot and gently rubbed the cold metal of his ol' dragoon, as though it were a harmless kitten.

The old woman picked up the bottom of her wide green dress. She carefully ripped a strip of cloth from the worn edge. Crawling to the bottom step, she tied the strip from one railing over to the other. One way or another, Cecil had to be stopped. They had a gun, a trick and a prayer.

Sixteen

UNDER THE COVER OF DARKNESS, THE RICKETY WAGON clamoured along the snow-covered road, turning at the fork that led to Birchtown. The wind and damp cold gnawed through the man's heavy coat and gripped his thin body. Stabs of pain shot through his hands and feet. The slow haul from Roseway was taking longer than expected. There was just too much snow.

True to his word, if a rogue can be honourable, Boll weevil had made his way back to Cecil's store. He jumped from the wagon, a string of pointless banter flowing from his cracked lips. He was out of joint, still agitated from Cecil's heavy-handedness. Eyeing the premises, he approached carefully, stopping first to peer through the window. Inside, a lamp burned brightly. He saw Cecil with his head down on the counter having a snooze. He pounded heavily on the locked door

Down in the cellar, the captives nestled together for protection from the bitter cold. The hard thumps awakened Lydia. In the startled darkness, she rubbed her hands to soothe her aching joints and pushed against her empty stomach to stop the loud rumbling. Beside her Fortune slept, making noises that reminded her of a snorting horse. She shook his arm. "I hear someone overhead. Cecil has company. It must be Boll weevil," she whispered, "What are we going to do?"

"All we can do is sit tight," Fortune said, rousing Sarah who lay sleeping on his shoulder.

"He has come for us."

"Maybe so, but don't be scared. I am ready." Fortune patted his leg for his gun. He realized that the weather could mess everything up—his cold pistol might not fire. He pulled out the gun and stuck it down inside his jacket to warm it. The cold had stiffened his fingers. He wondered if he could even pull the trigger.

Sarah rocked back and forth. Her insides surged like incoming waves. How could anyone have thought of such a place as the Land of Milk and Honey, she wondered. Where would they end up? And would Reece look for her? She listened as the biting cold caused Grandmother's breathing to come in quick, short puffs matched by steady pleas to her Lord. Were they going to die here, unbeknownst to anyone? Maybe it was better to die now, here in this stinking cellar, and be through with it.

Upstairs, Cecil finally bolted upright at the pounding. He stood up groggily, stretched and shook his head. "Who is there?"

"It's me, Boll weevil. Unlatch the door, man."

"You brought the wagon?" Cecil asked.

"Yes and a costly one it is. You can add that expense to my bill."

Cecil cut Boll weevil a nasty look as he brushed past. It was a strange night. The wind had been unrelenting, slamming the window shutters hard against the logs. There was a strange howl in the wind, a nor'easter with an eerie pitch. The lamp had gone out twice. Strangely, Cecil was glad to see Boll weevil. It meant the end was now in sight. Though the Redmonds were secure with no means of escape, he anguished over having them in the root cellar. Once Boll weevil placed them on the ship to Boston, his worries would be over. He had considered alternatives, such as burning them out, but this way was best. No one could connect him to the plot and his problem would be sailing south with no chance of ever returning. "The Lord does work in mysterious ways," he laughed.

He glanced around the store. Yes sir, he was doing well. He owned this store. He had a good wife and two grown lads in the British army. After tonight, he could focus on getting back to business as usual. In the faded light, he sized Boll weevil up as he dashed about the store, helping himself to food. He hated the look of the man's chops and his brash attitude. His behaviour was growing insane, but then he was always a little unhinged, always seeking some crazy adventure. No matter, it would all end soon.

Boll weevil sat on a barrel chewing strips of dark beef jerky and crunching hardtack with his rotten teeth. "I ain't had a bite to eat in two days," he said. "I can't work on an empty stomach. You could have cooked up a scoff on that fancy stove and had it waiting."

"I don't recall saying that the job came with meals. I didn't indenture you." Cecil laughed as he let out this last retort.

Boll weevil did not reply. He was too busy eyeing a huge block of yellow cheese. He pulled out his knife, leaned across the counter and cut a big chunk. Piercing the chunk with his knife, he held it up and took several bites, and then pointed the knife towards Cecil. "At least a servant has a contract. That's more than I have," he sputtered.

"Come on, man. You are wasting time. There's work to be done," Cecil snapped.

Boll weevil took a long look at the man rushing him. "Hold on," he snorted. He went to the back and got a small keg of rum, and after gulping several mouthfuls, he drawled confidently: "Now tell me, Cecil, we had a deal, didn't we? I don't plan on moving this lot until we settle our business and you have met my terms."

"When I have proof that you have done the job, then we will talk."

Boll weevil's face darkened to a deep blue hue. "That is not what we agreed on. What now, another lie, Cecil? You keep changing the terms, going in circles, backtracking to cheat me. Remember the old days when we were like brothers. Is this how you treat a friend? The deal was to settle the account before I took this bunch to Roseway."

"I had to rethink the offer. I'm just making sure everything goes as planned."

"For a desperate man, anxious to rid himself of a bunch of meddling Negroes, you have forgotten one thing. There is a dignified fee for such a miserable job. That's all I ask."

Cecil laughed. "A dignified fee for a dignified man." His laugh ceased when Boll weevil waved the knife in his face. "Of course," he said, stepping back, "I will pay you. But first, you must show me proof that you have done my bidding, that everything went as planned. I cannot afford to throw my money to the wind. No, Boll weevil, money is too scarce to be foolish. Bring back a statement from the captain in Roseway if you want your pay. It will be a couple of days before he sails."

Boll weevil did not answer. He stood for a moment, staring at Cecil. In an instant, he drove the knife blade deep into the counter. "That does not set well with me. No sir." The vein on the side of his neck throbbed, sticking out like a long snake. His eyes bulged. "You are a fool if you think I'll be running back and forth out here in this weather!" he screamed. "What if I come back from Roseway and you have changed up on me again? What then?" His voice resonated throughout the store. "Will it be papers from Boston I'll need? I treated you fair and square. I came back and I told you what happened. I agreed to take on this lousy job again, despite the weather. Do you think I am a fool? Pay up now or there's no deal. You can figure out how to get rid of that bunch yourself."

Cecil moved closer to Boll weevil and raised his clenched fist. His voice was loud. "The likes of a man like you to question my integrity." He grabbed Boll weevil by his coat lapels. "You are no more than filthy scum, Boll weevil. I know your past and there's not an honest bone in your body. You do not scare me with your wretched chaff nor will you twist a coin from my hand." Boll weevil slid from his grip while he panted hard, like a dog returning from a long chase.

With a hard tug at the knife, Boll weevil freed it from the counter. He grabbed Cecil, and put an arm around his throat and the knife to his temple. "I mean business," he yelled. "Show me where you keep the money."

Cecil yelped, his face pressed into a nasty scowl. He stumbled as Boll weevil dragged him across the store by the neck. "There, by the back wall." He pointed to the floor.

Boll weevil was insistent and screaming now, "Lift the boards up!"

"You can't do this. How can you rob a friend?" Cecil protested.

Boll weevil hauled back and gave Cecil a hard slap to the side of his head. Cecil whined like a kicked pup while he slowly lifted the boards. He retrieved a large tin box, heavy with his cherished spoils, and placed it on a bench by the back wall.

Boll weevil swallowed when he saw the box. He pushed Cecil to one side with such a hostile thrust that the man staggered and fell hard. Working the edges of the box with his knife, he forced it open. He reached in and started pocketing handfuls of coins, then, inspired, stopped, shut the lid and made his way towards the door with all the plunder.

"What about the Negroes?" Cecil moaned. His left arm and leg ached from the fall. He gripped a barrel and pulled himself up. The thought of losing the money heated his blood. "Come back you filthy brute. You will not get away with this. I will hunt you down, Boll weevil. Oh yes and I'll see that you suffer like the dog you are." He made a mad dash after Boll weevil. "I'll be damned if I will let you leave with my hard-earned cash."

All was quiet. In the root cellar, the three waited and listened. Their bodies trembled from the tension and ached from the savage cold. They heard the men tussle for several minutes. Then, without let up, there came a rush of lively blows followed by a loud scream, a heavy thud on the floor and a scurrying of feet towards the door.

Seventeen

BEFORE BOLL WEEVIL HAD COVERED A MILE, HE GAVE A fierce yank on the old mare's reins to steer the cart around and head back to Cecil's store. He was in a pickle and he knew it. He had only planned to get what Cecil owed him, not to kill him. Was there any fault in that?

He pressed his lips together. As his witching stirred, a grin spread across his face. It would be obvious to all of Roseway who the murderer was: Fortune. Yes, that brazen lot was out looting after dark when he stumbled upon them. He would turn them over to Sheriff Beauford. His spurts of laughter steamed the air and demons danced in his wild eyes. It was almost too easy. The Redmonds, still tied up, could offer no resistance. It would compensate for all his troubles.

Lydia and Sarah snuggled together as Fortune stumbled about in the darkness looking for a means of escape. "I'll have to try the trap door," he said, extending his arms and pushing with all his strength on the sealed cover. Then came the unmistakable creaks of the wagon. He eased back from the stairs and sat quietly, feeling anxious … waiting.

Above the trio, the lamp flickered with an orange and eerie glow. Boll weevil quickly helped himself to barrels of flour, kegs of rum, salt fish, tobacco and rope. He made several trips to the wagon, nearly forgetting to leave space for his passengers.

He took two muskets from a wooden barrel and loaded each with a small ball and black gunpowder. He threw one behind the wagon seat and kept the other with him. "These items should fetch a good price. The coin will add up. Who knows, maybe I'll own this store one day."

Cecil's body lay sprawled near the door. Boll weevil pulled his knife from the man's chest. He gave it a quick wipe on Cecil's blood-soaked shirt and shoved it into the leather pouch tied to his belt. Before moving away, he looked at Cecil and raised his foot, kicking him several times in the head to release his hateful venom. "A little send-off," he chuckled. "A dignified pay for a dignified man."

Boll weevil grabbed a small crow bar from the bunch of tools lining the back wall. He worked it around the edges of the trap door, puffing and rushing wildly with enthusiasm, like a lunatic. He was eager to end this forsaken day, eager to get away from the colony. He drew a long breath and finally lifted the cellar door. The curfew in Port Roseway was a blessing—no one would be out at this hour. It would be clear sailing once the captives were in the wagon and secured. With the lamp in one hand and his gun in the other, he commenced the short climb down into the cellar.

The three Redmonds sat quietly. Fortune was ready, his dragoon loaded and pointed at the top of the steps. He stared, wondering which man was approaching. A foot hit the first step, then the second. Fortune was biding his time, hesitating to fire until he at least knew who he was dealing with. The stranger stepped slowly, cautiously, off the third step, the fourth and fifth.

With the lamp he carried casting a dim light, the man peered into the blackness below. He strained to make out the forms, listened for breathing. He kept descending, carefully planting his right foot on the sixth step. As his left foot came slowly down on the last step, the strip of cotton caught his ankle and he tumbled and hit the frozen ground. The air was heavy with the smell of whale oil from the lamp, but the flame held. He let out a loud, lengthy groan and then, losing consciousness, lay in a silent heap.

Fortune's hand shook. Strange whimpers emerged from his lips as his anguish withdrew.

Lydia picked up the lamp and held it to the man's face. "It be Boll weevil," she gasped.

Fortune scooped up the rope from the floor and tied Boll weevil's hands and feet. He untied the rag from the stairs and stuffed it in his pocket.

Upstairs, Lydia and Sarah warmed themselves beside the stove while Fortune secured the trap door. They stood in stunned silence as though the whole world had fallen into the shadowy Atlantic deeps.

"Boll weevil...he...he...killed Cecil," Grandmother finally stammered.

"Will Boll weevil be all right?" Sarah asked.

"He is dazed from the fall. He should come around," Fortune said. "We best make our way home while it's still dark and no one is about."

"We can't leave yet," Lydia said. "I got one more piece of business. Cecil had my Certificates of Freedom, Fortune." Their eyes connected and held. "I ain't leaving till I find my papers. They are in a small brown pouch."

"We got to hurry," Fortune ordered.

They searched every container, drawer, nook and cranny. When after half an hour the papers did not surface, Lydia turned to Cecil's body. She searched all of his pockets, but in vain. She staggered about and found an old rag behind the counter, wiped her blood-soaked hands and put the rag in the stove. She reached for the lamp and climbed the stairs to the loft. When she finally descended, there was a smile across her tired face. "We are done here," she said. "We can go home."

Eighteen

Port Roseway shivered. The news of Cecil's death engulfed the settlement in fear. Fuzzy details became solid facts as the gossip spread. Who could do such a terrible deed, the settlers wondered. How quickly they had dismissed the death of Isaac Haywood when his body was found in the Birchtown clearing, but the murder of one of their own, a prominent business man, had them all steaming like a pot of boiling soup.

Fortune paced back and forth. He could not rid himself of the fact that they left Boll weevil in the cellar. Nor could he forget the image of Cecil's body lying on the cold wood floor. The man had stolen his mother's certificates and had hired Boll weevil to kidnap them and take them to Boston. That much he understood. But why? Was it for the money and pride, as his mother insisted? She was guarding an important piece of information, another secret, and he wanted to know what it was and who she was protecting. She had not been herself this morning. He had never seen her so distraught. Getting to the truth would take more than one round of questioning with her.

When Lydia returned from her visit with Beulah, Fortune waited until she had swept the floor, put on some soup and made a pretence of ignoring him. He could tell that she was wound up, but this pressing mess could not wait. First he asked about Beulah—and found she was well—then about Prince, who by the sounds of it was getting stronger by the day. Then Fortune poured two tankards of tea and said, "Come and sit here at the table, Mama. We need to talk. There are things we must take care of and things that need saying."

"Do you want to talk about Cecil?" she asked. "Everyone knows now. I hear the sheriff was at the store early this morning."

"It's not about him. We didn't finish our talk last night. I don't like secrets. I'd like to know who your child is in Roseway."

"It's not my right to spread her business."

"If I have a sister, shouldn't I know?" He reached over and held his mother's hands.

"It's not our place to get into her business."

"Our place?" he asked. "Is that the problem? Staying in our place?"

The two stared at each other. In Fortune's mind, all this worry about who was who and where you fit was pointless. He had seen and heard enough about race in the war. The fuss over skin was just foolishness to keep the races apart, to put one above the other. "Place," he shouted. "Can this colony afford to worry about place when death waits to claim any one of us?"

"It's the way folks think. I wish it didn't have to be that way."

Fortune laughed. "It didn't matter about the skin when it came to breeding. No worries about the Negro's blood then. No sir. Not then." His eyes strayed to the fire. "How many drops do you think she has?" he snarled. "Reverend Ringwood says all the races come out of Africa so everyone has at least one drop of *Negro* blood."

The old woman stared at Fortune. "He said that? Oh my Lord, ain't that a yarn. Well, as far as I can see, Christians do not pay any attention to that. They make up their own rules. There is no loving the neighbour if the neighbour has a drop. Love is a poor person's dream."

"People believe such nonsense about race, and Cecil, well, he just hated most everyone. I saw the way he treated you. Oh, Mama, I am not blaming you. You had to obey him or lose your life. I could see that you were afraid of him. We all were. I understood how slavery worked."

"There's no need for you to fret over this, son. This is not your concern."

"We are free now, Mama. Cecil is dead. He can't hurt you anymore."

"The hurt will never leave. It holds me back sometimes. I cannot let anything come between me and my child. I don't want to upset her with things I might say or do. At least I can see her and feel her kindness. I had five and I only know what happened to three of them."

"I know it's painful, but when you let it out, the weight will fall from your shoulders."

Lydia stared into Fortune's eyes. Let the truth out, he was saying, but she was the one who felt cornered. She wanted to pounce like a cat and swallow up all the misery. Her silence was long and weary, but in the end, she knew Fortune was right. It was time to lay her burden down. "I suppose I've carried this long enough." Her admission felt awkward. "I must speak with her first. It will not be easy to bring this up. Lord knows if she has any idea of her background." The old woman smiled and relaxed a little.

"Well, when you're ready, Mama, I'm here and the Lord knows I won't judge you or anyone else for no good reason."

"That business can wait. We got bigger troubles, Fortune. The sheriff found Cecil but there's been no word of Boll weevil. He must still be in the cellar. What are we going to do about that? We were part of it. We got to do what's right."

"I know. I could not sleep. I worried all night over what happened."

"We can't leave Boll weevil in the cellar. He could die."

"Worse, if they find him, he could say I killed Cecil and that I tried to kill him."

"Oh, sweet chariots. Oh my, yes. A devil such as that does not know truth. His tongue always waits to give birth to a lie. He would do anything to save himself, but the Lord looks to us to do what is right, even if Boll weevil is a sinner. We cannot leave him there, though he gladly would have left us."

"If I report this, it's going to catch me up in a whole lot of trouble. They will never believe a Negro. Never."

"What if he's dead? Then what?"

"They could still connect me to the murders."

"How could that be?"

"Everyone knows he tried to kidnap you and Sarah. They might think I wanted revenge. The wagon was full of goods. They might think Cecil caught me robbing the store and I killed him."

Lydia's eyes glazed over. She fell on her knees right there on the floor and went into wild praying. She kept it up for a long time. When finally she got up, she said, "The Lord is good. You do what your heart tells you to do, Fortune. The Lord will protect his own."

SHERIFF ANGUS BEAUFORD USHERED FORTUNE INTO A SMALL office at the House of Corrections. "Take a seat," he said, moving over to a large desk strewn with papers, worn books and tobacco. He sat tall in his chair looking at Fortune, meeting the man's eyes with a frown.

"What brings you here, Redmond?"

"I have some information regarding the death of Cecil MacLeod."

"How did you come by this news? Gossip, I suppose. That's all you Negroes do."

"I was there at Mr. MacLeod's store ... when it happened."

Sheriff Beauford rapped his white knuckles lightly on the oak desk. "Well, well, is that right? It is such a tragedy. A Birchtown Negro by the name of Sam stopped by to bring me the news earlier this morning. He saw the loaded wagon and grew suspicious, knowing at that hour in the morning Cecil would not be at the store. He glanced through the open door and saw the body on the floor." Sheriff Beauford was staring at Fortune, watching him shift uneasily in his chair. "I hated to tell Cecil's wife, Annie, the news. I took her with me when I went out to the store this morning." He shrugged his shoulders. "It was a gruesome job, identifying the body, but what else could I do?"

"It must have been hard for her, Sir."

"Yes. Yes it was. It appears Cecil had quite a struggle. His face was bruised and swollen. There was one deep stab wound to the chest. The wagon from the livery was outside the store. Sure was peculiar how it was loaded with supplies and left behind. Looks like a robbery gone wrong. The Negroes are getting desperate. They'll do you in for no reason."

Fortune could feel trouble in the air. He wished he had stayed away, but his sense of duty had gotten the best of him.

Sheriff Beauford sensed his discomfort. He stood up and looked out the window. The snow was light and it covered the dirty banks with a fresh white layer. "Hunger is causing so many crimes that I'm losing track, but none as brutal as this. Only a Negro could do such an evil thing," Beauford said. "Isaac Haywood's death proves that. But this, to stab a good citizen of Port Roseway." Now he was staring at Fortune. "What can you tell me about this crime? What happened out there?"

Fortune paused. He would have to choose his words carefully. A nerve moved up and down the side of his face as he chewed away on the inside of his jaw. How much of the story could he tell without putting himself and his loved ones in danger? Thick drops of perspiration gathered on his brow. He sat still, his back straight, staring at a spot on the wall beyond Sheriff Beauford. Even now, he felt condemned. Misgivings tormented him. He despised the way a Negro had to suffer the contempt of the law. It had all seemed clear earlier when he felt compelled to visit the sheriff. As he sat across from the man now, cold eyes staring at him, he became unravelled.

"Well, sir," he began, sitting up taller in his chair, "I went to Mr. MacLeod's store, as he asked." Fortune held the sheriff's eyes. "He told me to come by because he had a job for me."

"What type of job?"

"He said he wanted to add a small piece to his store."

"When was this?"

"Yesterday morning, Sir. When I got there, I did not see any lumber, so I asked what his plan was, thinking he did not need me. He said to check with a man standing near the back of the store. He said to ask him when the lumber would be arriving. I recognized the man right off. It was Boll weevil, the slave catcher."

"Yes. Go on. You Negroes dawdle so. What did he say?"

"When I asked where the lumber was, he didn't answer. That is when he and Mr. MacLeod grabbed me, Sir. I tried to get away, but they overpowered me and the two of them took me down into the root cellar. They tied me up and put an old rag around my mouth."

"Is that it?"

"No, Sir. They had already captured my mother, Lydia Redmond. She was there, tied up in the cellar. Later, my daughter, Sarah, was put with us in the basement."

"What was the purpose of taking the three of you captive? You are free citizens according to the law."

"Well, Sir, I heard Mr. MacLeod and Boll weevil talking above us. As you know, they are rounding up Negroes and shipping them south. There is good money in it. I heard them talking about taking us to Port Roseway, then putting us on a boat for Boston."

"Nevertheless, why you Redmonds? You folks have a decent name hereabouts. It is common knowledge that you were a soldier. Your mother and daughter have their certificates. You were not among the Negroes we wanted deported. Something is not adding up." He shook his head. "There's more to the story, I believe." He stretched back in his chair now, lit his pipe and blew perfect rings of smoke.

The sheriff's questions made Fortune jittery. He knew a piece of the story was missing, but he could only tell what he knew and all he knew was how it happened. He continued with caution, knowing that his presence during the murder would be suspicious, his role, a foregone conclusion. He was dealing with the lives of two white men. He did not know quite how to tell what happened without bringing trouble to himself.

His story unfolded slowly. He told how the two men had an intense argument, how he heard the howl and the thud on the floor, heard the wagon leave, then return. He believed that it was Boll weevil making the trips in and out of the store. He was very careful not to accuse the man of stealing or murder.

The sheriff's hostile frown affirmed Fortune's fears. He took his time, weighed his thoughts carefully, considering all the ins and outs before speaking. He told the sheriff that Boll weevil tripped on the cellar steps and tumbled down onto the frozen floor, and that once they managed to get themselves free they tied Boll weevil up and left him in the cellar.

Sheriff Beauford studied Fortune closely. He twisted in his chair and mulled over the story. These Negroes, they act like children when caught, bend under pressure. It must be the weak blood in them, he thought. He was going to have to satisfy the townsfolk who wanted a taste of blood and he knew it. Not everyone would believe this man.

Fortune scratched his head, "Well, Sir, to tell the truth, all I could think of was getting my family out of there as fast as I could."

"Yes, I suppose. I can understand your fear, but the question is: Was he injured? Was he alive when you left the store? Answer the question, man."

"He groaned and passed out, Sir. I believe he is alive. I can't say for sure."

"There's no telling how he is. There's a good chance he's dead." His head bobbed up and down, taking stock of the information. He finally said, "I was out there earlier, never thought about checking the cellar. This calls for another trip to the store. There is a chance the man is still alive."

"I hope you are right, Sir."

"You had better pray that the man is dead, Fortune."

"Why would I wish such a thing, Sir?"

"Can't you see that if he's alive, he will not admit to anything? He will happily pin the murder and theft on you. There will be folks, perhaps many, who will choose his word over yours. If he is alive, they will rally to his lies. If he is dead, they will have to weigh the evidence without his influence and judge for themselves. That is where your chances lie. It could go either way. It's all in the way the dog's tail wags. But from what you have said, he likely didn't sustain deadly injuries. You are trapped."

"You could be right, Sir."

Sheriff Beauford liked that response. The case would be easy. He would set Fortune up now by pretending to be sympathetic, take his side to help him relax and then wait for the confession. His false smile and mellow tone were soothing. "Boll weevil was just following orders to get the riffraff out of here. He could try to link the murder and the theft to you, condemning you in the process. To avoid more heartache and rattling this good community further, you may as well confess and I suggest you plead for sympathy. Begging may be your best option."

"But I didn't take anything. The goods are still in the wagon."

"True, true." Sheriff Beauford laid his head in his hands and stared at the inkbottle on the corner of his desk. "There's a lot at stake here. However, I will tell you this: If folks have to make a choice between you and that thug, they will choose the thug. There are folks here who will stick by their own, regardless. Do you understand?"

"I thought I could earn a little money by doing honest work for Mr. MacLeod. I hate killing, even during war. I would sure as heck hate it now, unless I had to protect myself. And I hate a thief. I have never laid my hand on something with the intention of stealing it, even though I had to do without food and clothes, even the land promised to me. I never took anything that did not belong to me. I ain't that kind of man, Sir. I am not a murderer and I'm not a thief."

"Better be careful speaking thoughts like that in such a tone, Fortune. It could be dangerous. Folks don't appreciate hearing you people express yourselves forcefully."

"It is a horrible crime, but it was not my doing and folks need to know that."

"All this talk is not going to do us any good." The sheriff grabbed his hat and coat. "I have to get back out to the store and see what has happened to Boll weevil. Either way, this will lead to an uproar. Prepare yourself."

"Do you want me to go with you, Sir?"

"No. No. You will have to remain here in leg irons. You are now a suspect."

"A suspect? There's no proof I did anything."

"Folks will question why I let you go when they get wind of this."

"For how long, Sir?" Somewhere in the back of Fortune's mind, he had seen this coming, but foolishly, he dared to hope that the sheriff, once he knew the full story, would let him go free. Disappointment blanketed his face and his head fell to his chest.

"I can't say. It will be some time before a decision can be made in this case." He injected a thimble of compassion in his tone. "I'll have to keep you in custody until Justice Moody makes his way here for the Spring Session. We shall see what happens when I meet with him privately. I dare say that he may lean towards a trial, though it is not the practice with Negroes. Most prefer a quick sentencing and a good hanging."

The overpowering fear made Fortune queasy. He asked, "Could you stop by my place, Sir, and pass the news to my mother?"

"I will do that."

After his business at the store, Sheriff Beauford took the long way around to Lydia Redmond's cabin, passing by the maze of crude shacks, questioning why Negroes stayed in such shanties and misery, not wanting to better themselves. He did not look forward to the task of informing Lydia of her son's arrest. Such weeping and screaming the Negro women get on with, as though the world is about to end. He would be glad when his role in the matter had ended, for it was one crime after another in these parts and a thankless job for the sheriff. Arresting Fortune would make his job a lot easier and quell any uprising. Then the decisions were all up to the court. He didn't want a riot or a lynching on his hands.

He tapped hard and fast on the door, declining Lydia's invitation to step inside. Instead, he stood back, saying, "Your son, Fortune, asked me to come by with the news."

Lydia stood in silence in the doorway.

"I found Boll weevil Carter in Cecil MacLeod's cellar."

"Yes."

"I thought you'd like to know."

"Is the man alright?"

"His memory was cloudy and his behaviour so irrational, I had difficulty making sense of his story."

"But he's alright."

"There were no injuries as far as I could tell, but he walked with a limp. He's alive, at any rate."

"What did he tell you about that night, Sheriff Beauford?"

"He kept saying something about the Negroes stealing and how they lay in wait for him."

"This can't be. The Negroes rarely go out at night. Did he say who these men were?"

"He didn't name any names."

"I see," was all Lydia said.

"It all makes sense," the sheriff said, tilting his head at the harshness of the woman in the doorway.

"Will he be charged?"

"I see no need. He had a knife, true enough, but he said the blood on the knife was his, from being attacked. His memory was grey. I think the fall down the steps scattered his mind. I took notes and let the poor soul go, for in his state he could not harm himself or anyone else."

Lydia could feel disgust creeping through her bones. A favoured soul, she was thinking. No matter what a white does, he is always innocent. "What have you done with Fortune, Sir?"

"I'll have to hold Fortune in corrections for two months."

"Why so long, Sir?"

"We have to wait on the spring session of the court."

Sheriff Beauford nodded and mounted his horse. As he was about to leave the yard, he looked back and waved his hand. "You may visit your son between the hours of one and three."

Lydia made her way inside and dropped down on a chair. She wiped the sweat from her hands on her wide blue skirt. "Locked my innocent son up and let that crazy man go. No different from what we left behind." She threw her hands up in the air and sobbed. "Oh Lord, have mercy."

Nineteen

THUMP. THUMP. THUMP. SARAH BOLTED FROM A DEEP sleep and shivered in the frigid cold of February. The loud rapping on the thin wooden door awakened her. Her feet stuck to the frost on the floor as she ran to the narrow window and pulled back the heavy canvas sheeting. She blinked hard at the sight of Colonel Septimus Black and wondered what he wanted with them at this early hour. She grabbed a stiff, blue dress, petticoat and apron from a hook and dressed quickly. After washing her face in a basin of icy water, she rolled her hair up with a long ribbon and tied a kerchief over it. She hurried to the kitchen where Grandmother was folding laundry.

Gossip about the single colonel poured through Birchtown like warm syrup. He had his admirers and, of course, his critics. Some said because of his refusal to stand up for the indentured servants when they sought his help in challenging the laws in Roseway that he sold out the Birchtowners. More than a few accused him of cheating them out of their rations. There were those who said he liked the young girls a little too much. Others thought him more of a peacock, strutting about, showing off because he was the newly named Birchtown magistrate and because he had a nice home and garden.

Grandmother insisted he was just getting his rightful due, not unlike white folks. She dismissed the bitter gossips, saying they should feel proud that one of their own was doing so well. As head of the Black Pioneer Company, the colonel helped find work for the skilled tradesmen — the caulkers, carpenters, rope-makers, sailmakers, boat builders, millers, shoemakers, tailors, gardeners, cooks and others — by supporting the proposals from the military and magistrates of Roseway to create work. He drew up petitions to get their land surveyed. He distributed food and clothing and often kept them from a whipping by sending petitions for compassion to the magistrates.

"Oh yes. These folks can pull you down quicker than a jackal can wrestle an antelope to the ground. Oh my, calling the poor man a traitor to his race, saying he be supporting the white folks, all for trying to raise himself and us up out of the squalor. Lord, they should look at themselves. The desperate riff raff would all steal a louse from a dog's back, if no one be looking." Not that Grandmother supported stealing, but she hated the gossip of sinners. She looked at him and flashed a kindly smile. After all, to sweeten the pie, he was single and book smart, just the young man for Sarah, in her estimation.

Colonel Black bit into a small flat piece of skillet cake served on one of the good plates. Sarah sat opposite, understanding she was to be seen and not heard. She had summed him up as cold hearted at the indentures' meeting months earlier, but she liked the tea-brown skin, the freshly shaved face and the crisp Pioneer jacket that bore neither a stain nor a tear.

"So glad you come by, Mister," Lydia said. "We don't get much company out here." Her face was all smiles and her voice was sweet butter.

"Why thank you, Ma'am. I heard the news about your son. I understand that they are holding him for the murder of Mr. MacLeod. Can this be true?"

"Yes, it is. I hope you know that Fortune did not kill Mr. MacLeod. He's a good man."

"He is that. As you know, he served in one of the units I commanded. He was a good soldier. I will use my influence, Ma'am, to petition the court on his behalf. I cannot promise that it will do any good, but I can try. Justice is a cruel master most of the time."

"I hope my boy gets justice. That's all I want."

"It's all we can hope for," he said. He leaned back from the table and smiled. "I meant to come by earlier, to tell you folks about the new school."

"New school?"

"Yes Ma'am. Our children need to be educated. So few of us can read and write. I believe an education can help us find our rightful place. The associates of the Late Dr. Thomas Bray, a Church of England charity, have provided us with a free school. As long as the aid comes, we can keep the school going."

Sarah listened carefully to his moving words. They were soft and charming. He was a talker, just like the people said.

Lydia said, "I wish I had some learning. I got papers I would like to be able to read myself."

"Well, Ma'am, there is not much I can do for you, but the children …"

The colonel watched Lydia move to the fire pit, wondering if the old woman understood what he was saying. She came with the teapot a second time.

"There is a lot of work ahead of us. The promises the British made to us must be honoured. There are laws here that need to be changed. We must demand to be equal citizens in this colony. The war is not over, Ma'am. It's just that now we must arm ourselves with words instead of weapons."

Goose bumps dotted Sarah's arms. She knew what wanting to read had brought the slaves who dared to defy the law on the plantation. Was the colonel insane to suggest former slaves should get an education? Maybe folks would be too scared to consider such a thing. She shook her head. The very idea of going to school seemed unnatural.

"It sounds impossible, but this is not a dream. Mr. Winterbottom of the Bray Associates has assured me that they are determined to educate Negroes in America and the Bahamas. His members have been hard at work soliciting money and supplies. I am proud to say that we are now ready to begin this mission right here in Birchtown."

Unable to hold her tongue, Sarah stood up and said, "It's hard to believe we are to be encouraged to get an education."

Colonel Black patted his mouth and continued, "You are not alone in thinking this, Sarah. It's taken me some time to convince the community that this is a good thing."

Lydia spoke up, "The old ways have a charm on us. Yes, they do." She scratched her head, for she was thinking of how the past held a grip on her. "Mister, are you looking to see if Sarah can go to school?"

"The students must be aged five to eleven, so she does not qualify as a student. By the way, how old a girl is she?" He cast his steely eyes on Sarah, taking in the full length of her where she stood by the window.

"Seventeen," Sarah answered softly, feeling uncomfortable when the colonel's gaze lingered.

"Sarah didn't get much schooling, Mister, only what her mama taught her." Lydia paused before continuing. "But she's a smart girl, just as quick as a whip. She can read a little and counts her numbers off. As for me, I can count to ten."

"Well now," the colonel said. "Perhaps, Sarah, you might assist me with instructing the younger children."

"She's indentured, but maybe we could work something out," Lydia said.

"It would be a shame, Ma'am, for her to miss this chance to learn and grow."

"Yes, yes. It would be a blessing." Lydia laid back her head and chuckled as her chins rolled like waves. "More molasses cake and tea, Mister?"

"No thank you. I was not expecting cake in these hard times."

Sarah smiled. What if education could make a difference? Being a servant held little promise for one so independent. She had not thought about teaching. It seemed like a good beginning.

Colonel Black said, "Education is a key. There is no telling what you can do once you learn to read and write. They are necessary tools."

Sarah could not argue with that, but she was not thoroughly convinced. She said, "Do you think an education will make us full citizens of the colony, Colonel Black?"

"I can say that it allows me to have a better life than most. Being a Negro, well I am a long way from being equal. The law and attitudes limit me. That is why I fight for education. With education, we can fight against those things and hopefully it will bring about change. It has brought respect in some quarters and a steady income." He looked down and his eyes squeezed together. "My position as an overseer has caused some in Birchtown to resent me. If the people backed me, I could do more."

"Let them talk. This learning ... it's a good thing."

When Sarah returned to the table, Colonel Black took her hand, and gently rolling his fingers around in hers, he said, "No need to worry, Sarah. You are right to be concerned about how this will affect our relationship with the white community. Sure people have fears and rightly so, but this is progress and some folks cannot handle change. They will fight back any way they can."

Sarah slipped her hand from his. What Colonel Black said was beginning to make sense and her doubt softened.

"There is always an angry mob of men roaming about looking to destroy things and cause trouble. However, don't forget to look at the kind folks who have no part in all the violence. Education is a good thing. The school will soon be ready."

"Hallelujah. This place needs something besides another meeting house."

"Yes, Ma'am. It's a joyful day. Will you give your consent for Sarah to work with me?"

"I sure will. I never thought this day would come. The folks up in Glory must be rolling in their feather beds. Oh Lord, I cannot believe slaves will be getting learning with the white folks' blessing."

Colonel Black extended his hand to Lydia. He put his arms around Sarah and said, "I will see you in five days. There will be a small sum of money each month for your efforts."

Grandmother stood at the window and watched as he drove away. "Look at that," she grinned. "That mister. He has a new carriage and a shiny, black gelding. This learning, I know you're afraid and so am I, but don't you live your life bowing down, staying in the shadows, all bottled up, like I have. You go to that school and learn all you can." She placed her hand on Sarah's face and stroked it gently. "You be a bird. Soar high and as far as you can and I'll be right here looking on."

Twenty

L YDIA REDMOND'S BLOOD WAS READY TO BOIL. ANOTHER frigid morning, and though the fireplace was burning lively, the bedroom was freezing cold, as were most upstairs rooms in the Roseway homes. Lydia sat uncomfortably in a chair in Mrs. Cunningham's bedroom bundled in a bright head scarf, an ill-fitting wool coat and her worn black boots.

Fanny, who worked the odd days when Sarah was at Beulah's, had greeted her saying, "Missy Cunningham is not feeling well today, a touch of the cold. I see nothing to fret about, but she's gone back to bed. Wait here." Fanny had returned with instructions to take Lydia to Mrs. Cunningham's room.

Lydia and Margaret exchanged light talk about Fortune and little Prince while they waited for Fanny to return with tea and biscuits. Margaret's smile was like her father's, warm, yet with a chip of ice. Lydia detected that now, as she had a lot of things. She chuckled inwardly, reflecting on what you can see with your head up. She yielded now to the pressure to make things right. To do that, she had to face the unrelenting demons. This she found hard, but she had to try. As she listened to Margaret's idle chatter about the weather and Fanny and the mister and the new settlers, a voice in her head said, *She knows alright*. It was the tender smiles and hugs, the offering of food at her table, the slipping of extra money and the concern over her wellness. Lydia had seen the knowledge in her eyes, the kind warmth in her face, even the startled fear that sometimes held her back.

The wind was high and strange sounds filled the room as the roof rattled. Roseway was frozen under the blustery snow, but Lydia in her determination to right the past now sat waiting for a suitable time to find the answer to a fiery question.

Lydia looked at the fine furniture, linens and paintings with the awareness that even in a place like Roseway, where many a rich soul lived high above the rest, money had sway. For a moment, her confidence retreated, for how could she be part of such a life? She twitched and shifted uneasily. The hot tea cup Fanny passed her jiggled in her hand. She was thinking that the pretence had gone on for so long and the truth had been buried so deep, it may not surface without help. After two long breaths, she looked Margaret square in the face and said sternly, "You have a good life here in Roseway. You are well respected and fit in. You wouldn't want any trouble to change all that."

"Yes, this is true."

A huge swell in Lydia's throat caused her to cough and she tried to choke it back, but suddenly a rush of words tumbled out her mouth. "The past has caught me, Missy Cunningham. I'm tired of pretending and trying to forget about what happened years ago. I need to get things right between you and me. You should know the truth about your true family."

"If you mean my relationship to you, there's no need to worry. Mother told me everything. She died regretting what happened."

"Bless the dear soul," Lydia said. "So you know?" Lydia looked at Margaret with a pained look and the little voice said, *There, you see, you were right.*

"I've known since I was sixteen." Margaret sat up straighter and reached in the drawer beside her bed and retrieved a thick journal. The pages were worn and yellow. "I think it's time to bring the truth from these pages to the light. This is mother's journal. There are several things she wrote in here that I think you should hear. Should I read them to you?"

"If you like, Missy."

"Here, near the beginning, mother wrote:

The yearning I have for a child runs deep. It never ceases. I have spoken to Edward about the emptiness. I have been told that it is common to take a light Negro child for one's own. I am tempted.

"Further on, about a month later, I find that she has done just that:

Myself and Edward met with Mr. Carter today. He says he has no problem with keeping an eye out for a light-skinned baby. He said to be patient. I can't wait. This will be a special child since I cannot have one of my own. We promised to pay him handsomely for one.

"Well, well," Lydia mumbled. "For the money ... of course."

"And this:

I received my special gift today from Mr. Carter, just as he promised, a sweet baby girl of five months, so fair, no one would question her blood lines. I have my wish. A beautiful child with big brown eyes who seems to fancy her real mother when she enters the room. She is such a joy and my heart has never been happier. She is Lydia's child. Mr. Carter says he believes the father is the overseer from the Hartley place. He prefers sneaking around with the slaves from another farm, so as not to get caught on his own. I dare not say a word.

"There's more." Margaret flipped to the middle of the journal.

And now my sins have come home to roost. I find little peace at night for worry. This beautiful child, Margaret, has been brought into a world of shame. This great plantation spreads for miles and miles and produces much wealth. Our dream in coming to America has been fulfilled, but it brings no happiness, for I now carry a secret that threatens everything. I cannot mention this fear to Edward. He has so little time to console me.

Slavery is a terrible business. I see whippings and hangings most every day. I witness the suffering the slaves endure: the hard work, poor food and little clothing. I hear the terrible things they say about Negroes—how they are no more than an animal, incapable of learning or reason or feeling, how even a mulatto child is a Negro, no matter how fair. Slaves have no right to their children. As a mother now, that pains me deeply. The laws are cruel and hateful. Worse, my child may suffer from this hatred if her true identity should ever be discovered. Dear Lord, watch over us.

"On my sixteenth birthday, she wrote:

And now the real worry begins for my dear Margaret. Her coming out as a young woman worries me more than words can express. She is a fine educated woman, but a Negro, nonetheless. The Cunningham lad has expressed his intentions of marriage. This is my burden, to bear the news to her of her mixed blood. I pray that her children will not expose her Negro lines, for their lives will be intolerable, though we have raised our girl to be strong.

Margaret closed the journal with care and slipped it back in the drawer. She turned her back to Lydia. And Lydia, though she reached out an arm to console her, did not hold back. Like airing the quilts in spring, this was the time to get it all out into the open. And so in a pitiless, heated tone, she said, "You knew that I was your mother all this time, yet … you said nothing."

Margaret hung her head to the side with her eyes cast downward. She stared at the floor a long time while her shame searched for an explanation for her behaviour. Finally she said, "Yes, I knew. I was selfish and vain. Money can do that. It made me feel superior, not just to Negroes, but to everyday folks. I didn't want to be an outsider or suffer the scorn like other Negroes. At first, I could not tell anyone, not even William, but my guilt continued to pick away at me." Margaret looked at Lydia. "Losing everything, our home, my parents, it taught me a lesson about arrogance. I'm so sorry, Lydia, so, so sorry."

"Enough child. You said your piece. I have carried this burden since you were born. It's done with now. You are grown and happy."

"Can you ever forgive me?"

"Yes, the good Lord forgives and so do I. You are my child," Lydia said nervously. She sat with her eyes fixed on Margaret's face. It looked grey, drained from the golden tone, her eyes red-rimmed and swollen.

"Oh Lydia, I'm proud to call you my mother."

It was those words that put Lydia's anger to rest. She moved to the edge of the bed, reached out and hugged her daughter. They wept for a long time in each other's arms.

Suddenly the wind whipped against the windows and they rattled like dishes. It carried away the warmth in the bedroom and the women shivered. It was Margaret who disturbed their happiness by asking, "Will you tell me who my father is? I have wondered for a long time if Mr. Carter told mother the truth. She mentions later in the journal that she doubted his word."

"He lied, yes he did."

"Then who?"

Lydia halted. She saw a shadow on the wall facing the bedroom and shouted bravely, "Did you want something, Fanny?"

Caught, Fanny said, "Just finishing the dusting," and before anyone could speak again, she scooted down the stairs.

Margaret said, "You don't have to worry about Fanny. She has a nose for news, but she knows how to hold her tongue."

All the same, Lydia's face knotted before mumbling, "Cecil MacLeod."

"Cecil MacLeod?" She repeated it as though it could not be true. "Cecil MacLeod, the overseer? But he named someone else, the Hartley overseer."

Lydia nodded her head. "Yes, it was Mr. MacLeod. He kept his evil ways to himself."

Margaret fell back on the bed. "And now he's gone."

But Lydia was not finished with her business. "You are my child and so I marked you with the ring. Mrs. Redmond let you keep it after I told her it was a gift to her beautiful child."

Margaret rubbed the ring gently with a new sense of pride.

Lydia felt a sudden spark of joy, but in her heart, there was no calm. "Do you remember a child called Amelia?" she asked.

"Yes, I do. I remember when Cecil brought her to us. Mother said she was to be my companion, but Father kept reminding me that I was not to get too attached to her."

"She was my child," Lydia said. "Your sister."

"My sister?"

"Yes. And there's another boy besides Fortune."

"I am numb. I don't know what to say."

"I got to find my children before I go to Glory. Do you know of Amelia's whereabouts?"

"Father sold her to Mr. Pinkham when she was twelve. I begged father to let her stay, but he shoved me aside, saying it was all Mother's fault, raising the two of us like we were sisters."

"I had a few words with her before she left. Did you ever see her again? Did she stay on the Pinkham Plantation? Do you know if Master Pinkham was a Loyalist?" Lydia's face filled with torment as she continued, "Do you know if she's here in Nova Scotia?"

"Oh, Lydia, I know how anxious you must be to find her, but I can't say. I never saw her again."

Twenty-one

ALL WAS QUIET UNTIL GRANDMOTHER INVADED SARAH'S sleep with a loud shout. For several minutes, Sarah ignored the call and let her thoughts linger on Reece.

The *Cape Blomidon* had returned from the North Atlantic two days earlier and Reece had visited her at Mrs. Cunningham's. She could see that he was torn when he told her he was leaving again, going back to Carolina to try and find the Redmond midwife, Rose. For how long, he hadn't been able to say. Sarah lay quietly thinking of how she had pinned her hopes on marriage instead of herself. He was a part of her life, not the whole of it, but his leaving—it had felt as though her world had collapsed without any warning.

Now her thoughts turned to the morning ahead, of assisting Colonel Black at the new school. Imagine the children of Birchtown gathering and partaking in the thing denied them for so long. The idea still felt peculiar. She wondered how the folks in Roseway would take the news. Buildings had been burned down for less. She let out a sigh and tossed about under the heavy coats.

The cabin was just beginning to warm when Sarah rose and dressed, taking a moment to twirl in her flowered dress and admire the black leather boots with brass buckles—all donations from the missionaries. How different from the tattered rags of the little slave girl in Carolina, she thought. She draped a coat around her shoulders and sat at the table. Grandmother, anxious to create a special look for the occasion, was already standing with the bone-handled brush in hand.

"It's a very special day for this family. Now, hold that head still, Sarah." The thick hands clasped the sides of her head and pulled it back until her neck stretched like a goose.

Sarah was happy to let the old woman deal with the task, but it was her non-stop comments that irritated her so. Sarah interrupted her by saying, "You have to hurry this morning. I cannot be late." Then with a mindful mumble, she said, "I am past braids."

"I see you are not past giving Lydia orders."

Sarah wrestled with mixed feelings. Having a respectable job gave her a measure of pride, yet she worried. It was Colonel Black's smile. In it dwelled something sinister that had sown the seeds of mistrust. At the same time, she was flattered to have his attention. Not that it mattered, for her heart belonged to Reece and one day he would return to claim it.

"Hush now, Child. Hush now. You are right. You are too old for braids. You are ready for a Lydia look this special day." With that, the old woman broke into a long flow of broken lines from one of her hymns. Grandmother seemed unusually happy.

Sarah sat as still as she could. Her long mass of curly hair did not slow Grandmother's hands. She greased her palms and rubbed them through the hair to make it shine. All the while, she kept shifting Sarah's head up and down and from side to side. With her pipe stuck to her bottom lip, Lydia worked her magic. She wrapped a twisted roll once around Sarah's head and fastened it with a beautiful mother-of-pearl clip. It was a thing of beauty, a gift to Sarah from her Carolina odds and ends.

"If Fortune was here, he would burst with pride, and your mama, too. Who would have thought this day would ever come? It is a blessed day. Oh, sweet chariots." She looked down at Sarah and laughed. "There you go, peach blossom. You are ready for the colonel." Then catching herself, she added, "And the children. You best hurry. Your lunch is waiting on the table."

It was a long walk in the fierce cold. All around the snow lay in a thick covering over Birchtown. The school building was a small wooden structure with a pitched roof and four glass windows. The men of Birchtown had done a fine job. Inside she found the room crowded and noisy. The worn desks were of various sizes and arranged in neat rows. The shelves along the back wall displayed an assortment of donated books from the Associates.

The date on the chalkboard said March 2, 1785. She stood in the midst of it all: the smell of new wood and paint, books, desks, screams, chatter and laughter. Colonel Black greeted her, then read aloud her duties from a list. He gave three piercing rings of a brass bell to signal the start of school.

From her chair beside the colonel's desk, Sarah saw among the oldest students the familiar faces of her neighbour's children: Mary Browne, Stewart Jones and Priscilla Haywood's little sister, Bella. Colonel Black checked his pocket watch. The noise coming from the youngest children, to her left, was like a gaggle of wild cackling geese. Snatching a long rod, he struck the desk and screamed, "Come to order!" Then, ever so gently, he said, "Good morning, dear students," and they said, "Good morning, Sir."

The lessons began with the issuing of the first of many orders. Sarah chuckled silently. He was very much the colonel issuing orders to his troops: "There will be no cursing and no fighting, no lateness, no liquor, no loose comments and no talking back. Cleanliness will be the order of the day."

Frost nipped at Sarah's toes and fingers and she wished the new pot-bellied stove would provide more heat. She listened as Colonel Black stated, "A strong Methodist education will serve you well. There are three important qualities a former slave needs to survive in this new land: dedication, discipline and determination." He instructed the children to repeat the three qualities twice. Then he said, "These qualities will assist you in the attainment of perfection and in pleasing the Almighty God."

It was obvious to Sarah that the lofty words and high ideals confused the students, but their smiles blazed like golden flames nonetheless. Colonel Black turned to Sarah, put his hand on her shoulder and squeezed it. His glance was flirtatious and his voice soft as he said, "Please assist me with the next task, Miss Sarah."

She followed as he strode up and down the aisles handing out worn Bibles and hornbooks consisting of two sheets of thick, rough paper. A thin sheet of transparent horn protected each sheet. One page contained the alphabet and the other, the Lord's Prayer. The pages fastened to a wooden tablet with a handle.

Time was a long yawn. Sarah envisioned countless days and months of scripture, recitations and prayers. Already she disliked the colonel, whose long stares and touching felt uncomfortable and indecent.

Lunchtime came as a welcome blessing. She and Colonel Black discussed Fortune's upcoming trial. He assured her that he was doing what he could in meetings with the magistrates over the growing list of charges against Birchtowners, many of which he said were just plain foolish. Sarah devoured a piece of bread filled with molasses and a small leg of chicken. The food was good. After lunch, she led an embroidery lesson with the girls. Lots of cotton fabric, coloured threads, needles, scissors, tweezers and frames. The colonel struggled with meagre supplies for the boys to learn woodworking. Through the clamour, the children's eagerness was a pleasant surprise.

All went well and when the day ended, she was more than happy to accept Colonel Black's offer of a drive home. They made their way down a snowy country lane in his grand carriage. Sarah smiled, imagining herself a well-to-do woman touring the countryside. She glanced at the colonel. He was all of the things the gossips had said—dashing, showy, smart—and yet she saw another side of him that was demanding, impatient and rigid. As they further discussed her father's fate, she sensed that he had a genuine concern for him. Perhaps Grandmother was right about the colonel. He was a man trying to rise above the squalor and move the community forward.

They were nearing the cabin when the colonel slowed the gelding and stopped the carriage. He reached for Sarah's hand and looked at her for a long time, then said, "I hope you enjoyed your work, Sarah. This has been quite a remarkable day, one for history."

"Yes it has, Sir," she said, careful to avoid his eyes. He was facing her now, edging closer until his breath was warm against her cold cheek. "Your embroidery lesson went well." Leaning still closer, he said, "I admire your skills, Sarah."

Feeling flushed and unsure of herself, she thanked him awkwardly.

"Are you spoken for, Sarah?" Colonel Black asked.

She hesitated. She thought about Reece. "No, Sir."

"I'm surprised." he said. "Then you are fair game."

"Fair game, Sir?"

"Ready for courting, Sarah." He chuckled. "You are an innocent."

She was not sure what to think. His tone was kind and caring, but shallow and crafty too. She moved to the edge of the seat. He reached and pulled her to him and attempted to press his mouth on hers. She was quick and she gave him a strong heave with her elbow, pushing him back. She stared directly into eyes. "You have no right!" she screamed. "I am not your girl."

"I meant no harm," he stammered, regaining his composure quickly.

"Colonel Black, I am a free Negro woman and I am not for the taking."

"I lost myself, Sarah. Please understand. I don't know what came over me."

Sarah spoke sharply. "I thought you were different, a man with fine manners."

"I apologize. Men have to learn new ways. I didn't mean to frighten you. Please, let this be our little secret. I could lose my position, my good name. Please understand—your smile encouraged me."

Sarah looked at him for a long time. Her words were sharp. "A man who preys on young women does not need any encouragement. His instincts are those of a dog."

Colonel Black turned his face from hers, wearing his shame like a heavy coat.

Lydia was standing in the doorway when the carriage arrived at the cabin. Her head bobbed back and forth like a piece of cork in water. She was hoping the colonel would come in and sit for a spell. To her surprise, he waved his hand and was quickly away. The broad smile left her face. Later, when supper was over, Grandmother grilled Sarah about every detail of the day, probing deep, knowing something was amiss. Sarah held back, sensing Grandmother's intuition at work. The last thing she wanted was one of the old woman's sermons. To satisfy her, she said, "It was a wonderful day. The children were eager to learn and it was not at all what I expected."

Sarah watched as Grandmother stood warming herself by the fire. It came to her that there were many things to learn in this new place and the old woman's words were beginning to make sense.

Later that evening, deep under the quilts and coats, she wondered about Colonel Black. All that insisting that others have the holy virtue of discipline, yet he could not apply it to himself. A man so polished and trusted, but oh, like the jewellery the poor women were wearing of glass and paste, he too was a fake.

Twenty-two

SHERIFF ANGUS BEAUFORD STOOD BEFORE JUSTICE Nicholas Moody and read the following request:

Port Roseway, March 10, 1785
Justice Nicholas Moody,

I ask your favourable permission to solicit the release of Fortune Redmond from his present confinement. I am content that he had no part in the crime of murder against Mr. Cecil MacLeod, on the ninth January 1785, nor in the attempted robbery of goods from Mr. MacLeod's store. It is my belief that he himself fell victim to a crime and that he went to Sheriff Beauford with honest intentions to declare the truth of his situation. I am content that he is an admirable Negro and a good citizen of Birchtown, having fought in the King's army. I am, with due submission, Gentlemen,

Your most obedient Honourable servant,
Birchtown Magistrate
Colonel Septimus Black

As the Birchtown magistrate, Colonel Black had intervened in Fortune's case by petitioning Justice Moody, just as he had promised. The Redmonds were grateful for his interest in the case, while his efforts brought him renewed respect in Birchtown.

Fortune sat to their right, his legs in irons and his hands in chains. He was thin, unshaven and his face was drawn. He did not look at his mother or daughter, but kept his eyes fixed on the magistrate. Lydia, Sarah and Enos listened intently as the sheriff read Colonel Black's letter. When Sheriff Beauford reached the part stating Fortune served in the king's army, the Judge's eyes widened and he nodded his head in support.

Outside the courthouse, the small gathering of black and white citizens swelled, soon spreading out across the yard and down the road. Raw emotions charged the air as opinions see-sawed back and forth.

One man said, "That Negro killed Cecil. We don't need to wait to convict him."

Another shouted, "We would be murderers if we did not wait for justice."

A tall woman in a floppy bonnet screamed, "We have enough proof."

"We need to hear his side."

"You know Negroes never tell the truth."

"He fought for the king and that alone makes him a good man."

"I say we are getting soft on the Negroes and this proves we need more laws to keep them in line."

Neither side gained enough strength to take the lead. It was not quite a mob, but all it would take was one forceful speaker, a shepherd, and the majority would fall into step, march to one beat like a herd of sheep.

Beulah kept her eyes fixed on the door to the courthouse. She could not bring herself to enter. She was listening to all the remarks and growing nervous. She kept her ears tuned for trouble. It was not until she heard ol' Brown say that if the judge found Fortune guilty and Fortune would be found swinging from a tree, did she realize the horror of the situation. She moved back to the fringe, and then further until the loud chatter became a muffle.

Margaret Cunningham placed her hand on Beulah's shoulder. "Any word on how this is going?"

"No, Ma'am. The magistrate arrived but an hour ago."

"Did Lydia make it? Is she inside?"

"Yes Ma'am. Enos drove us here and he went inside with her."

"I'm glad of that. From what Lydia tells me, they were all victims of that terrible Boll weevil. Who knows what would have become of them?"

"That's true, Ma'am. They are lucky to be here. Do you think the magistrate will believe Fortune?" She faced Margaret with a lump in her throat so large it felt like an apple.

"That is a good question. I have faith in Nicholas. He is a good man and an excellent magistrate." She paused a moment, not wanting to fill Beulah with unreasonable hope. "His position on Negroes has always been fair. I know that he will do the right thing."

"I can only believe what Mother Redmond says, that the heart of a man will always show its hand. If the magistrate is a good man, we will have Fortune back."

"There is much to consider and not one witness. All the judge has is Fortune's words and the sheriff's evidence. There are no statements from Lydia or Sarah."

"What about Boll weevil?"

"I heard that Boll weevil lost his memory and cannot recall that night."

"I dare say that he came up with such a trick to keep from being found guilty."

"A trick?"

Beulah moved closer to Mrs. Cunningham. She kept her voice low. "He's a smart one. If he cannot remember, then no one will question his guilt. He wants sympathy. He knows exactly what he is doing. He's betting that everyone will assume Fortune is guilty. If you ask me, there is not a thing wrong with that man. Anyway, it all rests on the credit of Fortune's story."

"That's true. Mr. Carter thinks he is a wise fox, but do not give him too much credit. Nicholas is a far wiser man who has seen the best and the worst of the criminal mind. I dare say that thinking yourself too smart can lead to tripping yourself up."

"I do not doubt that. I hope that Sheriff Beauford found a clue, something to help the magistrate reach a decision."

"It won't be long before we know. The facts are as plain as the nose on your face and, by God, I think the facts are on Fortune's side."

"I hope so, Ma'am, I surely do."

Margaret hugged Beulah. "It will all go well, just you wait and see."

In the courtroom, the heat from the wood stove filled the crowded space. Onlookers twisted and turned in their seats. Sarah could feel their anger and she moved closer to Grandmother. Her heart raced as she reached for the old woman's hand and silently prayed. Grandmother squeezed her hand hard. She wished she could squeeze away all the nervous energy that was keeping her on the edge of her seat.

Justice Moody sat with an odd look of displeasure on his face. He removed his monocle, wiped it with a large white handkerchief and returned it to his face. After clearing his throat several times, he raised his gavel and struck the bench twice. Reading from some papers, he said:

On this day, the twelfth of March, seventeen hundred and eighty-five, I hereby state that the facts pertaining to this case are clear and concise. There were no witnesses to the crime, therefore my summary and judgment are as follows:

Cecil MacLeod was murdered. The murder weapon was a hunting knife. That part is clear. The weapon used to kill Mr. MacLeod was on Boll weevil Carter's person when found in Mr. MacLeod's cellar. Having failed to remove all of the blood from the knife handle, and having blood stains on his hands, jacket and pants at the time he was rescued, I hereby declare Boll weevil Carter to be the murderer.

He paused for a few seconds, and then continued.

An attempted robbery appeared to be in progress at the time of or following the murder. The murderer failed to leave with the stolen goods, therefore no robbery occurred. It is known hereabouts that slave catchers, such as Boll weevil Carter, were in the service of their employers or the local authorities to retrieve Negroes from this province. That fact may be connected to this horrible act of murder, but that remains to be proven.

Grandmother held Sarah, clinging to her like a frightened orphan, waiting anxiously for a decision that would either liberate or condemn their beloved Fortune.

Justice Moody discharged yet another loud snort. He raised his eyes from the page and stared at the family before he continued:

I hereby issue a warrant for the arrest of Boll weevil Carter.

Turning to Fortune, whose face was stone cold, Justice Moody forced a thin smile.

I have concluded that Fortune Redmond is guilty of… nei-
ther murder nor robbery. Fortune Redmond, you are free to
go. This case is dismissed.

Justice Moody struck the bench with one thunderous blow of the gavel. He rose and turned to face Lydia, Sarah and Enos. He nodded and left the courtroom by the back door.

No one stirred for several seconds. The onlookers were numb and bewildered. It was Fortune who first rose to his feet. Within minutes, the sheriff had removed Fortune's irons and chains, and he hobbled to his mother, lifting her from the chair and hugging her passionately. Sarah watched, thinking that at any moment her heart would stop.

The Negroes outside stood stock-still when the magistrate's carriage flew past them in a cloud of dust. A group of them immediately burst into the courtroom and, upon learning that Fortune was innocent, raised him to their shoulders.

Outside, the whites wandered about, restless and impatient, perplexed by the sudden departure of the magistrate. Their anger rode high on a wave of smugness. Their confidence in a favour-able verdict—one that found the Negro guilty and that would put Negroes in their old place—showed in their faces and slid from their tongues. "This will teach them," a rough-looking man shouted. "He'll hang by nightfall and we'll drink to that." All were ready for a celebration but for the few who stood together off to the side of the road praying for sanity and compassion. The remaining Negroes waited patiently, barely uttering a sound. Fear was their master, striking them hard with a vicious sting. They wept, not just for Fortune, but also for themselves. They waited quietly, drowning in wild emotions and watching the rowdy crowd carefully, knowing it was a dangerous animal that could lash out at any second.

When Fortune came through the courthouse doors carried on the throne of shoulders, the Negroes stood transfixed for several seconds. Could this mean he was free, an innocent man? It didn't take them long to figure it out, and when they did, they let loose and filled the air with rejoicing. Their laughing, singing and dancing in gratitude brought many to the ground. It was a spectacle that the residents of Port Roseway would remember for a very long time. For the Negroes, it was a happy, unforeseen ending to a very bad dream and a wonderful taste of justice in their new country.

For their part, the Redmonds glowed. They walked with their heads elevated, not superior but proud. The hostile comments and flying debris could not shake their confidence. When Enos finally managed to gather them up, they sat in the back of his cart like heroes, smiles stretching from ear to ear. Fortune threw his hat to the wind and let out a lifetime of restraint in shouts. Enos sat tall and stiff on his seat like the grand master of a parade, leading the throng of revellers back to Birchtown to continue the celebration.

Twenty-three

THE RUN-IN WITH THE LAW HAD NOT SOURED FORTUNE, BUT he was disappointed that Boll weevil was still at large, with not a word surfacing about his whereabouts. At last, on April 3, 1785, the surveyors arrived and marked off but a handful of the remaining land grants for the squatters. The rest of the men in the Black Pioneers received their lots by rank, the same as the white folks, while the other squatters came last. The original land grant, now reduced in size because of the generous allotments to the white Loyalists, could not accommodate all the Negroes. Happily, Fortune got his.

Fortune scrutinized his rocky plot in Birchtown with disbelief. The one hundred acres promised had dwindled to fifty. In spite of that, he convinced the surveyor to measure off two ten-acre lots from his grant so that both Lydia and Sarah could share in his stake. Receiving any amount of land, he supposed, put them among the lucky. From squatters to landowners—their dreams were coming true.

Every day presented a face-off between endurance and defeat. Nothing made him angrier or destroyed his confidence more than feeling betrayed and desperate. He was not alone. All the poor settlers were without their needed provisions. Upon arrival, the Royal Bounty of Provisions had filled two storehouses on Commissary Island, close to the shores of Roseway. Thousands of pounds of flour, bread, pork, beef, rice, vinegar, oatmeal, butter and countless gallons of molasses and rum had been brought in and distributed as rations, but the demand soon outstripped the supply as greedy individuals, able to pay for supplies, took from those in need. The bounty of provisions, extended twice, was now restricted to a few and reduced to one-third rations to the people who settled on farmland and improved it—but it was too late. It had taken so long to receive the land that it could not be cultivated in time to feed anyone. Requests to the king asked for two more years of provisions.

The promise of prosperity was now a joke. Birchtown was thinning as the crushing weight of poverty drove folks away. Some of the residents fled to other parts of Canada or back to the American colonies. Some talked of finding a way back to Africa. Fortune's resolve was strong. He refused to leave. What he had was just enough. After all, what had he known but a hard day's work, one pair of shoes, raggedy overalls and two squares a day? He had as much here and more. The Birchtowners who stayed sank to scrounging, begging, re-making items or putting up with what they had. Every day the number of deserted shacks added to the increasing despair. Some folks roamed from place to place looking for work or liquor, whichever came first.

Fortune knew that his soil was poor, and without proper tools and good seeds, his crops would be undersized and the hay sparse. He had one old ox, a horse, four cows and a few chickens. It was not much, but as Lydia said, "It keeps the wolf from the door." He often walked the surveyor's lines. He delighted in knowing his property stretched beyond the horizon. It felt vast. He found joy in being able to work the land, in shaping it, nurturing it and claiming it. To him, it was not just land, it was *his* land. All of it was his: the trees, the fields, the swamps and the rocks.

He thought of Beulah often. Prince had been the lucky one, assigned to breed her right off. Though he longed for her himself, Fortune made sure the other men kept away from her. That was before Dahlia came along. But now there was a chance and he might try testing the waters. He was ready to move forward and a partner would make life sweeter.

For her part, Beulah was getting better with each passing day, finding her will to step away from the past. And so on this sunny April day, he set out to Beulah's with a wide grin on his face. He found her sweeping the floor. She greeted him shyly, pulling the rag from around her head and smoothing the front of her ragged dress.

Fortune handed her a bag. "I brought you a beef heart. It's not much."

"Thank you, Fortune. Care to sit for a spell?"

"I don't mind if I do." He lifted Prince from the floor and tickled his chin.

"I got a pot on. Just beans. Stay for supper?"

Fortune looked at the small black pot hanging over the fire. "I'm thankful for whatever you have. We are lucky to have a pot."

"That we are."

"It must be hard, you being on your own with a son to raise. Are you lonely, Beulah?"

"Is that pity I hear in your voice?"

"No, no. It's just that I care about you." There, he thought, something simple, a start. But his next words had no time to form. The door to Beulah's shack flew open with a heavy kick. Both sets of eyes went to the plump white man standing on the wobbly step, a rifle pointed inside at them.

"I'm looking for the Negro, William Hampton, a runaway servant from Roseway."

Beulah snatched Prince from Fortune and held him tight. "There's no runaway here!" she screamed.

"Step to the side while I look about this hole."

Fortune jumped to his feet. He thought of the dragoon in his boot, but quickly changed his mind, saying, "We have nothing to hide. Go ahead and look and then leave us in peace."

The man stepped inside the one-room shack and glanced about. Satisfied with finding no one, he walked to the door saying, "You people have no regard for the law. Harbouring a runaway will mean a hanging. Just letting you know."

"Wicked, wicked," Fortune said, after the man left. "They hunt us like foxes. They want every ounce of blood in us if we do wrong."

Beulah brought tea to the table and sat down across from Fortune. He looked at her and felt what he thought was affection. "As I was saying before we were stormed, I care about you Beulah. I am thinking of taking a wife, if you would have me."

"Good Lord. I cannot think about being a wife or having more babies. I am done with that kind of aching. I had my share. It would take a deep love to change my mind."

Fortune was confused. He wanted to get on with living and could make no sense of her reaction. This courting business, could he ever get used to it? In slavery, breeding was the reason for mating. Was she saying that love was now the purpose? To his way of thinking, it was simple: A good man and a good woman got together. Love was a luxury in a place desperate for the basics of life. Did love matter when you were destitute, wanting just the warmth of a body to share your bed, a good woman to share the load? It wasn't that she hadn't caught his eye and it wasn't that he didn't want her company, but refusing him based on love alone when she was having it so hard … He scratched his head, trying hard to understand Beulah's hesitation. He said softly, "I wish I knew how to make this right. You mean the world to me. I have a job on the new road to Annapolis and soon I'll have enough to start a small farm. It is not much, but you and my nephew are welcome to it. I will be good to you. That I guarantee."

Beulah was anxious and trembling. She could not explain why she felt the way she did, other than her heart was empty. She faced Fortune now and looked at him intently. Her mind was drifting back to Prince. That had been a good match. They had found happiness. Neither she nor he had known much about marriage, but it came easy in their short time together. Sometimes, late at night, she would think of all the things they were going to do to make their dreams ripen sweet—and then he was gone. "You have been so kind these past months. I could not have survived without your help. I don't mean to be ungrateful."

The tears welled up in Fortune's eyes. His throat was tight.

Outside the wind was blowing, howling like the pain in his heart. He longed to tell her that he ached for her, that life could be sweet if she wanted it to be.

A FEW WEEKS AFTER FORTUNE'S VISIT WITH BEULAH, he came to realize how true it was that life could come at you hard. Lydia had turned in early after a busy day. Fortune was watching Sarah hem a dress when Fibby opened the door after two faint taps. She was grim-faced and puffing. She held Prince Junior in her arms and a large sack on her back. They looked at her in alarm.

Sarah went to the door, taking the child and handing him to Fortune, then taking the sack and placing it on the cot. Fortune looked at the woman and immediately he sensed the grief in her eyes. It was unlike her to venture out by herself in the darkness.

After she joined them at the table, Fortune said, "What brought you here with Prince at this hour?" He was already assuming there would be bad news.

"I brought the boy to you because I didn't know what else to do," she mumbled.

"What do you mean, Fibby? What on earth has happened?" Sarah asked quietly.

"Beulah got sick." Fibby said. "I tried to save her. I tried. I thought she would get better, but the cholera took her. You know it is raging through the colony, taking us down fast, showing no mercy. She was sick only for a few hours. Went into shock ... she couldn't move or speak and then ... just like that," she said, snapping her fingers, "she was gone. I would have come sooner, but I could not leave her in that state. She passed but a few hours ago."

"It's all right," Fortune said, wiping his eyes on a rag he pulled from his pocket. "You were her friend. We thank you for caring for her and brother Prince and the babies."

"What's all the chatter out here?" Lydia asked, appearing from behind the canvas sheeting and bundled in several heavy sleeping gowns and a nightcap. "What's happened?" she asked.

"Beulah passed this evening," Fibby said. "Cholera."

Grandmother fell back against Sarah's chair. She looked from one to the other and shook her head. "It doesn't seem right. Prince and Destiny, now Beulah ... gone. One by one, the hunger, filth and strange diseases are taking us. What is this juju that shows no mercy? What's to become of the rest of us?"

Sarah held onto Grandmother's arm and let the tears flow down her cheeks.

After some time, Lydia said goodnight to Fortune, Fibby and Sarah, kissed little Prince, and made her way to the back room. Her sobs were loud and without let-up.

"Don't worry, she will be alright," Fortune said.

Fibby turned and made her way to the door. "I wrapped her up as best I could ... Beulah. She is at the hut waitin' on burial. I'll stay there overnight. Tomorrow, you come by and do the rest."

"We will be there in the morning," Fortune said, pushing back the lump in his throat.

"I hated to bring bad news. You tell Prince that his mama loved him and his papa, too. Tell him every day. And now ol' Fibby has to get going."

Twenty-four

IT WAS A BEAUTIFUL AND JOYFUL JUNE SATURDAY. WILD
cherry and apple blossoms sweetened the air with a dream-
like potion. Sarah and Fortune were out in the yard slicing the
eyes off sprouted potatoes, getting ready for the spring planting.
Prince, now nine months, babbled away, watching from a small
seat made from black ash by a local Mi'kmaq.

Fortune scanned the ploughed field. It was far from a perfect
job with the crooked rows and clumps of hard sods. Breaking
the ground had been a backbreaking task with a horse and a
dull, homemade plough made from scraps of metal. The rocks
were unforgiving under the thin soil and there was no knowing if the weather would cooperate during the short growing
season.

Sarah was in good spirits. Two jobs kept her busy — one during weekdays at the school and the other on Saturdays at Mrs.
Cunningham's home. She thought of Reece less frequently. He
had been gone since February and time had slowly eroded the
earlier feverish feelings. Like a smouldering fire, she was confident the desire would flame again when he returned.

"Hello, Fortune. Hello, Sarah. It's a great day for sorting
seed!" Mr. Cunningham roared as he flicked his whip and sped
by in the carriage.

Fortune gave a shout back, "Aye, it is," and waved.

It was not long before Grandmother came to the door and let out a holler. "Come in! Mr. Cunningham left us a trunk."

"A trunk. I cannot believe it. Come on, Papa. Let's go see," Sarah yelled.

"Likely it's all women's things. No need for me to go. I'll finish up here."

Sarah hurried, skipping like a child wild with excitement.

"The Cunninghams always think of us," said Grandmother. "I heard the supply ships were on their way. Oh Lord, everyone wants a trunk from the British missionaries. I bet everyone flocked to the wharf in Roseway. I never thought we would ever see one."

Grandmother threw back the lid. Such beautiful things: bedding, dishes, shoes, skirts, blouses, men's breeches and shirts. That was not all. Sarah reached into the black trunk and pulled out a red wad of chintz. Her jaw fell. With fine detailing, puffed sleeves and a flared skirt that spread out like an inverted bowl in perfectly even gathers around the waist, it was no ordinary dress. The seams were practically invisible and the stitches regular and delicate. She held the dress to her shoulders and looked down the full length. In an instant, it came to her. Dresses such as this were difficult for the women of Roseway to get. She thought about ol' Briggs, the man who made the clothing at the Redmonds. How she had helped cut the fabric and sew the pieces. She loved watching yards of cloth become wonderful garments. It came to her that she could create lovely dresses to wear to the weddings, embroidery parties, coffee houses and literary meetings. A Port Roseway tailor.

Grandmother was less enthusiastic after hearing the plan. When Sarah held the dress up and proclaimed it the most beautiful thing she had ever seen, the old woman looked at it as though it was blasphemous. "That's not a dress for us to wear," she scowled.

Sarah squared her shoulder and gritted her teeth. "We have just as much right to feel grand. We are worthy."

So harsh was Sarah's tone that Grandmother stood silent for a moment. "I know how the dress makes you feel, Chile." She chomped down hard on the end of her pipe. She was not about to let Sarah off easy. "But red brings trouble."

Sarah's eyes flashed. The idea of red bringing trouble was no more than a superstition. She remembered how the slaves wore clothing of the brightest colours to defy such notions. She smiled. How good it felt to forget so many old beliefs and wondered why Grandmother held on to them.

"Trouble finds us no matter what colour we wear. We may as well save it the time and the effort."

"You could be right about that." Grandmother let out a soft turkey chuckle.

Sarah snatched up the dress and whisked it away to tuck safely into a trunk at the foot of her bed, leaving the lid ajar. She sat on her bunk staring at the red roll. She hoped Birchtowners were ready because she intended to go out in the dress, attend a dance or two, maybe turn some heads.

Grandmother approached and stood beside the bed until Sarah looked at her. "One of these days, you will understand why all of the things I say can put your life in danger. You got to watch every step. There's always someone ready to strike. I know there are times when you think I don't want you to enjoy yourself, but that's not why I say these things."

"Then why, Grandmother?"

"Because I want to protect you, Sarah, to keep you safe from all the hardship I've seen. You and Fortune mean the world to me. I guess I worry too much."

"We must let our spirits fly."

"You are a wise one, for sure, but watch yourself, Sarah Redmond."

SARAH STOOD IN THE WINDOW WAITING FOR GEORGE Washington Brindle to arrive. She dazzled like the beautiful crimson clover in the fields of Carolina in the red dress, ready for the dance at ol' Brown's shack.

"You and that Fortune make a fine pair of roaming owls. Your late hours fill me with worry."

"Stop worrying. We have the right to a little merrymaking."

"Oh Lord, you know the law forbids such a thing. Some of these folks get a little crazy in the head when they get that poison in their bellies."

"You don't find the law unfair, only applying to Negroes? Everyone else can have a good time. Roseway has enough ale houses for three colonies." Sarah turned away from the window. She stood for a moment with her eyes mashed together and her teeth clenched. Then, like an angry cat, she growled, "The law makes no sense. It assumes that drunken Negroes will act differently than drunken white men. We are no more shameful or brutal than they are. Such laws make us out to be the brutes and to further separate us."

"Chile, I hate the laws, they are not fair. We must continue to fight against them, but all I am saying is that for now, you watch yourself. Your name is all you got. Remember that."

Sarah held her tongue. She had heard Grandmother's sermons so many times before. She thought about Colonel Black. The old woman had a point, but she needed to stand her ground. "There's no need for you to worry. Besides, George will watch out for me."

"And who will be watching out for George? You have a lot to learn, Girlie." The old woman had had enough. She sighed and said, "Lord, put some sense in that chile's head."

Day or night, there was always a good time at ol' Brown's place. The laws strictly forbid Negroes from gathering to dance and drink. Frolicking they called it. Ol' Brown said he was just waiting for the sheriff to poke his nose through his door. He was a free man, and that was that. He did not fight in the white man's war to end up treated like he was the enemy.

When Sarah and George arrived, the party was well under way. Ol' Brown sat in his usual spot, to the left of the open door, with his Winchester Flintlock across his knees. Already fights and arguments were filling the yard around his shack, but ol' Brown just sat back and watched, content as long as they kept it outside. Sarah saw two men boxing, two others pushing each other and three women screaming back and forth.

Sarah looked at ol' Brown, who sported a Pioneer jacket, beat-up and filthy now, along with a raggedy shirt and breeches. Ol' Brown was a leech of sorts. He knew nothing of earning an honest living—partly because he lost a leg during the war, but mainly because he did not have an honest twitch in his body. Sarah found him amusing. Grandmother did not. She called him "Half-penny Brown" because, in her estimation, he fell short of a whole penny. It was hard for Sarah to refrain from calling him that when she greeted him. "Hello, Mr. Brown," she giggled.

A smile burst across his grubby face. "Jambo, Miss Sarah."

The thick ether from Brown's foul brew hovered in the air. George dropped two shillings into the small keg on the floor beside the chair. There was always music: washboards, spoons, homemade violins and banjos. And Brown always had a pot on. Tonight was no exception. The steam from the tripe drifted throughout the shack. Getting on midnight, he would drop some vegetables in and when it was ready for the eating, his yell would fill the room: "Grab a plate!" That was the one kindness ol' Brown seemed to possess—that and looking after his Flintlock. It sparkled, even in the dim light.

Tonight, Rod was drawing his bow across his hand-made fiddle, stirring up the dust. The rickety boards trembled as the crowd stepped wildly. Sarah made her way through the clamour to a group of people standing near the stove ol' Brown had constructed. In their midst was Medley, the Birchtown handyman who could not find a woman in the whole of the colony desperate enough to be his wife. Priscilla Haywood was the one currently slapping his advances away. Spotting Sarah, she ducked under Medley's arm and headed in her direction.

"Well, well. It's Sarah, though in that get-up should I call you Missy Sarah, the Queen of Birchtown?" Priscilla's taunting was loud. Rod stopped playing. Heads turned for the show. Folks had grown accustomed to watching the feuds of Birchtown and so they stood back with their ears alert for any signs of a showdown. All eyes focused on the pair.

Priscilla smirked, "I see Grandma has let you out again tonight."

"I let myself out, thank you."

"Are you sure that the old woman is not hiding around the corner, ready to yank you home by the hair?"

"You should worry about your own hair." Sarah smoothed down the front of her wide red dress. She looked at Priscilla, gave her the once over, then cut her eyes. "At least I do not look like yesterday's news."

"You know, Miss Teacher, this is not New York."

"And what would you know about New York?"

"New York has a lot of women in red dresses. I know they're not school teachers."

The place swelled with laughter.

"Don't be jealous, Priscilla. Your ugly dress matches your ugly spirit."

"Same old Sarah, always quick with words."

"Well, there's nothing quick about you Priscilla."

The laughter turned into a roar this time. Ol' Brown let out a yell from his chair by the door. "None of dat foolish talk. You can take that one-upping somewhere else. Do you hear me in there? First thing you'll be in a fight and me place gets all broke up." He let a shot go from the Flintlock up through the ceiling. Dirt fell from the sod roof onto the floor. The place fell into dead silence.

Sarah moved on. Having gotten one up was good enough for her. George reached out with a cup of liquor. She hesitated, then took a sip of the horrible concoction. At first, her lips tingled and her throat burned. The brew slid down into her stomach and set her gut on fire. For an instant, her vision blurred. She handed the cup back to George. "Wicked, wicked, foul stuff," she said. "How can anyone drink such poison? Who knows what ol' Brown puts in this stuff? It could kill us."

"It will loosen you up," George laughed.

"And mess us up," Sarah added. She could see that there was a sickening power in liquor by the way it took hold of the people. It would not control her. She passed the cup back to George. It was the music and dancing that lifted her spirits, not the liquor. She followed George to the middle of the floor. They were shoulder to shoulder with the crowd. Rod played a wild, jubilant kind of music, making it up as he went. Music made the dancers come alive. Made them want to step and whirl. Made them feel free from the world with nothing holding them back. Sarah created new steps and twirled in her red dress. The music picked up in tempo. This was living, she thought. It had been hard to survive without music and it felt good to hear it now.

Midnight was fast approaching and the pot would soon be ready. Sarah made her way to the bench by the back wall. A man in a white ruffled shirt and brown waistcoat approached her. His hazelnut skin glistened in the dull light and his smile astounded her.

"Hello, Sarah," he said, extending a hand. "I inquired," he said when Sarah looked at him, puzzled.

"Pleased to meet you."

"You are striking in your red dress."

"Thank you," she said and in a sugary tone asked, "And your name?"

"Thomas Cooper."

"And where are you from, Thomas Cooper?"

"Philadelphia, born the son of free Negroes."

"Free?"

"Never free. A Negro is a Negro. The laws that applied to the slaves applied to us as well. For awhile, I was indentured to old Mr. Brunhoff who taught me to read and write and how to keep ledgers. A good man from Germany. Then I worked for my father, importing and exporting goods to Barbados and Jamaica until the war started. Our business closed and so I left."

"What brought you here?"

"In New York, I heard about Nova Scotia. I thought it would be a good place to find work, but the poverty is the worse I've seen."

"So you won't be staying."

"I'm leaving for Halifax, then going back to New York."

"I guess there's not much here to offer anyone, but I plan to start a business. A tailor's shop."

"A tailor's shop. Hmmm... And are you spoken for, Miss Sarah?"

Sarah managed a half-smile, "I thought I was."

"Which means?"

"It's not working out the way I expected."

"What happened? What did you expect?"

"I had big dreams. I was looking forward to settling down, but sometimes dreams do not work out. It has been four months since he went away and I'm doubtful that he's going to return."

"Then you are free, as far as I can tell."

Sarah smiled and she let herself enjoy the happiness overtaking her, though it troubled her that she had dismissed Reece so easily. Was she finding an excuse to abandon him? Had she just admitted that her future with Reece was becoming increasingly uncertain? For the moment, none of it seemed to matter. "I am a free woman with no obligations," she finally said.

The music slowed. Thomas led her to the centre of the floor. He smelled of sweet cedar wood. She felt like a million yesterdays tucked away inside a double-happiness jar. As they danced, Priscilla watched from the sidelines until she could stand it no longer, then she strolled over to the couple and with devilishness she said, "Well Sarah. With Reece away you seem to have found yourself a new sweetheart." She laughed and said, "It must be the dress leading you astray."

Thomas withdrew his arms. A pained expression swept across his face. Sarah looked at Thomas, then turned and gave Priscilla a short, cold sneer before she managed to say, "No, I did not." She turned and headed to the door.

Outside, she stood under a huge hemlock. She was not obligated to wait for Reece, to pine away, hoping for something that might never be. She twisted her face. It was good that she left, for surely she would have taken a swipe at Priscilla and embarrassed herself and Thomas too.

It took Thomas a second or two to come to his senses before hurrying to the door where ol' Brown was slumped down in his makeshift chair. He was drunk, but not so drunk that his one opened eye could not follow the young women about the room or watch out for any commotion. Between the snorting and grunting, Thomas broke in with his question: "The young woman who just walked past in the red dress, which way did she go?"

"Dat way," ol' Brown said, pointing to the right side of the shack.

Even in the dark, the red dress drew Thomas's eye. He made his way towards Sarah, thinking on what had just happened.

"I believe you, Sarah Redmond. Please don't be upset."

Thomas's sudden appearance startled Sarah. She took a deep breath. The truth was Priscilla's remark was a blessing. Deep inside, where all the lingering doubts held up her expectations, there was a cleansing going on. She let the remnants of past dreams fly away. She faced Thomas and, oddly, felt a deep sense of respect for this stranger. He seemed to see clearly into the nature of people and to have a few things figured out.

"I am fine," she said. "It's been quite the night." Sarah thought about Grandmother's bad juju and was sure she felt its hold on her evaporate as she looked up at this handsome stranger and allowed her face to crinkle into a smile.

Twenty-five

THOMAS REMAINED IN BIRCHTOWN FOR ANOTHER TWO weeks. He and Sarah shared a joyous time: talking, laughing and dancing. His love was a healing potion, nourishing Sarah's emptiness, leaving room in her thoughts for only him. At first, she hesitated, trying hard to maintain her feelings for Reece, trying to figure out how such a thing could happen, but this new fire and passion sought her out and devoured her.

It may have been his smile or his confidence or the way he thought about life, she wasn't sure. Perhaps it was something that happened on the evening they went to the clearing to a boxing match. The strongest Negro men in Birchtown lined up in pairs to fight each other. By the fifth round of the first fight, Thomas had turned to her and said, "Such brutality. The Negroes fight for a few coins to please this senseless crowd and the white men from Roseway who come to drink, take our women and make sport of the men who tear each other apart. We're always for their amusement and never their equals. These men who cheer for us at night will jeer us during the day." Without asking permission, Thomas took Sarah by the arm and said, "After coming out of slavery, we should never have to witness such brutality again." And with that, he led her away.

On another occasion, he stopped by the cabin and carried her buckets from the well. Instead of sitting on a stump and watching her do the wash, like most men would have done, he pitched in and helped, not giving it a second thought. She grinned, thinking of how in an instant the idea of women's and men's roles could change. He brought a fresh view of life. There was a lot to like about Thomas Cooper.

On the evening before Thomas left, Sarah took out the red dress and put it on. They stood in the moonlight holding each other as though bound by some syrupy tonic. "Sarah," he said, with her face in his hands. "You and I belong together. I have never felt so certain about anything in my life. I love you deeply. More than I could ever have imagined."

When she did not answer, he continued gently, "Come to New York with me. This life here has nothing to offer but lost dreams and misery. We can have a good life in New York. We will have a chance to grow there."

In the unforgiving chill of the Birchtown night, Sarah found no easy words to answer a question that demanded such quick action. Hadn't she dreamed and longed for a better life, wanted to fly like a bird, be her own person? She looked down at the dress, admiring its showiness and defiance. Her smile grew narrow and her eyes closed. Nothing was ever clear-cut. What was holding her back? It was the timing and all the tangled bits and pieces of her life and, just as importantly, family. She could hear Thomas's voice pleading with her to answer. It sounded far away and desperate. She opened her eyes.

"Sarah, don't turn away from me." He was shaking her gently with both hands. "Come away with me. We can leave in a few days. I have enough money. We can take your things with us. I have thought about this. I have a plan."

Sarah did not answer. She kept staring away in the darkness. She was searching her heart, trying to grasp what was happening. She studied his eyes, not wanting to turn away from the passion in them, but she did, suddenly, uttering, "No. I can't. It would not be right to leave. I have family here, hopes and dreams. I could say that I do not love you and put an end to this right now." She shook her head wildly and continued, "But no, that would not be the truth."

"Then what is the truth? What is it, Sarah?"

"The truth is … I care deeply for you."

"You love me, I know it. Say it!"

"I do love you."

Thomas hung his head and stammered, "What can I say that would change your mind?"

"I can't say … just that I know I am where I need to be."

"I understand your need to stay, but I can't stand the thought of leaving you behind. I will not try to persuade you against your will."

Her eyes held his and she knew what she felt was as true as the moon above, but still … Unexpected thoughts of Reece surfaced and it came to her mind how her faith in him had been dashed by his sudden leaving. She ran her fingers along the edge of the puffed sleeves of her dress, feeling the fine detailing, the expert stitching: steady and even, like she wanted her life to be. She would help raise young Prince and follow her dream of becoming a tailor. If Thomas loved her so much … She wanted to scream it out loud, but it would have been selfish, and so what she said was, "Let's not be sad. Some things are not meant to last forever. We found joy in each other's company and maybe we should be happy with that."

"Perhaps. But if you should change your mind, you come to New York and find me. I will make my name known in every Negro quarter." He reached for her hand and this time she did not push it away.

Later that evening, she carefully folded the red dress, smoothing the wrinkles as though she were erasing the troubling lines of life. She wondered who it had belonged to, if it had been part of another romance, part of a lavish ball with handsome gentlemen. She wasn't feeling at all like the child who needed Grandmother to speak for her or the one who needed direction and advice. She was in charge, looking out for herself. Blessings and curses, joy and sorrow, all at once, like a thunderstorm when the sun was shining. What was this mixed-up crazy life really about? Sarah had worn the red dress for perhaps the last time. She gazed at it for a long time, then gathered it up in her arms and placed it in the trunk at the foot of her bed saying, "Guard the memories this dress holds dear." And she closed the lid.

Twenty-six

IT WAS EARLY JULY 1785. SARAH SPENT HER TIME WORKING at Mrs. Cunningham's, Mrs. Atkins' and at home. There was little time to think about Thomas. She had Prince to care for and, more urgently, Grandmother, who had fallen ill. The old woman lay in bed for three days, suffering delusions that caused her to cry and, sometimes unexpectedly, erupt into fits of laughter. Peace refused to settle across her troubled brow. Sarah worried that she might have smallpox or cholera and she kept an eye on her fever. Fibby was certain it was neither. She spread a thick paste of black mustard powder, flour and hot water between two pieces of cloth and laid the poultice on Lydia's chest. After several applications, the congestion had not loosened.

Grandmother lay on her side, her eyes wide as her raspy groans and deep breathing intensified. She called out saying, "Just a little glass of water, Sarah, and I'll be all right."

Sarah held the water to her parched mouth only to watch her barely swallow it. She knelt on the floor beside the bunk. There was a dullness in the old woman that was unfamiliar. Sarah searched her eyes for signs of hope. What she saw was troubling.

"What is it?" she asked. "What is troubling you? Is there something more I can do, some way to comfort you?" She wondered what was so heavy on the old woman's mind that she could not speak it.

Grandmother forced her head up on the thin pillow and sipped a tiny bit of water. Her scratchy voice came in weak spurts, "I got to make ... my peace with God. Do you hear?"

"Yes, Grandmother," Sarah replied.

Grandmother spoke again and her words formed a plea. "Where is Fortune? Can you get your Papa, please?" The old woman spoke with an unsettling urgency. "There is something I got to tell him."

"Papa is out at the woodpile. I'll get him."

After Fortune took his place in the chair beside his mother's bed, pulling off his cap and hanging it on his knee, he said simply, "I'm here, Mama."

The old woman turned to Fortune, squinting. She stretched upright on her elbows. "I'm so glad that you found us, Fortune." She opened her eyes wider. Her words evened out. "I never told you this before, but you surely are a blessing and, oh Lord, I need you now, son. I got to make this journey to Glory with pride, without any regrets. I got to gather my children now. I got to try."

Grandmother's eyes strayed from Fortune's face. She looked towards the light streaming through the thin canvas draping. "It is true. I was keeping things from you, waiting on the right chance. Oh the guilt and shame I felt over the loss of my children. It seemed like some evil spell stole my life." She slowed, taking deep breaths. "I did not want the burden on no one but myself. The time has come to speak the truth ... all of it."

"You don't have to talk about it now, Mama. Sometimes the past is best forgotten and things left alone."

"Fortune, you have to listen to me, now. I must get it all said. I have to stop waiting on time. Time is running out."

He brought the chair closer to the bed. The time had finally come for the telling, "the freeing of the soul," the slaves called it.

Fortune wished Reverend Ringwood was there, but he was not about to suggest that.

And so, between catching her breath and the raspy coughing, Lydia unfolded her sad story. So many births, too many to count for a breeding slave. Most of the babies had died, leaving her with five children. Boll weevil and Cecil had guarded her newborns like soldiers, one of their jobs being to decide when the children would go to sale. They would cart the babies and children off like cattle to auction. Some remained to learn skills or work the fields. She recalled how Cecil took the three light babies, saying she had no right to them.

She assured Fortune that she had kept her promise and spoken with Margaret Cunningham. It was all out in the open now, how Cecil had sold her back to Master Redmond to bring up as a Redmond. She told them too about Amelia and another son who had been taken. And when her head fell back on the pillow, with not an ounce of breath left, both Fortune and Sarah felt her sadness right to their core.

Fortune showed no evidence of surprise. Looking at his mother, he said gently, "Well. Margaret Cunningham. The secret is out at last. It all makes sense. It wasn't hard to figure out after thinking about it. I heard the fondness in your voice when you spoke of her. One time ol' Tally, the wood carver, told me the slaves were marking their daughters with the rings he carved. It sure did raise my curiosity when I saw Margaret's ring, just like yours. Well, mama, I'm happy for all of us. It's what you have prayed for, to bring your family together."

"Here in Scotia we can put this family back together. We can know our real kin. There's no shame in that."

"There is no shame in that," Fortune repeated. He paused. She had kept the secret for so long. Pride and guilt, he thought, it stole her joy all these years. If only he had found the courage to say something when he first suspected, when he wondered where the babies went, when he saw the creamy tint in Margaret Cunningham's skin and his mother's attention to her. No matter, you can't change the past, but you can enjoy the moment. He kissed his mother on the cheek and grinned, "It feels good to know she's one of us."

"Son, I can't rest until I know what happened to my other children, my boy and my girl." She looked away, her bones telling her there was only a little time left to do anything.

"Do you have any idea of what became of them?"

"The girl stayed with the Redmonds for awhile, a playmate for Margaret, and then she was sold to Mr. Pinkham. I let him do that, Fortune! Let him sell my child without a word. Oh, Lord, please forgive ol' Lydia."

Fortune reached for her hands and rubbed them gently. "You could not stop it. Cecil would have beaten you … or worse."

"One day she came back to Master Redmond's, grown, almost a woman. I wanted to mark her like I did Margaret, but there was no time for ol' Tally to make a ring. Oh, Fortune, I pray that I will see her again!"

"I wish there was something I could do."

Grandmother let out a long sigh. Her bedclothes were soaked and her lips dry.

According to Chance, the local healing woman, Lydia had pneumonia. How long she had to live was anyone's guess. Each day an endless parade of well-wishers descended upon the little cabin. Margaret came to sing a round of hymns, bathe her mother and help change her gowns. She said it was strange how the tables had turned. It was her turn now to look after dear Lydia, just as the old woman had looked after her. Having dragged on for over two weeks, the sickness finally cleared, but Lydia remained weak and bedridden.

When finally she regained enough strength, Lydia called Fortune to her bedside once again. "I believe that Amelia is in Scotia. Margaret has told me she found the Pinkham name in one of the books listing the military men who came here. The Pinkhams headed to Yarmouth shortly after they arrived. Her name is likely Amelia Pinkham. This is the only lead Margaret has. I have to try to find a way to contact her and tell her this ol' woman needs to see her one more time."

"Don't fret, Mama. If she is in Nova Scotia, I'll find her. I will do my best. What about the boy? Do you know where he is?"

"I kept the boy but a short time. He looked so much like Margaret when he was born. That Cecil, I believe he knew where he was, but he would not tell me. I have searched every mulatto face in Birchtown, but I can't say for sure that he is here."

Fortune said, "Asking questions is trouble, but I'll stir the pot to see what I find."

Fortune's eyes clouded. He stood out in the fresh air, taking a break from chopping wood, and scanned the land, thinking of how far they had come since Carolina. He was grateful. They were finally landowners. Sarah could read and write. Prince Jr. was doing fine. Mama had realized part of her dream with the reconciliation with Margaret.

For some reason, the idea of going back into the past made him anxious. Fortune picked up the axe, brought it down hard and buried it in a thick block of hardwood. His worry now was how Amelia would react to being found. Oddly, it was not just light-skinned ones who were afraid to acknowledge their mixed heritage; many Negroes were running away from their past and their families. The colony was wading in a flood of shame and frightening memories that made talking about slavery difficult. Neither did the white folks acknowledge their role in the horrible practice, though it was ingrained on their tongues and minds, like a permanent scar. They were all acting like a little time could wipe the slate clean with no side effects. It made not an ounce of sense to Fortune. It was to him like holding onto another secret of which no good or peace could come. He prayed Amelia's reaction would not be one of the remaining barbs in his mother's crown. Misgivings aside, Fortune vowed to honour his mother's wish. That was all he could do — give an old woman a promise to help her make peace with herself and God.

After supper, Fortune lit a candle and placed it on the table. He looked at Sarah and said, "Can you write a letter for me?"

Sarah went to the trunk and got some paper, a quill and black ink.

"Okay, Babygirl. This letter is to go to my old friend, Fred, down in Yarmouth. We served together in the Pioneers. He worked on the Pinkham plantation, so address it to Fred Pinkham. Tell him I need a favour. Ask if he can find an Amelia Pinkham." He scratched his head, wondering what to say next. "Write out a special message for Amelia and put it in the letter to Fred. Tell her that we have need of her … tell her that she has a very sick mama." His words were thick and burdened with soreness. "Tell her to come to Birchtown as soon as possible. Remember to put it separate with her name on it." He finished by saying, "I would sent it by pony express, but it might take too long. I will see if I can find a boat heading to Yarmouth in the morning and someone willing to take it."

Fortune watched as Sarah wrote the letter. Her writing amused him. "Babygirl," he said, "Grandma's life has been a long journey burdened with the kind of misery we can't even imagine, though we seen a lot. We got to send her off happy. We got to pray." Sarah bowed her head. Fortune turned his face upward. "Sweet Lord." he said. "The one who the pastor said delivered Moses out of Egypt, the one who delivered us up to Birchtown, I am asking for a little time to see this through, before Mama is delivered up to Glory. We put our faith in you. Amen."

Twenty-seven

I T WAS MONDAY, JULY 19, 1785, WHEN REECE JOHNSON
stepped off the schooner *Julie Anne*, in Port Roseway. The
port was hectic with several schooners tied up and men unloading fish, molasses, dry goods and rum from the West Indies for
the King's Bounty and shops. The air smelled of mud flats and
fish and rang with loud chatter and laughter. By luck Reece came
across Enos loading his cart with fresh cod.

"Are you going to Birchtown?" Reece asked.

"That is where I'm headed, lad."

"A lift would be much appreciated."

"Hop aboard. Just one more barrel to fill. You come from
afar, did you?"

"All the way from Carolina."

"I believe I've seen you before."

"No doubt. I have a little place in Birchtown."

"Yes, yes." What is your name again?"

"Reece Johnson."

"Well, well. Carolina you say. It sure must have changed since
the war."

"The name has changed from Charles Town to Charleston.
They are rebuilding parts of the city and plantations. It is a far
busier place, for sure, than when we left."

"Folks can't leave anything alone, always changing everything," Enos said. "Port Roseway is called Shelburne now, but most of the people refuse to call it that. Stuck on the old name, I guess." He climbed up on his make-shift bench in the wagon. "I'm through here. Giddy-up, Doris," he shouted, then continued, "Did the war change anything in those parts?"

"Not much, Sir. The land still sweats its tobacco, rice, indigo and cotton. The port was busy with the hustle and bustle of merchants, planters and slaves, all making it a wealthy place. There's nothing but a sea of black with so many Negro slaves. They say they are equal to the population of the white folks or greater. There's a growing concern over the slaves."

"I knew that was coming. What are they fired up about now?"

"There's a lot of talk about creating new laws, the Slave Codes of South Carolina. That much has not changed as far as I could tell—how to control the Negro, keep him as chattel with no rights, keep him from mixing with them and now fearing them as rivals for jobs."

"Oh yes. Fear is the rich man's tool all right. The war set many of the slaves free. Surely those who are free have it easier."

"It's dangerous for free Negroes and worse for the slaves. There is no real freedom yet, though the air was thick with talk. You know the war got everyone talking about slavery. The newcomers from Europe need to work. The abolitionists do not see the jobs as just slave's work. Nor do they approve of selling the Negro against his will. Their ideas are met with hatred."

"Oh, slavery will die in time. Birchtowners talk about having their freedom, but a Negro still has to fear the laws and the hateful conduct and attitudes. Be careful, lad. Free is a double-edged sword. The slave catchers followed us here to reclaim lost property. You could be going back before you know it."

"Ah, Enos, a Negro spends his life trying to avoid the quicksand."

"And bad women," Enos laughed.

The cart slowly jogged along the road and headed out to Birchtown. "Which end of Birchtown are you be headed to, lad?"

"Out the road to Lydia Redmond's place."

"Lydia's place, ah?" He snapped a short whip. "Giddy-up, Doris."

"I suppose not much has happened since I left in January," Reece said.

"Well, let me see now. Folks are leaving faster than they are coming in now. It is thinning out. And then there was Fortune Redmond's trial a while back."

"Trial? What happened?"

"Well, I imagine you knew Cecil MacLeod, the one who owned the store. Murdered. Fortune was a suspect. The judge let him go because they found Boll weevil Carter, the slave catcher, with the knife that killed Cecil. Boll weevil, well, the sheriff had let him go because he seemed a little crazy, and the man skipped town. Folks are still talking 'bout how lucky it was for a Negro to receive that kind of justice. They still cannot believe it. I was there in the courtroom when the case was dis … dis …"

"Dismissed?"

"Yes, that be it. Folks had poor Fortune hanging, but it wasn't to be."

The cart jogged down a side path lined with thick bushes and trees. The smell of sweet pine and smoke from the shacks blotted away the strong fish odour from the barrels in the wagon. Enos made five stops before saying, "We'll head over to Lydia's now."

When Enos pulled up beside Lydia's step, he said with sadness, "Lydia's off her feet. She is doing poorly. I hear she ain't got long! I am going to miss the dear ol' soul. There is no one here like Lydia. I'll have to drop by soon."

Reece took a deep breath, jumped down from the cart and said, "Thanks for the lift, Enos. I'll do you a turn one day."

"We had a long yarn, didn't we? Give Lydia my best wishes."

IT WAS MID-AFTERNOON WHEN SARAH PULLED OUT A box from under her bed with the intention of sorting through the thread, buttons, ribbons and odd bits of cloth she and Grandmother had been collecting for their quilt. A gentle tapping on the door startled her and thoughts came rushing back of the night her father returned. The tapping came again just as she was making her way around Prince, who was happily rocking on a horse her father had made from wood. "Oh, Lord, my hair," she drawled and flung a small white bonnet on her head before answering the door.

She cracked the door and stepped back in amazement. He looked much the same, only thinner. She waited before speaking in hopes that her emotions would take hold— force her to cry out his name, fling herself at him, something. She was surprisingly empty and there were no emotions to guide her next words. When they did come, they were not at all with the fervour she had imagined. "Reece. It's good to see you. Come in. It has been a long time," she said with the excitement of receiving an old friend. Guilt kept her from looking Reece in the face, forced her to deny it was Thomas Cooper she longed to see come through the door.

She had not changed much, perhaps in height and in some places a little weight. Reece noticed more than anything her discomfort, but the cool welcome did not bother him. He expected to find her a little distant—as he was, what with the news he was about to deliver, news that would alter everything. To avoid telling her, he had even thought about staying away for good, but returning was the honourable thing to do. A man kept his word! Besides, his news needed telling to make things right.

The awkward silence was difficult to bear. He watched her scurry about, fussing with Prince and setting the table with a confidence and maturity he had not seen before. He waited until Sarah had bread, scanty vegetable soup and tea in front of him before he said, "Enos told me that Lydia is not well."

"She has not been herself for awhile. When did you get back?" she asked.

"Today. Enos was at the wharf and gave me a lift. I came straight here."

"He must have greased the wheels on the cart! There was no squawking today. I'm surprised he and Doris are not deaf from the noise."

They laughed. The air felt thinner now.

Sarah asked, "Did you find Rose?"

"Yes, eventually. It took a long time to trace through records of slave sales. She was on a large farm in Kentucky." He looked at Sarah kindly, knowing that his news would come slowly now, piece by piece.

"Did she know you?"

"No, she did not. I was a child when she last saw me. She is old and worn out. The poor old soul had too many babies, one every year and several at a time to suckle. Her memory is not what it used to be. She hobbles along with her stomach, back and feet giving her torment and she still must earn her keep. The one blessing is that there are fewer chores expected of her."

"Were you able to find out anything about your childhood from her?"

"It took awhile. I had to paint a picture to jog her memory, take her mind back to the Redmond plantation. Take her back to the night she received a baby from Cecil MacLeod to tend.

She never forgot the Redmond overseer. That 'son-of-a-one-toothed demon,' she called him. At first she couldn't remember where the child came from, but then she recalled he mentioned a slave by name."

"What was the slave's name?"

Reece stared at Sarah. He was silent for a full minute, stalling. He struggled with wanting to tell her the truth, but he had trouble wrapping his tongue around the words. He reached across the table and took her hands.

"Did she tell you the slave's name?" Sarah asked again.

"Yes. Rose said the slave's name was … Lydia."

"Lydia?" Sarah's mouth fell open. Her mind was galloping so fast she could not keep up with the pace. "My grandmother Lydia?"

"Yes, our Lydia …" he stammered.

"No, Reece." Sarah bit her lip. "Such a thing cannot be true!" Sarah slumped over the table. "To think," she said, "you and I could have married. Tell me you are not my uncle. Oh Lord, tell me this cannot be true." Her eyes dulled with embarrassment and she sat whimpering over such a tragic thing. For surely the hungry gossips would love such a scandal. She could see them gnawing on the news like a bone until there was nothing left but the splinters. It was a moment, if ever there was one, for tears. She kept her head down, waiting for the tears to come, but none did. This family has enough secrets to fill Birchtown Bay, she thought.

Reece withdrew his hands and leaned back in his chair. "Are you all right?" he asked. "It hurts me as much as it does you, having it all come at once and knowing that we can never be together. I know this is difficult, Sarah, but I cannot change it."

Sarah raised her head and met his gaze. "Reece Johnson, you are Grandmother's son, my uncle," she said. "There is no choice in the matter."

"No, none, but cheer up, there's a bright side to what's happened. We will forget this disappointment with time," Reece said, a smile breaking across his face.

"Yes, I suppose there is. Grandmother will be surprised and so happy to hear the news. She always speaks of her missing son. Never in my wildest dreams did I think it might be you."

Like with Margaret, they would all have to face the truth. Sarah looked at the fire pit, avoiding Reece's eyes. He was not the only one with news. As she slowly turned and held his eyes, she filled with a small measure of regret, and an overwhelming amount of guilt. "I have a confession to make, Reece," she said. Her words stretched. "You will hear about it soon enough, so I think it is best if it comes from my lips."

"What is it?"

"You were away so long … well, things changed. I … I became involved …"

"If you have found someone, I have no right to question it."

Sarah cut him off. "I was seeing someone, but as is my fate, he has gone away, back to New York. I don't think he'll ever come back to Birchtown."

"I am sorry, Sarah. Sorry things didn't work out for either of us."

"I'm not sorry. I found a wonderful friendship, more than anyone could ask for in these times. You and I, Reece, we will always be close because we are family."

"I know that when folks find out about this, their tongues will feast. I hope their stony comments will not worry you. We will just have to remind folks that any of us could be related, seeing the way families were separated."

"So true!" she said. "I have Grandmother to think about now. She is not well, Reece. She has taken to her bed. Her last wish was to see all of her children before she passed. You will be surprised to learn that you have more family, not just Papa, but two sisters."

"Sisters? Here?"

"Yes! Margaret Cunningham in Port Roseway is one of them."

"Surely you are joking. Margaret Cunningham?"

"It is true and we have sent word to Yarmouth in hopes of finding the other one, Amelia Pinkham. You are the last of Grandmother's lost children." Sarah smiled and her face lit up as if the sun entered the cabin through the window. "Today has brought us all a blessing. Papa will have a brother and Grandmother will see her lost son. Are you ready to tell her?"

Reece nodded. He followed Sarah into the back room to greet his mother with the news.

Twenty-eight

THE HOUSE WAS THE KIND OF QUIET THAT COMES WITH grief. Not even young Prince fussed or went about looking for the usual kind of attention or getting into mischief. Sarah's thoughts were in limbo. There were days when she was a hummingbird, going from task to task as though seeking a sweet nectar that would satisfy her. Lydia's illness, Thomas's leaving, Reece's return, the lost children—it was all, for Sarah, a full plate to digest. She turned to filling her life with work and attending to Grandmother. Whether she liked it or not, deep down her loyalty was first to family and then to herself. If only she had known that the pot was being stirred.

For weeks, Thomas Cooper had wandered the muddy streets of Halifax, bags in hand. He found lodging and food wherever he could. He worked at the docks, loading and unloading goods. The pay was good. The ships came and went from the eastern states. He could have boarded any one of them as a hand and returned to New York, but his desire to leave was defenceless against his heart. It was Wednesday, the twenty-sixth of July 1785, when he boarded a schooner and headed back to Roseway.

The sky bulged with masses of fluffy, luminous clouds. On this bright summer day, with the sun warming his spirits, he knocked on the Redmond door. It was a joyful *tap, tap*! Sarah opened the door and stared in wide-eyed silence. There she stood with doughy hands, in a pale blue dress and her hair a tangled web, and he, all decked out, looking fresh and clean, his smile breathtaking.

"Do I get a hello?" Thomas chuckled.

"Thomas," she finally whispered.

"May I come in?"

"Yes, of course. I cannot believe my eyes."

"Have I surprised you?"

"You are supposed to be in New York." She looked at him again and her heart quivered with joy. "Where are my manners? Come in," she said. "Let me finish cleaning the table." Her words were gushing now and she could not stop babbling. "There will be fresh bread soon. I will put the tea on. I must look a fright. Will you excuse me while I freshen up?"

The cabin warmed with the aroma of fresh bread cooking in a heavy black skillet over the fire. Thomas hoped that all would go as planned. He ached for the joy of having her in his arms. He turned his thoughts to Birchtown. It was a cold, hard place, all right. He figured he could settle for the simple joys of life, master the elements with a little preparation and skill. Perhaps his education would lead to a job. And equality, well now that was the never-ending storm for the Negro.

"There," Sarah said on her return. "I feel better now."

"Good," he said. "Seeing you again is pure happiness, with or without the flour," he laughed.

She stood back and held his flickering brown eyes. Her face glowed as though she had swallowed the sun. She looked at him curiously, thinking of Reece coming and going in and out of her life. Was this going to be more of the same? With hesitation, she asked, "Are you back to stay or are you leaving again?"

"I'm here to stay." His tone was firm. "No matter what the wind blows in."

Thomas reached in his pocket and pulled out the case from Murphy's Jewelers. He removed the ring from the case, reached across the table and took her hand. He slipped the ring on her left middle finger. "A gift for a new beginning," he said.

Sarah's smile broke into a series of giggles and howls. She held up her hand and gazed at the sterling silver ring with a centre emerald surrounded by tiny pearls. Rising from her chair, she threw her arms around Thomas's neck and kissed every inch of his face, uttering a million thanks. "It is the most beautiful gift in the world."

After lunch, Sarah said, "I want Grandmother to meet you. I want her to see the ring. It will make her happy to see that her family is moving along."

Two days later, Thomas accompanied Sarah down to Roseway to deliver the laundry to Mrs. Cunningham. Thick grey fog blanketed the settlement, leaving it cold and damp. They skipped over the ruts and hopped over the holes in the muddy streets. As they left Dock Street and cut through a side alley that took them down a hill to Water Street, an abandoned fish hut caught Sarah's eye. She scrutinized it carefully as they passed. She looked at Thomas. "Do you know what I've been thinking?"

"No." he chuckled, "That's too big of a job for me."

She gave him a nudge and ignored the remark. "We should be planning our future. And there are things I want to talk to you about."

"Such as?"

"Getting that shack over there."

"That bait shack? What on earth for?"

"I have found my calling, Thomas. I want to be a tailor. We could turn that hut into a shop. Nothing fancy, but something useful." Her face lit up with a warm mahogany glow.

"And what would you sew, Miss Sarah?"

"You're not making fun of me, are you? I am serious."

"I am curious, that's all."

"I can do repairs and I can make clothes, plain or fancy dresses for the women of Port Roseway. But, that's not all. I want to make a quilt to retell the story of our journey."

"I know you're serious. You have that look."

"Do you think the hut can be saved? Fixed up, I mean."

"Have you thought about what the reaction will be in Roseway? Have you forgotten why the Negroes live separately in Birchtown?"

"It doesn't matter," she hissed. "All my life I had to keep thinking about what others wanted. It was you who said that I should see myself the way I wanted to be. I want a shop and if I can find a way to have it, I will. Papa says change comes from a need. If there is a need, nothing else will matter."

"You will require a licence from the Sessions Court. Are there Negroes here who have been able to get a licence?"

"Not that I know of."

"Then what makes you think you can get one?"

"All I can do is ask, like everyone else. I have enough money for one."

"And if they turn you down?"

"Then they turn me down. Damn it, Thomas. Whose side are you on?"

"I am just asking, Sarah. I'm not against you, but you have to think ahead … know what you are dealing with. Being prepared is the best way to get things done. No surprises."

"You sound like Grandmother. Just worry about today, never tomorrow.'"

"She knows what a day can bring. It can bring a lot to handle."

"How many times have you expected one thing and gotten

another? I know what you are trying to say. Every day of my life reminds me of the fact that I am a Negro. It feels like some kind of a death sentence."

"Stop and think, Sarah. We are charting new ground and anything can happen. Hatred is as thick as the mud here. Try to prepare for all possibilities."

"Every step forward will be a new step. Should we stop stepping, stand still? Keep using fear as an excuse to do nothing?" She was not prepared to give up, not without trying. Thomas was just being cautious, but her dream to break with the past was too important to be afraid. It was time to get to stepping. Her life would be different, not like her mother's and grandmother's. She would go it alone if she had to, but she would not sit idly by wishing for change and she would not depend on charity.

They walked briskly now that Mrs. Cunningham's was in sight. There was something else to share with Thomas. She told him that Margaret Cunningham was her aunt, and how they had come together as family. "I'll run the subject of the hut by her," she said. "She can judge how folks will react."

In the kitchen, Sarah introduced Thomas. Margaret Cunningham smiled pleasantly. "I am pleased to meet you, Thomas."

"Thank you, Ma'am," he said.

"Grandmother sends her love. She's holding her own, waiting for Amelia to arrive."

"Amelia? My goodness, were you able to find her?"

"Not yet, but Papa sent a letter to Fred Pinkham in Yarmouth to see if he could help us."

"Yes, that may be just the thing."

"This is her last child. Hopefully, we will get a reply soon."

"So much good news. Lydia has found her son, Reece, and now maybe another daughter. It's a lot to take in. Come, this calls for tea." She brought tea and sweet treats but Sarah's uneasiness stole her appetite. Exhaling, she said, "There is more good news since I last saw you."

"I can see that something has changed." She took Sarah's left hand and looked at Thomas. "Well, well! It's a lovely ring. Maybe a wedding soon … something to bring a little cheer."

Anxious to keep the conversation moving in a certain direction, Sarah said, "You would need a new outfit. I suppose the women of Port Roseway have their pick of dressmakers. I saw two shops."

"There's only one good tailor in Port Roseway. That would be Martha Lewis. I would not mind engaging her, but oh my, the chatter that woman gets up to … just sinful. I would make my own clothes but my eyes aren't what they used to be."

"I've been thinking long and hard about something … something I would like to do."

Margaret looked puzzled.

"I am not complaining about my job, Ma'am, but I long to have something to call my own." Sarah continued, "I am not a slave or a servant. I am a free woman … free to follow my heart. All I need is a chance."

"And where is your heart taking you, Sarah?"

"It might sound like a dream …" She looked at Thomas, her eyes narrowed.

"Let me be the judge of that. Whatever it is, I will help in any way I can."

"Well, Ma'am, I've been thinking about setting up a tailor shop. There is an abandoned hut down on Water Street. It would be big enough to take in some sewing, but, 'I got de worries,' as the old folks say."

"Worries? Why you were taught to sew when you were just a girl."

"It is not about that, Ma'am. I'd have to purchase the hut and I need a licence. That could mean trouble."

Thomas smiled flatly, wondering what the response would be.

"Sarah, you put that thought out of your head. This nonsense about who is entitled to what has to stop. We are all the same under the skin. I am a witness to that. Let the people decide if they want something made well by a trustworthy person."

Sarah nodded, watching the way Margaret pulled her mouth to the side in a half grin, not quite a smile or a frown, just like her grandmother.

"We humans are shameful creatures. There is no excuse for us not knowing how to get along together." She rubbed her head. "But now we must think about this."

"It could present some problems," Thomas said.

Margaret glanced at Thomas. "It could, but we won't let that stop us." She turned and looked deep into Sarah's eyes. "I know who owns that fish hut and I will make you a promise that I will ask about his intentions for it. Do not worry about the licence. In that regard, I have a little influence."

"I am grateful, Ma'am."

"You know, Sarah, there's nothing I like better than to remind the good Christians of Roseway of their Christian duties to bring about fairness and justice! Perhaps the ladies of Roseway will come for a special tea to look into ways to stop this hatred."

"Well, as long as they do not turn on you, Ma'am," Thomas interjected.

"It is Sarah who will need the protection. Try to have faith and courage. You have to trust me."

Sarah looked at her aunt and puffed a relieved sigh.

It was one week later, on August 4, 1785, when Sarah cut away from Dock Street and manoeuvred down St. Patrick Lane.

She was about to turn onto Water Street when she spotted a group milling about the smouldering remains of a building. It was the fish hut. The charred wood and ashes lined her nose with stench. Ordinarily, there would have been a long line of men with water buckets attempting to put out the fire, but it was too late for a rescue. The crowd stood idly by, watching.

"There's the Negra girl who wanted to set up the shop." A flat-faced man with salt-and-pepper hair and long whiskers pointed in her direction. "Did you ever hear the likes?"

"How do you know this, Ramsey?" someone in the crowd shouted.

"Why that Margaret Cunningham was nosin' around, askin' about the hut. She confided in me missus that the Redmond girl wanted it to do some tailoring. I guess that will not be happening now." Ramsey Lewis laid his bushy head back. Laughter rained from his bearded mouth.

The taunts and laughter made Sarah's skin crawl. Feeling small, she stood back, not wanting to get near Ramsey. She smelled the group's hatred on the edge of her own fear and tried hard to ignore it, but it stuck like dry bread in her throat. She wanted to lash out.

"Look there, it's Margaret," Ramsey shouted.

Margaret Cunningham approached the ruins. She scanned the crowd and when she saw Sarah, approached her slowly, shouting, "Who did this terrible thing?"

The crowd watched to see what the tiny woman would do. Margaret extended her arms and hugged Sarah. "Believe me, Sarah," she said, "I never thought this would happen."

"Why did they have to burn it down? It meant nothing to them. It was in shambles. No one was even using it."

"You have to understand hatred. It's like a poison that attacks the mind and the heart. It keeps them from feeling or understanding. Some people have the poison in them. In some minds, Sarah, you are not as good as they are. That makes you less deserving." Margaret bent her head and shook it several times. She could not look into Sarah's eyes. "You deserve better. We all deserve better. I can't change that, but we can't let it stop us." As mounting tension swelled the air, Margaret, in a voice so loud that Sarah could not imagine where it came from, faced the crowd and bellowed, "Can anyone here tell me who did this cowardly act?"

"Margaret, are you taking up for the likes of that one, that Negra?" It was Ramsey.

"I'm just asking for information. I bought that hut. No one had the right to burn it down. If anyone thinks that by burning it down, it will end the matter, they thought wrong."

"You bought it for that Redmond girl. You tried to make it look like it was for yourself." Ramsey Lewis walked over to where the two women were standing. Sarah could smell the liquor coming off the man. "You tried to sneak a Negra into our midst. You love them Negras, always takin' up for them. You thought you could get away with it, didn't you?"

The commotion grew louder as the gang cheered Ramsey on. The noise drew Thomas from his job at the wharf. Seeing Sarah and Margaret Cunningham in the centre of the confusion, he ran as fast as he could to get to them. He knew trouble was riding on the air and it sent chills along his spine. When he reached Sarah, he shouted, "Say nothing. Let Mrs. Cunningham do the talking. I'm going to get the sheriff."

"What gives you the right to decide what I or anyone else can have?" Margaret screamed. She was standing tall, wanting everyone to hear.

Ramsey glared, not at Margaret Cunningham but at Sarah. He approached her and raised his hand, pointing his finger in her face. "I don't want no uppity Negra thinkin' she can come down here and pretend she's one of us. You ain't nothing but trash. First thing, you will all be down here, actin' like you own the place. You hear me now, girl. You keep your place. Go back to Birchtown and be a good girl or you'll get yourself hurt."

The words cut deep, right to the centre of Sarah's heart. She glared at the liveryman, moved within inches of his face, pushed back her shoulders and said, "I am not a girl, Mr. Lewis. Not yours, not any man's. You do not own me. Those days are past. Who are you to decide what a Negro can have? We won our freedom and have rights as citizens, the same as you."

A hush fell over the crowd. They had never seen such brazenness—a young one standing up to a white man as if she had the right to question him. It beat all.

Mrs. Cunningham stepped between Sarah and Ramsey. Her wide-brimmed hat was teetering on the side her head as she frantically pulled on Sarah's arm. "Step back. Let it go, Sarah. Let it go. The hut is not worth it. We can get another one."

Ramsey's blood was white-hot. He threw one hand in the air and clenched his fist. His eyes blazed and flashed like lightning. "How dare a Negra say such a thing to me? I owned a hundred Negras like you before the damned Patriots came. You were only good for the plough and a damned good whippin'." With that, he spit on her, then pulled his hand back and struck the right side of Sarah's face. A loud gasp rippled through the crowd.

Sarah did not stop to think, did not need to. She raised her hand and without a word slapped his face with a swift blow in return.

The crowd went wild. The air burned from the heat of their rage. Within minutes, the men who had been watching from the alehouses filled the street. Their jeers and slurs gave rise to action. They readied themselves for battle, gathering sticks and

rocks. Their anger so disfigured their faces that Sarah was sure
they were demons come from hell. She stared at the men and
their wives, these grand gentlemen and ladies of the Empire
whose foul mouths filled the street. She and Margaret ran to the
other side of the street.

Thomas came running fast. "I couldn't find the sheriff," he
called.

A man with a cane was screaming, "You Negroes better get
out of town."

Margaret shouted, "Come on. You can go to my house."

Thomas roared, "No. Ma'am. This trouble you do not need,
they will burn you out," and he grabbed Sarah's arm. "We must
make a run for it, while they're still plotting what to do."

He and Sarah turned and ran down Water Street. They had a
good start. They ran as fast as they could and turned up Maiden
Lane with the wildest of the men in pursuit. Sarah ran until
her exhausted lungs ached. She sucked the air hard, so hard
she nearly suffocated. She kept running—faster and faster—
and when they cleared the town of Roseway, sheer exhaustion
pushed her down into a pile on the Roseway Bridge.

Her body stopped, but her mind kept racing. Grandmother's
warning pounded in her brain. "This skin will hold you back
and keep you down, only letting you rise so high. Some things
will always be too good for a Negro," Sarah tried to get up, but
the words overpowered her. "Some folks will treat you right and
give you a chance. But others, they would just as soon kill you!"
Until today, it all seemed like crazy talk. It had not mattered.
Now, here it was, all playing out, all stacked up against her.

"Come on, Sarah, we can't stop now." Thomas screamed.
"We have to keep going. Get up. If they catch us, they will beat
us to death."

In the distance, she could hear the uproar. A mob was on

their heels. They wanted revenge. Thomas helped her up. She thought of the shortcut to Birchtown. "This way," she said.

From somewhere deep inside came the strength she needed to run like hell.

Twenty-nine

F OR DAYS, SARAH REMAINED LOCKED IN THE HOUSE IN FEAR of her life, not knowing what each hour could bring. It was clear to her that Ramsey Lewis was at fault with his hatred of Negroes and his fear of change. His slap left a bitter bruise that covered the left side of her face. Grandmother spoke often of the laws in Carolina. To strike a white person meant a severe whipping followed by a burning with a hot iron. Sarah cringed. Here, there were similar laws and there had been whippings at the scattered whipping posts. She had witnessed 110 lashes to a young Negro for stealing a pound of butter. Would this be her fate?

It had been four days since the incident in Port Roseway. Grandmother, permanently bedridden now, was humming a hymn and Prince was napping. She and Fortune were having lunch when a heavy rapping on the door pummelled through the cabin. Though she had prepared for this moment, her nerves nevertheless made her tremble. Fortune rose from the table and cautiously opened the door to a tall, gangly man in a felt hat with a flat brim holding a paper in his hand.

"Mr. Redmond?" the man asked." I am the county bailiff, Mr. Gordon."

"Yes."

"Do you have a daughter by the name of Sarah Redmond?"

"I do."

"I have a court order here for Sarah Redmond to appear before the Court of General Sessions of the Peace on August 15," the bailiff said, "on a charge of assault. May I leave this with you?"

"I'll take it. Thank you, Sir." Fortune closed the door before the man could speak again. Tears rolled down his face, dripping off his jaw and onto his blue shirt.

The cup in Sarah's hand fell to the floor and the hot tea splashed over her skirt. She trembled violently. It took a long time to stop, even with her father holding her tight.

The next day, Thomas came with good news. He had found lodging with Steppin' John. Colonel Black had been helpful in securing him a job as supervisor of a Black Pioneer road crew. There would be work for a very long time. He could not have hoped for better luck.

"My news is not so cheerful," Sarah said. "The bailiff came by yesterday."

"I feared that. What did he say?"

"He gave Papa a court order. I have to appear in two weeks."

"Well, think of your father's case, Sarah. Didn't common sense prevail?"

"This is different."

"How so?"

"There are witnesses who may exaggerate the truth or lie to protect Ramsey. Besides that, I am a Negro woman. That makes me less valuable than a man. They will want to whip all the black off this skin."

"Stop it. You will get through this. You have to believe."

"And if I am beat to a pulp, will you still want what's left, a disfigured shell?"

"You could be disfigured on the outside, but inside … inside is where the pure beauty of your soul shines through. Blind is the man who cannot value that. I will kiss away the scars."

"What can I say to that?" She giggled.

Thomas put his arms around her and kissed her gently. "I'll be there forever and whatever! I won't let anything happen to you."

The next day Mrs. Cunningham, who came regularly to attend to Lydia, tried to console Sarah. "You must take control. You have to put your best face on. Appeal to their hearts when you are before the judge! Surely, they will consider that you acted in self-defence. Ramsey Lewis is an outsider trying to prove himself. He doesn't stand a chance."

On the morning of court, Papa pulled the wagon around to the step. Fibby got down and went inside to stay with Grandmother and Prince. Sarah grabbed her coat and sat up as straight as an eastern pine on the seat. She was numb and drained from all the worry and lack of sleep.

Hundreds of people lined the Birchtown Road. They stood in deathly silence like statues as the wagon passed, as though they were watching a funeral procession. Their screwed up faces were tight and filled with horror. What were the odds of two Redmonds beating the system? A lamb, she was, going to the slaughter.

Thomas was a welcome sight at the courthouse. He helped her from the wagon and steadied her with his arm. Amid the hundreds of onlookers, there were but two or three Negroes in the Roseway crowd. Fortune tied his horse under a towering fir by the courthouse step. The three kept their heads down, proceeded up the walkway and into the courthouse. Inside, Sarah sat at a small table facing a newly appointed judge, Justice Clarence Smithfield. Ramsey Lewis sat to her left with a strange-looking man in a puffy white wig. Spectators overran the room. It was hot and stuffy.

The ceremonious opening of the August 15, 1785, Sessional District Court began with a series of announcements. The judge stated the order of the proceedings, read the rules of conduct and announced the charge against her. There followed a bedraggled string of witnesses to answer a series of questions by the town prosecutor. Reports of the time of the event and the actual words exchanged varied. However, uniform and truthful statements emerged about Sarah's actions, and the actions of the acclaimed victim, Mr. Lewis. Witnesses told how the pair engaged in an argument, how Ramsey Lewis struck the accused first and how Sarah had slapped him back. Sarah straightened. The truth gave her a needed boost of confidence.

The judge called Margaret Cunningham to testify. She told about the shameless results of her desire to help Sarah, praising Sarah's trustworthiness and good manners. She complained about the lawlessness and un-Christian behaviour of some of the residents and ended with a plea for change and mercy.

Sarah could not bring herself to look up when Margaret stepped down from the witness box and walked past her table.

Justice Moody turned to Sarah. "Do you have anything to say for yourself?"

Sarah was terrified, but she stood tall and stated. "Yes, Sir, I do."

The room trembled with foot stomping and shouting. The judge slammed the gavel down on the bench saying, "Quiet. Order. I want order!"

Sarah was fearful. The floor seemed to waver and it seemed like an eternity to get to the witness box. With her damp hand on the Bible, she recited the oath and took her seat. When she finally raised her head to look out among the faces, she knew in her heart that her time had come.

In a clear voice, she said, "Today I sit in this courtroom after being insulted, slapped and humiliated for no reason, other than the colour of my skin. I want to be treated with fairness. You see me as the attacker, but I beg you, Sir, to see me instead as the victim."

The courtroom grew quiet. Sighs and a snicker or two drifted throughout the room. Sarah continued, "As a citizen of this colony, I continue to face the same conditions that my family and I left behind in Carolina. Here in Port Roseway, we are free people. We should be able to choose a life for ourselves, one that is not decided for us. The good citizens of Port Roseway are free to do as they please. They are free to choose their own jobs, and that was all Mrs. Cunningham intended for me, to fulfill my dream of becoming a full citizen and to choose my work."

Sarah looked at Thomas sitting in the second row. He was nodding his head in agreement. She smiled and leaned back with added confidence, then took a moment to examine the crowd. She had their ears now. "It was not my intent to take something that belonged to someone else, only to make a life for myself. I want to be as proud and as independent as any of you." She shifted to one side in the chair, then the other. "I am a Negro, Sir. Must I be condemned to a life of misery because of it?"

Some of the faces drooped like wilted flowers. In others, the anger deepened.

"Have you finished?" Justice Smithfield asked.

"I would like to say a few more words, if I may, Sir."

"As you wish."

"Sir, here is my Certificate of Freedom." She held it up for all to see. "This says that I am free. How many of you need a certificate to say that you are free? This paper does more than set me free, it returns me to the world as a human being. It should guarantee that I have the same rights as everyone else, including the right to defend myself and to receive justice. I hope that it will stand for that in this court."

Sarah looked sideways at the judge, then over to Margaret. There was one more thing to add, but had she said too much? Justice Smithfield had not given her any indication that she should stop. She repressed her fear by swallowing hard, and continued. "Sir, if justice is based on fairness, then I had every right to defend myself, did I not?" She turned and faced the judge, then lowered her head.

The judge made no reply to her question. "Did you finish, Miss Redmond?" he asked.

"Yes Sir!"

"Then step down and take your seat. I shall render a decision after reviewing the evidence. I ask this court to remain seated until my return."

Sarah could hear the judge and loud angry voices drifting from the room behind the bench. The voices came in rushes. She wondered what the men behind the door were saying.

The time dragged on, well past an hour. Fortune gripped her hands. The heat in the courtroom was unbearable and the spectators, fuelled with tension, argued amongst themselves. There they sat, debating and cursing, shaking their fists and holding their own court.

Thomas caught the fear in her eyes and gave her a reassuring smile and a wink. At the back of the room, she caught a glimpse of Reece. He smiled and nodded his head. She turned back and huddled down in her chair, unable to make herself as small as she wanted to be. She wrestled to keep her breath from leaving her body. She pressed her eyes shut, and waited.

Thirty

THE COURTROOM WAS EXCEEDINGLY NOISY ON THAT overcast day in August. Sarah counted every tick of the corner clock. It seemed as though time had left her stranded in a faraway place, waiting for someone to rescue her.

When Justice Smithfield arrived through the side door, his stern voice let out a command for all to rise. He remained standing, bringing his gavel down hard. Silence fell upon the room. Fortune gripped Sarah's hand. She feared her punishment. Would they banish her from the province, hang her, lash her with cat-o'-nine-tails or use the whip?

Without any emotion in his voice, Justice Smithfield said, "I have reviewed the evidence. I find the accused guilty as charged. I hereby order forty lashes to be administered at two o'clock on the twenty-first of August 1785, at the whipping post, outside this County Courthouse, to one Miss Sarah Redmond, on the charge of assault against one of our leading citizens."

Silence was an angry beast that stunned the crowd and carried Sarah down into a great void where all awareness deserted her until a sudden explosion of loud noise—cheers, whimpers, curses, crying and clapping—revived her. A circle of men surrounded Ramsey and shook his hand. His laugh was long and hollow. His scandalous joy filled the room.

This cannot be what justice is all about, Sarah thought. After her argument about fairness, she could only see that the judge, of all people, was no more than an arrogant, cruel slave master, protecting his own interests at the expense of others.

"Clear the courtroom," Justice Smithfield ordered.

The room soon emptied, the people spilling out onto the road and alleyways. Soon, music blared from the alehouses and folks drank and danced in the lanes.

The bailiff escorted Sarah down a narrow path to the local House of Corrections. She did not hear the chains that clanked and coiled about her ankles and hands. She did not feel the rocks the crowd threw out of anger, nor did she see the eyes that glued themselves to her or the mouths that spit on her. She walked with her head high, her steps steady and even.

When they reached the House of Corrections, the bailiff informed her that she was to work and earn her keep while there. Any surplus earnings went to the keeper for wages and for those unable to work. The place was small and full of Negroes: men and women, some in fetters and shackles on their wrists and feet. Their alleged crimes were numerous: robbery, murder, pilfering livestock or goods, assault, brawling, forgery and even counter-feiting. They were a pitiful lot, and later, when Thomas, Fortune and Margaret Cunningham came to see her, Sarah sat in silence at the back of the room with her back turned away from them.

Fortune found the courage to speak first. He said, "You come around now, Babygirl. You did what you had to do. Don't blame yourself for what happened."

Without turning to face him, Sarah said, "It is over, Papa! I have been judged!"

"It is not over." Thomas insisted. "You had the right to defend yourself from a raging man. The judge was heartless. We can't let the judge get away with this." Margaret Cunningham walked towards her. "Come here, Sarah," she said. "You need not fear us. We are family."

Sarah turned to face them. Thomas reached for her hands.

"Judge Smithfield was extremely harsh. From what I hear, Ramsey's gang cornered him in the back room. I believe that he gave in to their demands. I would wager that being a newly appointed judge, he felt pressured, but he's paid to uphold the law, not bitterness." Margaret spoke with a bitterness of her own.

Thomas looked at Sarah. "We have six days," he said. "Perhaps we can get his decision overturned by another judge, one more respectful of the law. We need a plan."

"You leave this to us, Sarah. Trust us," Margaret said.

Sarah stared down at the little woman. She was a mighty force in Roseway, organizing events, helping the poor and now she was preparing to take on the arrogant stiff-necks of power. She was firm in her resolve, fearless and confident, but Sarah understood that she was up against a force mightier than the king's army. She glanced away and said, "It's of no use."

"I will not let them do this to you, Sarah." Her tone was rigid and her face fierce. "We will find Justice Moody. He is hearing cases at this end of the colony. The people will not influence him."

Papa pressed his hands against his face. "If I could trade places with you, Babygirl, I would. How could they do this to you? How in God's name can this be justice?"

"I don't know," Sarah said, "but Mama did not give in when she was punished and neither will I. I will not be afraid. They can hurt my body, but they cannot hurt my spirit."

"They got no cause. No cause."

"It is the poison, Papa. That is what makes it right in their eyes."

Fortune turned to Margaret Cunningham. "Judge Moody was fair in my case, but do you really think he would help us?"

"We can try, Fortune. I will get Fibby to stay with mother and Prince. Fortune, you and I will go to Yarmouth, even up to Digby, if we have to. Thomas, since you have to work, you can organize a petition in Birchtown. Get as many as you can to sign it. If folks cannot write, you print their names and get them to put their 'x' beside it."

"It's not over yet, Sarah," Thomas said, holding Sarah's face in his hands. "We are going to be busy, working on getting you out of here. You must stay strong. Do not give up."

When they were gone, Sarah sat on the long bench twisting her hair. The whipping would be a show, like when Big Cain juggled the seven gourds and everyone gathered with their mouths hung open, amused with wonder. If only this show could be so joyful. She was the seven gourds that would dazzle the crowd, only the awes and thrills would come from the worst of human instincts, the thirst for another's blood. She inhaled deeply, then again and again.

Thirty-one

IT WAS EARLY MORNING, AUGUST 21, THE DAY OF THE whipping. The long days had dragged by for Sarah without a word from Margaret Cunningham or her papa. She awakened to an aching back and the sound of rain pounding heavily on the roof. Sleeping had been close to impossible in a room full of strangers on a hard, narrow bunk. She was exhausted. The remnants of her courage were fading fast. She realized that her destiny was in a race against time. What, in such a short time, could her papa and Margaret accomplish?

Praying became part of her daily routine to remain strong and hopeful. She wondered if fear had kept the Birchtowners away. There had been but three visitors. Thomas faithfully came by each day after work with updates on the petition. It was proving difficult to get signatures. Either the Birchtowners were scared of retaliation in the form of violence or loss of work, or they believed it would not do any good. To Sarah's surprise, Reece came by twice. It was comforting to hear him say that he supported her right to defend herself. He wanted her to know that he had visited his mother several times and that, in Fibby's care, she was holding on. The wait to hear from Amelia was keeping her strong. The third visitor was Priscilla Hayward. She came by, she said, to express sadness over such a crime against her friend. Though her sentiments felt genuine, she did not leave without letting it be known that she had finally caught Reece's attention. Happiness to them both, Sarah thought. They deserve it.

Noon came quickly and still there was no news from Papa and Margaret. Her stomach was about to explode when the keeper arrived with a plate of stew and tea. The gravy was cold and thick with a nasty scum, the bread was hard, not cut but torn from a loaf, and the tea cold. More pig slop, she thought, as hunger forced her to approach the table. In the end, she could not eat. She sat on the bench staring at the wall, the butterflies in her stomach caught up in a hurricane.

When the bailiff came, he stood with his face in a mocking grin. "Half an hour remaining," he said. Sarah's head felt heavy. She pictured herself tied to the whipping post before the jeering crowd. She thought of all the times Cecil had called the slaves from their work to witness some type of miserable act: the removal of a limb, a hanging or a whipping. She thought of her mother and that gave her courage. She would show them the willpower a slave could muster in the face of pain. She would not scream and she would not tremble! She closed her eyes and felt her brain do a dance of sorts. There was no way to track the time, but the hour was looming. What had become of Papa and Margaret? Where was Thomas? Had they been successful in finding Justice Moody or anyone who might believe her innocence and keep her from this punishment?

It was fifteen minutes before the hour when she heard the keys clang as the sheriff unlocked the door. He led her in chains down muddy King Street. Without her coat, she shivered as the biting cold of nerves nipped her courage. Her hope for salvation was retreating, but she walked queenly with her back straight to the rhythm of the clinking shackles around her ankles. She focused on the end of her ordeal now, rather than the beginning. He took her down Water Street to a spot the locals called

Stanhope Hill. The whipping post stood like a crucifix. She saw Reece and Priscilla at the front of the crowd. Enos was there, too. The three were rigid, expressionless, and she turned away.

At the whipping post, the sheriff said, "Step up to the pole. Turn your back to the crowd." He freed her hands.

She heard the loud jeers and slurs about Negroes, the name-calling and threats. Despite the apples and eggs that pelted her, she looked directly into the crowd before turning and retreating into herself. In these last minutes, she did not beg for compassion as she had seen slaves do, for she knew such wickedness did not know mercy. She stood erect and defiant.

A man wearing a black suit, black gloves and a three-cornered black hat greeted her with a quick nod. In his right hand, a whip curled like a serpent. His long white hair hung beneath the hat and framed his head like a fringe. Sarah turned her head and eyed him sharply. His eyes were barren. He was ready to perform his duty. He ordered her to remove her top garments. With her upper body exposed, her bare back facing outward, the sheriff tied her to the post with a rope.

She watched the whip unfold from his hand. The full length of it—six feet—fell to the ground. In a loud, ringing voice, the sheriff announced, "On the count of three … One," he screamed.

Sarah murmured, "Do not scream."

"Two."

Sarah murmured, "Do not tremble."

"Three."

Sarah stiffened. The first blow came down with a whistle.

The onlookers gasped as their eyes followed the rise and fall of the long whip. It bit into her shoulder and opened her flesh. Bright red splatters of blood flew past her face. The blood running down her cold back felt like warm water. The pain was scorching hot.

After the first taste of blood, a spasm jarred the crowd, making them cringe and fall into an eerie silence. Sarah squeezed her eyes tight and held her breath. She stiffened and gritted her teeth as the sheriff skipped the countdown and yelled, "Two!"

Again, the whip danced, making a loud snap as it caught the air the second time. She waited in fear for the whip to strike and when it did, she sprang from the ground. Her blood sprayed in the air like water from a fountain.

The whip whistled again and circled around catching the wind for the third strike. "Three!" the sheriff screamed. The leather came down with a thud and she felt the burn of the rope on her wrists as she slid a few inches down the pole.

Thirty-seven to go, she thought. The rest of the lashes meant nothing now. She was already weak. Her mind was floating away. She was nearly unconscious, hearing, seeing and feeling little. The sound of the whip whirling high above her head was faint. The muted cries ringing out in the crowd came from a distance. They were blurry and she strained and forced herself to hear.

"Stop it. Stop the whipping." And again, "Stop the whipping." The voices were louder now, sharper, clearer. Was she dreaming? Was that Thomas's voice?

Again the shouting came, "Stop this execution." The crowd stirred and, to her ears, sounded like the hum of a world of bees.

Justice Moody screamed above the uproar. "Stop it, I say. My God, man, stop. It is by order of the magistrate. Stop this butchering."

The man in black let the whip fall and asked, "Who be you to bring such an order?"

Justice Moody shouted, "I, Justice Moody, bring the order. It is an order from the Provincial Magistrate's Office."

The crowd swelled with noise and became unruly chaos. The sheriff raised his gun and fired twice. Justice Moody stepped forward and took the whip from the man's hand. He then shouted at the top of his lungs, making a declaration to the crowd: "Due to an error, Justice Smithfield's decision has been overturned. The accused, having undergone a wrongful conviction, will not undergo further punishment. Please go home now. Go about your business."

The show was over and the onlookers made their way to the alehouses where both disappointment and relief manifested into a rowdy night of drunkenness and brawls.

The sheriff untied the rope and unchained Sarah's feet. Her back and skirt were drenched in blood. After two steps, she keeled over and lay in a red puddle beside the whipping post. She could barely see Thomas when he took off his jacket and spread it around her shoulders. Fortune scooped her up in his arms and carried her to the wagon.

At first, the long, deep gashes would not stop weeping. Sarah lay quiet in her bed for three days suffering from the shock of her punishment. For weeks Margaret and Fibby took turns caring for the terrible lacerations, bathing them with wild herbs collected at the roadside and ointment from Mrs. MacLeod's store. The lashes would leave scars, thick rides as tough as rolled leather, but by the third week, when she was feeling somewhat herself, she knew they would become reminders for when she needed strength and determination.

Thirty-two

"IT'S HERE! IT'S HERE!" FORTUNE WAVED THE LONG-AWAITED letter in the air. "I picked it up at the Pony Express office this morning. Go ahead," he said, "read it." Sarah eagerly ripped the letter open as Fortune pulled up a chair and listened intently.

September 8, 1785
My Dearest Fortune:
I wish to inform you that I received your letter. I am much relieved now that I know what has become of my mother. I plan to journey by boat from Yarmouth to Port Roseway on September 24, 1785. I should arrive mid-afternoon. I look forward to meeting my family members.
With affection,
Amelia Pinkham

"This is it." Fortune said. "This is the last of her brood."

"Should we share the news with her?" Sarah asked. "Or should we wait?"

"It might be too much excitement." Fortune said, "Yet it amazes me how she remains so hopeful, even with death in search of her."

"It's her faith keeping her strong, Papa."

"She has been like a shepherd gathering her flock. One last sheep to come to the fold. This blessing belongs to her and she will not be cheated out of it."

It was just two days after receiving the letter that Fortune and Sarah, unable to keep the excitement to themselves, felt obligated to share the news. They stood at the old woman's bedside announcing they had found Amelia and that she would be visiting soon. Grandmother lay still. She stared at Fortune a long time before she smiled and said, "All my children will know of their mama's love."

On the morning of September 24, the early sun unfolded through layers of pink and grey sky. It slowly released its warmth over Birchtown, promising a beautiful evening for a reunion. Fortune stood by his mother's bed. "She's going to be here today. Amelia's on her way." His deep voice slipped into a mellow sweetness. "I have to go to Port Roseway to meet her at the wharf."

Grandmother struggled to raise her head. "Okay, I hear you." She turned to Sarah. "Get my good nightdress, the one with the lace, and a pretty nightcap." She bowed her head on her chest and murmured, "I'm counting on you, Lord."

Sarah pulled the old woman's hair back into a bun using the bone-handled brush. "You're as pretty as a Carolina rose, Grandmother."

"Come here, Sarah. Come sit a spell." The old woman's eyes were kind and they dazzled in shimmering amber. "I got something I need to say to you." She paused and said, "I was blessed with a wonderful gift."

"A gift?"

"Yes, Chile. You were the gift. You were mine as much as the rest, more like a dear daughter, a good friend. You and I and Fortune, we been through a lot together."

"We have."

"I want you to know that I heard about your troubles in Roseway."

Sarah stared at Grandmother and sighed. "How did you know?"

"I could tell you were not yourself. You never came in to see me or sleep in the room. I tricked Fibby into telling me all the news. You know that Fibby. She could never keep a thing. I wished I could have been at the trial. I am proud of you, Sarah. You've got fire and you did good."

"I tried to be strong, Grandmother."

She took Sarah's hand. "Do you see this black skin?" She ran her fingers up and down Sarah's chestnut arm. "You love this skin because no one can love it the way you can." She held Sarah's eye for a long time. "Sometimes our voices, our hair, our features, they are not pleasing to others, but you love them. You love your wondrous self." She was wheezing now, but she kept going. "I'm not long in this world. You and Thomas have a good life. I give my blessing." She took only a sip from the water glass Sarah raised to her lips and fell back on the bed. "I got one last chile to claim, my Amelia."

"You rest now. Amelia will be here soon." Sarah stroked the old woman's hair and planted a kiss on her forehead. "I love you, Grandmother. Thank you for all you have done."

Sarah sat idly on the cabin step. Her back was sore and the bandages so thick that she could barely fasten her gown. She watched the wind breeze the maple leaves and listened to the birds flitting about in the tall trees. The day was calm, just still and peaceful. She thought of Amelia. Another member to add to the family, more gold.

Suddenly she heard strange moans that took her rushing back inside.

"Grandmother," she called. "What's wrong?"

The old woman's face was a clump of flesh and the bedclothes twisted about her. "Did I scare you? I was just thinking out loud. I was thinking on what I was going to say to Amelia."

"You will know when the time comes," Sarah said. "Lie back and rest."

Sarah was busy with needlepoint when Fortune returned with Amelia. It was still light outside. A short bronze woman in a green dress and black jacket came through the door. Sarah expected to see a fair-skinned woman, creamy-coloured, like Reece and Margaret, but Amelia was dark-skinned with a round face and thick, short hair. How strange it was to mix black with white and produce such a range of colours.

"You must be Sarah," Amelia said. She reached over and squeezed Sarah's face. "My, if you ain't a picture to behold." Amelia's voice was loud and robust and the joy in it tickled Sarah. "Well, well," she said. "I'm happy to know that I have a family in Birchtown. I never thought I would ever see such a day. Your father has told me all about you."

"Welcome to the family," Sarah stammered.

Amelia looked at Sarah and said, "Well, thank you. I'm anxious to see my mother. Is she feeling better?"

Sarah nodded. She pointed to the back room. "She is waiting for you."

Amelia followed Fortune. As they entered the room, Lydia mumbled, "Tell Sarah to put tea on and set the table for my daughter."

Amelia approached cautiously and sat at the foot of her bed looking at the woman who came to the Big House every morning when the roosters first crowed. She remembered her with long, black braids wrapped around her head and a round face that rarely smiled. This was the woman, always with a big belly, keeping the fires, cleaning the house, making the meals and washing the clothes. She moved closer.

"Is that you Amelia?" Lydia smiled up at her.

"Yes Ma'am. It is Amelia."

"You are a godsend, Chile." With trembling hands, she reached over and gently patted Amelia's arm. "Your coming here makes me happy."

Amelia gazed at the tired face. She could read the years, like reading a book, not in words, but in wrinkles, scars and bleached white hair. Time, she thought, had left its mark, and yet there was joy in her eyes and a glow in her skin that magically erased the strain and worry of her long life. As she gazed down at her mother's face, there arose in Amelia a burning pain that came from abandonment. All this time, she had known when she was carried off by the Pinkham foreman that she was being taken away to a new family, and she went in silence, fear sealing her lips. How she had missed Lydia's kindness and Margaret's friendship. Those she would never forget. It was not until the letter came that she realized her mother's need to connect to family was the same as her own. Although time was snatching away the love she had regained, it was not too late to save some of it.

Lydia nodded slowly and moved her mouth. She wanted to speak, but Amelia pressed her finger gently on her mother's lips to prevent her. "Hush now, my dear. Fortune told me that you need my forgiveness. There is nothing to forgive. There is no reason for you to feel guilty. There is not a thing you could have done differently."

Fortune stood quietly to the side. He witnessed the closure of the long-held secrets, watched how it removed the weight from his mother's shoulders and left a joyous woman. All that balling up inside had found a way to escape.

"You did the right thing," Amelia said calmly. "I do not blame you. Rest now, knowing that the love of a child for her mother lives on in her heart." She stroked Lydia's cottony white hair. Their eyes met and held. She said, "I am blessed. I have finally found you and my true family."

Lydia tried to speak, but again Amelia shushed her. "Save your strength," she said. "All that matters is that I am here to comfort you."

Amelia cradled the old woman in her arms, rocking her back and forth. "I remained with the Pinkhams though they often sent me to work on other farms. There were many times when I wondered what became of you," she said. "My master's missus was a nice woman who liked me and so they kept me on their plantation."

"The Lord was good to you," Lydia said weakly.

"You are right, Ma'am. The Lord was good. Now, you must not worry any more. We are family." Amelia leaned over and tenderly kissed her mother's cheek.

Lydia leaned forward and whispered, "Ask Sarah to come in. There is a small wooden box under the bed. She knows which one."

When Sarah entered the room, she reached under the bed for the box, only to find when she stood up a look of disapproval on Amelia's face. Sarah glanced quickly at her aunt, wondering what sort of thoughts lay beneath the pleasant surface. With a slight raise of the brows at her aunt, she handed the box to Grandmother.

The old woman's jittery hands opened the box and she pulled out a sheet of paper. "Margaret wrote these names ... they are all my children's names." She unfolded the paper and laid it on the bed. In the box was a tiny wooden ring. She held it up and said, "This was your ring. I got Tally to carve one for each of my girls. This one was carved after you were gone, but I kept it, just in case." She stopped for a moment to catch her breath, then said, "You have a sister, Margaret Cunningham. You must get to know her."

"A sister?" Amelia asked. "Why I had no idea."

The old woman's mouth was dry. She rolled her tongue over her lips. "Margaret Cunningham, Amelia Pinkham, Prince, Fortune and Reece Johnson," she murmured, "all my children!" She paused a moment before whispering, "I love them all. I am sorry that I had to keep this secret … Lord, I am sorry." The old woman fell back into the soft feather pillows and closed her eyes.

Thirty-three

IT WAS MID-OCTOBER 1786. FORTUNE HELD THE REINS steady as he and Sarah travelled along the Birchtown Road. Their singing was spirited as the words of an old work song tumbled from their mouths. Sarah sat tall, sporting a green Sunday jacket and a flowered gown. Her wide hat flopped in the breeze.

"Are you sure that you want to do this?" Fortune asked.

"Yes Papa."

"Maybe you should wait awhile. I'm not feeling sure about this."

"I cannot give in to fear, Papa. I have to try."

"Getting a licence from the Sessions Court is no easy task." He looked over at Sarah and smiled. "Your courage is as big as the whole outdoors. I admire your strength to keep pushing ahead. You are so much like your mama and grandmother."

"I can see that you are worried …"

"No, not worried, just a little tired of the fight."

"Yes, and it's my turn now. There are times when I feel a hand around my throat, waiting to choke the life from me. I cannot give up. Sometimes I don't understand why our path is so rocky, Papa."

"If I knew the answer to that, Babygirl, I would be the Lord."

They laughed and their laughter echoed throughout the Birchtown woods.

Outside the Sessions Court, the line-up was long with a sea of unfamiliar faces. Fortune waited, head down, waging war with his decision to encourage Sarah to try this test. He wondered if he could bear to see the pain if she lost yet another round. He rubbed his forehead and spit yellow tobacco juice out onto the road.

It was nearly an hour before Sarah came out through the doors of the courthouse. Fortune slowly turned to get a glimpse of her face, hoping to get a hint of the verdict. Her expression was almost stony as she climbed into the wagon and slid over on the seat beside him. She reached inside her rag purse. Fortune watched her every move, followed her hand closely.

"It's a hallelujah day," she exclaimed.

"You got the licence?"

"I got it. I got the licence."

Fortune wrapped his arms around her and they rocked with joy. "You had me for a minute," he howled. "You are almost as good as your Papa! We'll have to find a building somewhere. I imagine the cost will be put up higher when they see our faces! But we will find the money."

"I have hoarded like a field mouse gathering up bits for a nest … every crown and shilling, every piece of jewellery or thing of value. Thomas has offered his help and, among us, I am sure there will be enough."

"You are a wonder, Babygirl. A true wonder."

The next morning, Margaret Cunningham pulled her carriage up to the Redmond cabin. Inside, after making herself comfortable, she turned to Sarah. "You have not stopped by in a long while for a visit. I missed you and I have been wondering how everyone is getting along."

"We are doing well. It is so different without Grandmother."

"Yes it would be. I miss her as much as you do."

Margaret caught Prince up in her arms and said, "My, my, he is growing up fast. He is looking more like his daddy every day." Then she looked at Sarah with concern. "We didn't have a chance to talk about what happened, Sarah. The whipping, I mean. It was a very cruel punishment. But that's the people here for you … it's hard to understand what they think, why they act the way they do, how deep their habits are."

"For them, it's like Ramsey said, we are of no account. We are no more than the rocks in the field."

"Not everyone is cruel and heartless, though sometimes that may seem true," Margaret said, "but many in the settlement are fair-minded. Perhaps disappointment has led to violence and hatred all around. It is time to make peace."

"Even if there is peace, the Negroes will still be treated the same way. These folks see no reason to change their ways."

"I believe in time they will."

"Perhaps. It is true that when they needed more men during the war, they had to change their minds about Negroes. Change comes from a need, Papa says, and the war opened the door a little wider, but why must there be a door?"

"A door can be taken down, Sarah."

"I tried. Didn't I try to have the law applied fairly?"

Margaret faced Sarah saying, "But in the end, Sarah, the law that condemned you was the same law that saved you."

"Even that required a fight."

Margaret searched for the words to console her niece. "Shame is on those who have no respect for justice. When a law is not rooted in fairness, we all become victims."

Sarah sighed. "I have decided that there is no gain in dwelling on what I cannot have or what I cannot do. I plan to take one day at a time and do all I can." With that, Sarah broke into singing one of the songs from the camp meetings:

I got wings, you got wings,
All o' God's chillun got wings,
When I get to heaven, I'm goin' to put on my wings,
I'm goin' to fly all over God's Heaven!

When she finished, she looked at Margaret and laughed, "I'm not waiting to get to heaven. I'm going to fly down here, going to fly all over Port Roseway. I will get a shop with a little faith ..." She moved to the trunk at the foot of her bed and came back with a piece of paper. She waved it high above her head, "and with this licence."

Margaret stared at the paper. "This is beyond words. I cannot believe it."

Sarah walked to the window and stood looking out into the yard. The trees around the cabin had been cleared. A path stretched to a barn where she saw her father coming through the doors. When Fortune caught sight of her in the window, he waved his hand, yelling for her to come. She turned to her aunt, saying, "Father needs us. Quick, we must go to the barn. Something has happened."

Once inside the barn, the two women heard strange sounds coming from a stall near the back. It was the sweet neighs of Betty, the mare. Beside her a tiny filly nestled in the warmth of her neck in the hay. Fortune faced them beaming like an August moon.

When the women returned from the barn, Margaret's voice became playful, saying, "Oh, and by the way, I have a surprise as well. You may as well know about the trunk."

"The trunk, Ma'am?"

"I have a trunk full of fabric and needles. It has scissors, thimbles and thread. I have been saving it for a long time. It will be a good start and there is more good news! Colonel Aiken's wife has another trunk filled with goods. She will give it to you, just as long as she can be your first customer."

"Oh Lord. Have I died and gone to heaven? A customer."

"A family has to pull together, doesn't it? Lydia wanted this family to be whole." Margaret's voice dropped. "Forgive me, Sarah. We kept the secret for so long. From now on, it's going to be 'mother.' No more 'Lydia'. I spoke with Fortune yesterday. He said you were searching for another place." She reached into her jacket pocket and handed a large key to Sarah. "This is for a building on Water Street, just a few buildings down from the burnt fish hut."

Sarah held the key in her hand and stared at it a long time. Her stomach felt like warm porridge on the coldest winter day. "I am grateful, Ma'am! You are the amazing one."

"Mr. Harris has offered it to you at no cost. Fortune told me you saved to purchase a building. Now you can use the money to fix up the place."

Sarah pressed the key to her bosom, letting out a long sigh.

"There is one more bit of news," Margaret said, reaching for the latch on the door. "They found Boll weevil's body on Maiden Lane a few days ago. He was badly beaten. The sheriff has questioned a lot of people, but there are no witnesses."

"I am glad it is over, Ma'am."

"From now on, you call me Aunt Margaret."

THOMAS COOPER AND SEVERAL FRIENDS WORKED TIRELESSLY for weeks in the shop on Water Street until the plain tackle shop resembled a place of business. It had long counters for cutting, hooks for hanging, drawers and shelves for goods and a place to iron. A pot-bellied stove stood centre floor to greet and warm the customers. Outside, the sign above the door read, "Sarah's Tailor Shop." The Roseway women cackled like hens when they saw the sign go up, clucking about the bold Negro woman daring to return and set up shop after what happened. Many of them did not like the idea of her competing with Martha Lewis. Some said they would cross the street because they feared walking in front of a Negro's shop. Others just quibbled for the sake of it. Yet others acknowledged that Negroes were people just like themselves, said it was time to work together for the common good. There were women who came to give away their fabric scraps. There were those who came for alterations and others who placed orders for winter clothing. As the work piled up, Sarah was so busy she barely had time for herself or Thomas.

Mr. Eldridge, an elderly tailor, volunteered to take Sarah under his wing and show her a thing or two about the art of sewing. This is when her real education began. She learned how to measure, the function of different types of needles, the correct stitches for the fabric and the names of the many varieties of fabrics. The most important rule was the need to conserve and extend the life of costly fabrics. Nothing went to waste. Alter, mend and remake.

Sarah carted all the leftover fabric home. "One of these days, we are going to make a quilt, Sarah, one that tells the story of our journey," Grandmother had said. The time had come. After many months of late nights and hard work, the quilt came together. The colours dazzled in a warm collage of greens, browns, blues, white and gold. Valued memories lay deep in the varying textures. In the smooth were the things of love, joy and plenty. In the coarse were the things of sorrow and betrayal. With every stitch and every decision, whether it was the colour, the size or the shape of the piece, Sarah heard Grandmother's voice. This was their legacy—the story of their journey to Nova Scotia. It became the centrepiece on the back wall of the shop, a sentinel keeping watch. The quilt could have sold many times over, but it was not for sale for all the money in Port Roseway.

Thirty-four

FALL ENDED, THEN WINTER CAME AND FINALLY SPRING rolled into summer. For weeks, the candles burned all night. On July 15, 1786, daylight welcomed a morning of feverish activity. The horizon brightened as golden rays filtered through the blue-grey sky. It was a honeyed day, one for making the sweetest dreams come true. It was a day for an enormous celebration.

Sarah scurried about the new house—a small, four-room home on the Birchtown Road on the edge of her ten acres. It was about a mile up the road from Papa's new place and a half-mile from the old homestead, where Aunt Amelia now lived. She was proud of the glass windows and thick door, but the delight was the kitchen fireplace that Thomas had built. It was fitted with hooks to hang pots and a recessed wall for baking. Reece made a three-legged kettle for cooking and Aunt Margaret gave her an array of cast-iron skillets.

The day began at six with the bell ringing in the new Methodist Meeting House. The bell would ring every hour until the wedding began. Several customers had secretly made beautiful paper bells and streamers to hang in her home. Food from the neighbours kept arriving. There were tables to set up outside and crates of donated dishes to clean. Savoury aromas drifted throughout the house from pots of chicken stew topped with mounds of fluffy dumplings and from the tangy apple pies. To liven up the festivities, three large tubs of spruce beer were chilling in a cold pool behind the house.

Margaret and Amelia were like tornadoes around Sarah. There was not a minute to relax—no time to think about the most wonderful day of her life. But soon her energy slowed and she lay sideways on her bed, taking a much-needed break. Thoughts of Thomas encouraged a smile. They would spend their first night together not in a small bed with a straw mattress, but in the big feather bed he built for them. Grandmother use to say, "Look at the heart. It rules the deeds." If that were true, Thomas had a good heart. He was the kind of man who would do anything to help a friend or neighbour. She wondered what her life might be like if they had gone to New York. No, she told herself, they were making good right here in Birchtown. He was a hard working, sweet home man and she was proud of him.

It had taken Thomas such a long time to propose that she had started to wonder if he ever would. The promise ring was one thing, but the actual proposal ... well, that took awhile. When it finally came in mid-May, after a long walk down to the Roseway River, it was entirely unexpected. There they were, standing on the wooden bridge, watching the rushing water, chatting about the usual things—their work, ol' man Johnson's house burning down, Reece and Priscilla—when Thomas stretched out his arms and hugged her. As usual, he had his own peculiar way of getting to it. Even his tone did not reveal his intentions when he said, "I came to Nova Scotia, never intending to stay."

"I, for one, am glad you did," she said.

"So am I," he said and turned to stare into the forest. "I believe our ancestors are watching us," he whispered. "I hear them directing us to join and celebrate all the good things we have found in this place."

"I feel them as well, all those who endured a life of slavery and have passed on. Their spirits have gathered here tonight on the bridge."

"They are telling us to move ahead, not to worry about what has been. And they want us to marry." The twinkle in Thomas's eyes told Sarah that he was taking delight in surprising her. Strangely, after waiting for so long to hear the words, she did not know what to say. She listened as the loons on a nearby lake wailed and the frogs croaked. She watched the steam rise off the water. Still she held back.

Thomas hugged her. "Will you have me?"

Sarah could not resist a little game of one-up. "You said the ancestors have decided for us. Are you sure you have decided?"

"Oh, yes! All of us in our wisdom have decided." Thomas knelt down on one knee and said, "Sarah Redmond, will you take me, Thomas Cooper, to be your husband?"

"I guess. I think so. Oh, why not?" She giggled and then shrieked, "Yes!"

With the ancestors as witnesses, they pledged their love. She closed her eyes and said, "This is the beginning of our flight. Can you believe it?" She smiled a heartfelt smile and in a creamy voice she said, "I believe that we have a chance."

The memory of that day came to a hasty end when Amelia's patience cracked Sarah's daydreaming. "Sarah!" she called, her voice worrisome and tired, "Are you getting ready? It will soon be time to go."

"Don't worry. I am doing fine … I am nearly ready," Sarah roared, although she had not done a thing yet to get herself ready. She turned over on the bed. Her aunts were chatting and laughing in the next room. She heard Amelia say, "I wish Mama was here. If she could see Sarah now, she would swell with such pride the seams of her dress would split."

Margaret laughed and said, "I can hear her whispering in my ear, trying to direct our every step. I can hear her telling us to hurry up and stop our jabbering." They laughed hard this time.

Everything had to be perfect. Sarah basked in her accomplishment of creating most of the attire for the wedding: Margaret wore a floral gown over a matching petticoat with sleeves in rows of frilly lace. Amelia decided upon a plain green petticoat with a beaded bodice trimmed with frills and a small lace ruff around her neck in a matching colour. And Papa, well, he looked just fine in a long, double-breasted black coat, short in the front to reveal a creamy waistcoat and long tails in the back. A new pair of black breeches and a white muslin neck scarf completed his outfit. Sarah had fussed over every detail, to the point where she became exasperated. It had been tiring work and now all of that effort was coming together for everyone but her.

The aunts found Sarah lying on her bed in a slumped heap. They gasped in disbelief and pulled her up with a rough tussle and a good shake.

"You have to hurry, Sarah," Amelia said. "There is no time to waste."

"I cannot do this." Sarah sobbed. "I'm just not ready for marriage."

Margaret and Amelia gulped in dismay. Amelia spoke harshly, saying, "What do you mean, you are not ready? After all the gushing about being in love and all the planning and hard work. You must be joking." She squeezed Sarah's face hard into a pucker. "What are you saying?"

Sarah slumped back on the bed, falling into a fit of sobbing, searching for assurances that everything was going to be perfect. Margaret gritted her teeth. "I do not want to tell you how to think, Sarah, but there is no time for memories or regrets or fretting and jitters. You made a decision and now it is time to honour it. Get up off that bed, Girlie!" Her voice was so demanding that it sent chills along Sarah's arms.

"Margaret's right," said Amelia. "Pull yourself together. It is not the end of the world, you know. It is the beginning."

Sarah realized there would be no gentle nudging and no sympathy, not this morning. The two aunts stuffed her into her wedding outfit: Grandmother's necklace, a sleeveless, red, brocade gown over a petticoat with a frame to widen the skirt, a handmade silver hair clip, Amelia's white gloves and Margaret's white straw hat with a bow of red ribbon.

Colonel Black insisted that Fortune use his carriage. It shimmered as he proudly held the gelding's leather reins. "I feel like a big brown puffball in this suit," he chuckled. Sarah was perched beside her father among a multitude of streamers and wildflowers. The horse and buggy led the way down the Birchtown Road to the church. Enos's cart dawdled behind carrying Margaret and Amelia with Prince Junior sitting between them. When they neared the church, Fortune cracked the whip gently, high above the horse's head and prepared for the grand entrance.

The sun beamed down on the folks who came from near and far. The churchyard buzzed with awaiting guests who amused themselves with worn-out stories and news from around the province. Many had travelled for several days, slept in wagons, crowded in with family and friends, though their weariness did not show.

Reverend Ringwood met the wedding party at the steps. He pulled them aside and outlined the service. In the vestibule, leaning against the wall, was a beautifully decorated broom. The long handle flashed ribbons of assorted colours, tied on by well-wishers. The pews overflowed. The wedding party quickly assembled while many of the guests hummed. Ol' Woman Westcott leapt from her seat and belted out a blissful song of her own composing, with everyone joining in with foot stomping and hand clapping.

> *Oh chillen, fare ye well, Fare ye well! Oh chillen, fare*
> *ye well, I say.*
> *Gonna sweep away de past today, Oh chillen, fare ye*
> *well, I say.*
> *Gonna make de Lord smile down on us, Fare ye well,*
> *fare ye well, I say.*

Sarah held her Papa's arm as he escorted her slowly to the altar. A tear that had been lingering in the corner of her eye let go and trickled down her cheek. Today Reverend Ringwood was performing the first wedding ceremony in the newly constructed meeting house. This wedding would be the first church wedding between two free people in a proper ceremony. Reverend Ringwood directed his discourse to Sarah and Thomas, proudly explaining that today's wedding was "history in the making."

"Let your love be strong!" he said. "Times are hard, food is often scarce, the weather is often frightful and tensions sometimes rise, but hope springs eternal! Dare to live, love and dream! Let nothing stand in the way of your happiness!"

Priscilla Hayward stepped forward wearing a beautiful gown of Sarah's creation. In her rich soprano voice, she rendered a moving song. The beautiful melody reminded Sarah of her mother's voice hovering above the cotton fields, bringing her needed calm.

The taking of vows followed. All was going well, but the stress of the occasion caught Thomas up. He was bewildered and stood with a faraway look in his eyes. For the second time, Reverend Ringwood had to ask, "Do you take this woman, Sarah Lily Redmond, to be your beloved wife?"

Finally, he blurted, "I do!"

Sarah held his eyes, promising to love and treasure her husband.

Reverend Ringwood said, "You are now …" but before he could finish the line, the overjoyed crowd enclosed the couple. They delivered hugs, kisses and warm expressions of good luck for a happy life.

Thomas held Sarah's hand as he reached for the broom. They followed Reverend Ringwood outside. They walked in silence to a spot beneath a huge birch tree. The crowd, which had been milling about, gathered around Reverend Ringwood as he laid the broom on a bed of wildflowers. The long, colourful ribbons wafted in the warm, summer breeze.

The reverend beheld the smiling couple.

"Let me remind you that the straws of the broom represent your families, the handle represents the Almighty and the ribbons represent the ties that bind you together. Being on the other side of the broom will change your lives. Jumping over will mean leaving the past and all that it encompassed. It means making a deep commitment to your future for a rewarding life together."

At that very moment, Sarah felt a light warm breeze flutter over her. The grass gently shimmied beneath her feet. Her skin tingled as an image of Grandmother drifted lazily before her eyes. The old woman's spirit was present. She remembered Grandmother's words, "We got to get this family here in Scotia started!" The sun cast scattered rays of dazzling light across the broom.

"Are you ready to take a leap of faith, my children?" Reverend Ringwood's words drifted softly through the balmy air.

Their reply came in unison and with confidence: "We are ready!" Thomas squeezed Sarah's hand and without hesitation they jumped.